PHANTOM REUNION

Hailey Arquette Murder Files
Book Four

REILY GARRETT

Acknowledgments

To Gunther... This series, as is the case with much of my writing, is inspired in part by my four-footed companions. Dogs have always been a part of the Garrett household. I recently met one who has reminded me so much of my long-coat shepherds that he deserves a mention. Gunther is a 200+ pound ball of love and fur who shares some of the same mannerisms as my fur kids. Yes, I used *who* instead of *that* because in our home, dogs are considered people too. Thank you, Gunther, for keeping all my fur kids alive in my memory.

To Rosie Amber for an in-depth assessment of character and plot, thank you for all your help. You can find her blog and services at rosieamber.wordpress.com/beta-reading-service.

To my editor RE Hargrave, tireless and always patient. Thank you for keeping me on the straight and narrow. You can find her services as www.rehargrave(dot)com.

To my readers, each one of you who selects and reads one of my books, thank you for the opportunity to share my work. If you've enjoyed it, please consider leaving a review. They are the best way to help your author share her work.

Copyright
Copyright© 2023 Reily Garrett
All rights reserved.

Chapter One
Casper

"Go to Texas," they said. "It'll be exciting and open your life to new adventures." Casper ignored the spirit's impatient hand gesture to exit her sleek Camaro in favor of finishing her breakfast sandwich. Her food was hot, and the victim's body wouldn't get any colder.

"Yamato, your body isn't going anywhere in the next fifteen minutes. I'm going to eat while I wait for Hailey." She needed the breakfast sandwich to boost her energy for the coming activity.

"*You need to contact Dante Rossi. This... Hailey, whoever she is, cannot help me.*"

"Dude, you need to chill out."

"*That's the point. My body and the trail to my killer are getting colder by the second. Meanwhile, you're sitting there stuffing your face.*"

"Unlike you, I need nutrition to get through the day. And Hailey's not coming to help you directly. She's coming to help me. Just wait and see. It's never too late to learn."

Hounding by the spirit since the rude awakening at one in the morning warranted harsh words to squelch his attitude.

She wouldn't tell him she needed the mental prep to deal with uncovering a body in an unknown condition. Yamato remained stingy with details, and she'd witnessed her fair share of gory demises, the memory of the most recent forcing her to toss the rest of her food out the open window.

Bayou territory held unparalleled beauty. Few would debate that fact. Then again, few residents had to traipse around in the swamps looking for a corpse tucked in a submerged compact car. At sunrise. On a Saturday morning.

December in Pennsylvania would've seen her huddled in a heavy down coat. Here, fifty-two degrees in Texas warranted nothing more than a light jacket when the promise of warming rays peeked over the horizon.

Despite the ability to remain dry when wading into the river where a killer dumped the vehicle, she found the idea of all the unknowns waiting in the dark and dismal depths unnerving.

Nothing cleared the remnants of exhaustion faster than a ten-foot alligator with jaws open wide inches from your face. Her ability to phase through an attack required constant focus. Her mentor, Nicholai, had proven how distractions could kill during their training sessions; a mantra he often repeated.

The morning had dawned clear, perfect weather for a leisurely ride in a canoe. Instead of sleeping to a decent hour before spending the morning with Noah, she now waited, parked on the side of a tertiary road with no traffic, to *find* a dead body.

Overhead, the screech of a red-tailed hawk asserted dominance over its domain. If her friend Kiera were here, her link with it would inform them exactly what the bird of prey saw and felt. It could also warn of any slithering or four-footed predators nearby.

She missed her family.

The spirit of Yamato Takahashi straightened to his full height of five feet seven inches outside her window with hands on hips and fingers drumming impatiently. *"The sooner you call Dante, the sooner I'm out of your hair."*

"I'm not calling him until I know more. When Hailey gets here, we'll go to your car, and she can tell us what happened. If you'd tell me who shot you, it would save a lot of time."

"As I've already told you. Sniper. From a distance. What part of that do you not understand?"

"Why would someone shoot you? What are you doing in Hamchet?"

"Enjoying a vacation. I hear y'all make great shrimp and grits." Black hair needing a trim blew to the side in the otherworldly breeze.

"Your sarcasm is duly noted, *doyle*."

"Idiot? You're calling me an idiot? How do you even know that term?"

"The guy I'm dating is from Connecticut."

"Figures. If you weren't so stubborn, you could've made one call and be with him now."

"Look, Dante is a pain in the ass with more control issues than Trenton Briner, AKA federal hemorrhoid. The less I have to deal with either, the better."

"Do it sooner and you can go back to bed. Maybe someone's waiting for you."

"First, Noah and I haven't knocked boots yet. Second, well, as if I could sleep now. Are you serious? I know you want justice, but you won't accept my help. That tells me there's a lot more going on here than you're letting on."

"I want Dante involved, and you're the only one I know who can act as a go-between."

"I'll call Dante after my partner takes a look at the situation and not a minute sooner." Casper had scrambled to wake up when the spirit tore into her bedroom like a class four hurricane. He could cool his heels for a few minutes.

"Just what I need. Responsibility for another mortal."

"Boy, are you in for a surprise." She smiled at the thought of Hailey's talent blowing through the victim's confidence after touching the car and corpse.

A thought occurred while she waited. Casper could feel the touch of spirits when wearing her amulet and concentrating. Others could see them, too, when holding her hand.

Hailey's touch instigated psychic visions. Would touching a spirit while connected with Casper provoke a vision? The theory bore testing.

Word had started to spread about H&C Investigations and how they obtained justice for murder victims. It wasn't just the living who'd taken notice.

Spirit traffic to her home had increased to the point she kept a list of cold cases in her office. Another thing she'd never counted on having. This job kindled adult-like qualities, habits, and worldviews she didn't like and didn't care to adopt.

Yamato's case jumped to the head of the line due to his death's timing and the fact he insisted she contact a man who delayed giving her vital information about her family.

The low purr of an engine preceded a familiar maroon truck pulling around the bend of the dirt road in her rearview. In the passenger seat,

Hailey's blue-eyed wolf dog bounced in the seat with a wide doggy grin. Gunther fostered smiles in whomever he met.

The truck stopped behind her car and Gunther hopped out after Hailey slid from the driver's seat. "Hey. What's up? I thought you and Noah were spending the morning in a canoe."

Gunther raced to Casper and sat, nudging her thigh. "Yeah, I know, boy. You want to say hello to Simon." Kneeling, she stroked Gunther's back.

High-pitched squeals of excitement from the spirit capuchin monkey perched on her shoulder elicited Gunther's play bow before hopping to the side in an invitation to play.

A dip of Casper's shoulder and the spirit rode the dog's back, much to their obvious delight.

"That was before my newest pain in the ass woke me up. Meet Yamato Takahashi, died last night via sniper. He won't tell me shit. Well, except that his body's in his car, and he wants me to call Dante." Casper held her hand out for Hailey, the contact allowing her to see the spirit during their conversation.

"Morning, Mr. Takahashi." Hailey took Casper's outstretched hand and adjusted her line of sight to meet Yamato's gaze. "I'm sorry we had to meet like this."

Casper snorted. "Damn. Look at you, all tactful and polite. I know what I wanna be when I grow up." She pinched her lower lip between her teeth to keep from smiling. If her theory about Hailey's talent proved correct, it would save so much time with future cases.

If Yamato refused contact with Hailey, it would lend proof that he knew something about them both. As with all matters, good timing would help.

She and her partner knew spirits didn't communicate well, and this one was new to the realm. He also didn't show any sign of recognizing Hailey, either by name or sight.

"He says he was shot yesterday evening just before twilight. That bridge over there seems to have the best vantage point. Whaddaya think?" Casper gestured to the old stone bridge several hundred yards away.

"Any idea on the shooter?" Hailey asked, then startled with the distant bellow of a gator.

From behind them, Gunther stalked forward.

"No, boy. Load up. You and Simon can visit there." Hailey loaded her furry partner in the truck.

He whined from the driver's seat.

"Our noncorporeal buddy doesn't want to involve the frail womenfolk who'd then need protection from evil incarnate."

Hailey huffed and crossed her arms over her chest. "Doesn't matter. We'll figure it out ourselves. It's what we do." Focusing on where the spirit's voice last emanated from, she said while gesturing to Casper, "We'll call authorities when *we* are ready."

"My sentiments exactly. I'm tired of that wily Italian stud holding information about my family and not forking it over. This could give me a bargaining chip."

"Yep, we'll have a worthy trade," Hailey agreed.

"Where's your manners, Hailey? It's polite to greet people with a handshake," Casper asked with her left hand on Hailey's shoulder while turning to Yamato.

Hailey frowned then twisted her lips to the side, obviously picking up the intent if not what lay behind it.

Yamato, all polite formality and perfect etiquette, didn't hesitate to take her hand.

The minute the trio connected, Hailey's eyes widened, a wistful smile betraying a secret held deep.

"You've just had your first child. A little girl. You and your wife would've made great parents and loved your farm in Lafayette. I'm so sorry."

Yamato snatched his ethereal hand away and floated backward with a lift of his chin and hands clasped behind his back. Small clumps of seeding fall grass provided a backdrop for the ethereal visitor.

Crap. Oh, well.

Her partner may not have gotten much, but they damn well learned something about her talent.

"*What? No. My wife is not due for another month, and we've only begun looking at property in Louisiana. We don't even know the baby's sex.*"

Hailey appeared as stunned as the spirit. "Oh, ah, sorry. Maybe we should try that again. Sometimes I get a little confused."

Yamato was having none of it, his translucent form floating farther backward and out of reach. *"No. Please, just call Dante Rossi and let him know my body is in this river."*

"Tell me, Yamato, do you have psychic talent?" Casper studied first her partner, then the spirit, one of whom just saw a future that would never come to pass. She hoped it was Hailey's talent expanding and not something issued from the spirit.

"Psychic talent? That's nonsense. Now, can we please proceed?" The slim Asian gentleman gestured toward the river.

"Whatever. Fine." Casper headed toward the water line, unsure if the victim spoke the truth. They could lie as well as any of the living.

"Okay, Casper, shall we go *find* his subcompact? Oh, and first... Yamato, are there any other vehicles here? Preferably ones without bodies in them?"

"Mine is the only one in this immediate vicinity. Follow the twin trails of smashed grass. Wait, there's an alligator swimming this way. You need to—"

"We'll be fine." Casper matched Hailey's steps down the short slope and into the water, phasing their bodies to remain dry.

Water meandered slowly around the bend, carrying a broken limb gained from yesterday's freak storm. Unseen objects beneath the surface created eddies of various sizes to warn them of larger objects.

Movement in her periphery caught Casper's attention. With partially webbed feet and a tail that could propel it forward at twenty miles per hour, an alligator opened its mouth and snapped down on water when reaching her position.

Its bellow likened to the rumbling of a far-away motorcycle.

"Sorry, fella. You'll have to look elsewhere for your next meal." Casper continued walking without breaking stride.

With the soles of their feet solidified, each would have to navigate the unevenness of the river bottom that necessitated caution for steady footing.

Forty yards across suggested the depth could be well over their heads. They wouldn't get wet while phased, but each would have to hold their breath until back stepping and clearing the water line. They would also feel the chill. Both equaled distractions.

"Ready?" Casper asked when the water reached her chin. Looking over, she noticed it just covered the band of Hailey's low ponytail.

"Yep. Let's get this done. Trent and I are planning on heading to Houston for some Christmas shopping. Maybe we can still catch a movie tonight if we get the ball rolling here."

The next step put Casper in a small rut with the water reaching her forehead. Murky details curbed her curiosity with the increased opacity from silt and debris.

Estimation of the distance they could visualize proved wrong. Anything farther than two inches equaled a black void once water closed over her head.

It was cold enough to steal her breath.

The sole of her right foot bounced off what felt like a tire in moving forward. She stopped and squeezed Hailey's hand, receiving an answering signal in return. Concentrating, she unphased the fingertips of Hailey's right fingertips.

Her lungs burned for air while waiting for her partner's next signal. When it came, they both backtracked until their heads broke the water line.

"Well? Need another go at it?"

"Might as well. It's a damn rental car, so everybody and their brother-in-law has touched it. Let's go to the driver's side. I want a crack at the steering wheel and the body."

This time, her partner led the way, having *seen* through psychic touch, the vehicle's position and now able to navigate to the desired position.

With Casper's talent active, nothing could attack or affect them, except for the soles of their shoes and unphased fingertips.

Whatever unseen creatures swam through their phased bodies left traces of energy in tingling sensations where they passed.

It didn't take long for the chill to seep into Casper's bones. Her lungs burned for air.

She acknowledged her partner's shudder, knowing something of interest entered the equation by the way Hailey's hand inadvertently tightened before giving the retreat signal.

The moment cool air brushed her neck, Casper could see excitement dancing in her partner's eyes. "Well, did ya see who shot him?"

"No, too far away." Hailey rolled her shoulders but smiled. "However, I do know he's connected with your school. He's looking into the same thing you are, and he knows a lot about psychics."

"Damn it, girl. You're not supposed to find out about that. Dante will kill me." Yamato floated through the water with his torso visible above the ripples created by a bull shark's dorsal fins. The sharks were adapted to survive in both salt and fresh water, and on occasion moved inland.

"I think that ship has already sailed." Casper didn't release Hailey's hand, instead tilted her head toward the spirit, hoping her partner would get the message. Now that his thoughts were where they wanted them, picking through specific memories would be child's play.

Hailey reached out to grasp Yamato's forearm.

The spirit was faster. He darted out of reach.

"Insufferable. No wonder Dante despises kids and psychics. Both are equally sneaky." The aura brightened to a brilliant soft gold, his anger lending strength to his luminescence.

Casper looked away from the blinding light. Her experience with the ghostly realm rarely included anger directed at her. Though they couldn't affect her directly, they could inflict harm on those she cared about through possession.

"Okay. All right," Casper conceded. "I'll give Dante a call if it'll make you happy. In fact, we'll call Trenton too."

The additional concession seemed to appease her newest haunter. His aura dimmed to where she didn't need to shield her eyes. Retrieving her phone, she swiped to call Dante, jutting her chin at her partner. "How 'bout you call your favorite pain in the ass."

"Who do you think will get here first?" Hailey chuckled. "At least those two seem to have lost their mutual animosity. I think they've called a truce."

Casper shrugged one shoulder. "Actually, I think it's becoming a little one-sided. Dante still acts wary but doesn't seem as hostile as he used to be, except when dealing with me. I think he really hates me—makes me wonder if I insulted him in a past life. Maybe a relative of mine hurt a relative of his. Who knows?"

"I thought he'd loosen up toward you eventually, but that doesn't seem to be happening. Maybe he just dislikes all teenagers."

"He gets along with Noah okay, well, at least a little better than me."

"Yeah, that part is strange. Maybe it's a man thing, though he doesn't say much to Noah."

Chapter Two
Casper

Regardless of Casper and her family's best efforts, Dante Rossi remained a giant black hole in the information world. Neither she nor Hailey could determine his goal, employer, or significant past history.

His presence requested by a spirit heralded a new dimension of scrutiny concerning students, teachers, and administrative staff at the Gifted Elite School where she attended classes.

Dante parked his BMW behind Hailey's truck and strode with purpose the instant he slid from his vehicle. "What are you into now, and why did you call me out here at this hour?" He looked around as if expecting something to jump out at him.

"Well, now," Casper began, "...I have information about Yamato Takahashi that you need. You have information about my family that I need. Seems to me we should make a trade."

Dante froze. Only for a split second, but long enough to connect the dots. "He's... dead?"

A brief flicker of grief crossed his expression, swept away by the light breeze and replaced with a hardened jaw and eyes that had seen too much in life.

"Yes," Casper murmured low. "Last night. I'm sorry. You obviously knew him." She wasn't so heartless as to not give him a minute to collect himself.

Dante didn't need it.

"Olivia, I told you I'd share what I know when the school situation is clear, and you've stopped endangering other students."

He was the only person who called her Olivia.

Thank God.

"What? I haven't endangered anybody. I'm just helping out a friend who happens to be a private investigator, until I graduate."

"And then...?" Dante's forehead wrinkled as if he could summon her thoughts.

"Then, I'll decide what I want to do."

"Yes, I'm sure you'll go to college and major in home economics." Dante kicked a loose stone in the dirt, then met her glare with one of his own.

"Nope. No longer good enough." Casper gave a two-finger wave when seeing Trenton drive by and park bumper to bumper with Casper's Camaro. "Oh, look at his expression. More harassment to come. How delightful."

"Hold on, maybe he's not as grumpy as he looks. Maybe he's got a bone to pick with Dante." Hailey smiled when Trenton opened his door. "Since when did you two get chummy?"

The federal agent paused to kneel when Gunther hopped from the truck and greeted him with a raised paw.

"We're not. We just realized after a few frank conversations that we share similar goals and working together became prudent," Dante replied, offering a treat to the canine when he greeted him after the federal agent.

"What's up, Sparkles? And what're we doing here?" Trenton nodded a greeting to the Italian dressed in a suit.

Casper harrumphed. "Not sure what that dog sees in you, Dante. Must be a predator thing." She poked her finger at Trenton. "Dante is here because our vic wanted him here. There's enough information to go around."

"But it's going to cost us, Trenton. Olivia wants information on her family." Dante shared a knowing look with the federal agent as if aligning common goals.

"Damn right I want information on my folks. I don't care what they did to you or your family. And if you want to know anything about Yamato, you'll fork it over, *Goombah*." Casper waited, knowing she had Dante over a barrel.

"So, we're to be friends now?" Dante asked, his tone smooth and calculating.

Trenton stepped forward to face Casper. "Who is Yamato? And for the record, Dante's not giving you anything until the school investigation is clear."

"Who put you in charge? You think—oh, shit. You're in cahoots with Clannahan now? Damn it. You can't trust anyone these days. Does Kiera know?"

Major Thomas Clannahan, her legal guardian, had recently given Trenton the green light to provide overwatch. That prerogative did not extend to Dante or anyone else.

She didn't know when Clannahan read Trenton in on specifics of her search concerning the school. The fed knew about her ability to phase through objects, and that Hailey spoke with spirits. Maybe it was a mistake to bring him into the fold.

Trenton merely smiled and faced Hailey. "Okay. You've obviously found a dead body, even if you haven't said how." He narrowed his suspicious gaze on Casper. "Nevertheless, you've obviously touched something. Let me guess, when we send in a diver, we'll find a car with a body in it?"

"Yep." Hailey said no more. One word would force the fed into action yet keep him in the dark without revealing tradable intel.

Not one to be sidetracked, Casper reiterated her offer. "Listen, Dante. I'll give you a name if you return like in kind."

"Fair enough. You first. I'll even throw in a bonus," Dante offered, deadpan.

"I don't trust you. Tell me something about my parents. Give me a name."

"Martie Schrader is a relative." Dante crossed both arms over his chest and waited.

"Is that spelled with a y or ie? Living relative? Is that a man or woman?" Casper sputtered, her legs suddenly feeling weak.

"Nope. No more, except yes, among the living," Dante murmured. "Now, your turn."

Hailey and Trenton stood stock-still until Casper nodded. "Go ahead and give him something Hailey, but not everything." She knew Hailey would understand. They'd talked about always holding something in reserve where Trenton was concerned.

"Okay. Yamato found a deeper connection between Vice Principal Jenkins and a student who's connected to a newly appointed board member." Hailey made the offering without giving away too much.

Kudos, partner.

"Most of the board members are new. That doesn't help a whole lot. We need more." Trenton's exasperation translated into a headshake.

"We?" Casper's jaw went slack, a thumb hooked over her shoulder indicating Dante. "He doesn't carry a badge. Yet you two are working together behind our backs and think we're just going to let that slide?"

"You don't have a choice. We're all in this together now. Not only that," Trenton sighed, "...but because of the trouble you two have found to date, the higher-ups are forming a task force, kind of in your honor."

"What?" Hailey and Casper said simultaneously.

"Yes. It's small. Leigh and Lt. Colson from Jefferson County Sheriff's department, me, and, unofficially, Dante."

"When did this happen?" Hailey ground out. "And why didn't Leigh tell me? We've been friends, like, forever."

"Maybe because you started holding out on her," Trenton replied with the patience of a monk. "Just like you're doing with me now."

"Not so fast, fed. If you think you're going to wheedle me and my partner out of this, you're wrong. Hailey and I are going to work this homicide to the end. So, if either of you have big ideas otherwise, might as well drop them now."

Dante turned around and paced away. "Damn it. We're trying to keep you two safe."

"Since when did the Italian stallion become your best bud, Trenton? And why in hell is *he* on a task force? We haven't even figured out who he works for! How are we supposed to trust him?" Casper all but screeched the last words.

Trenton sighed, reaching forward and touching Casper's arm. "Look. Clannahan regrets involving you in this now but knows you won't quit even if he gets you kicked out of that damn school, which he won't do."

"That's why you've been so cagey lately. Coming over but never touching." Hailey advanced on her target, one of her best friends for years. "You knew I'd figure this out."

Casper coughed behind her fisted hand. "TMI, partner. Boundaries and all that."

Hailey shot him a dark look and said, "You didn't answer my partner's questions, Trent. How is that, Dante?" She held both hands up in surrender. "Yes, you've been a big help and even saved my life, but we don't know how you fit into all this."

Casper added, "I know you've been talking with Clannahan, like, a bunch lately. What's up with that?"

Dante studied her as he might a panther crouching to spring. "He and I have come to terms, an agreement of sorts. That's all you need to know for now."

Trenton held one finger out to forestall the coming argument. "Look, Hailey, we care, and we're not trying to sideline either of you."

"Speak for yourself," Dante grumbled.

Trenton continued after shooting a dirty look over his shoulder. "We need to work together as a team. I realize Colson and Leigh aren't read into what you two can do. Hell, I don't even know much about your... abilities. But I do know this. We can work this out."

"Damn it, fed. You've just gone and complicated the hell out of our lives. Leigh knows of my connection to others in Pennsylvania. The more she learns about me, the more that could put my family in danger. Clannahan had no right."

Trenton met Casper's gaze. "Actually, he did. Kiera, Wyatt, Ouray, and Nicholai have spoken with Clannahan at length, and they all agreed. You just weren't supposed to find out this way."

"You're saying Casper's family betrayed her, Trent. How could you do this? I know they want what's best for her, but this isn't the way to go about it." Hailey rubbed a hand over her eyes. "I'm sorry, Casper. I didn't know."

Casper whirled on Dante. "What else do you know about my life down here? Spit it out before I hand you your intestines."

Dante took a step back. "Fine. I know your boyfriend is a shifter and that *his* family is concerned he's getting in over his head."

"Holy shit. How did the world just get so much bigger?" Casper sat on the ground, dumbfounded. Her world turned upside down in the space of minutes. "You know about Noah and shifters? You've met his family?"

"I've spoken with his parents. That's all," Dante replied, offering a hand up, then crouching to meet her gaze when she refused. "I'm sorry that it came out like this, kid. I am. But you're not trained to investigate. *That* puts other students at the school at risk."

"Oh, are you having a fling with one of the students? Good to know. Which one?" At least his words were starting to make a little sense. "You and Yamato were working together, investigating something about the GE school. Well, listen, bud, I *am* a student there, and I won't quit."

"The rest is not up for discussion." Dante stood and turned away.

"Enough. I'm done with both of you! I wonder if Noah is aware of your sneaky tactics." Casper bolted to her feet and headed toward her car.

"Now hold on, Casper. No need to go off half-cocked." Trenton caught up and spun her around before she opened her door. "We're going to talk this through."

"No. We're not. I've had enough of both of you. Especially you." Casper had to lean around Trenton's larger mass to poke a finger in Dante's direction.

"You don't mean that, Olivia. You need time to cool off," Dante suggested.

"And you know something else I've learned from my *family* in PA? Sometimes it's safer to *not* have contact with them. My *former* best friend's uncle tried to kill her, multiple times. Tried to kill me too." The last, mumbled low, brought home the entire situation.

"I know family members don't always have your best interest at heart but, Casper, Clannahan and the others... they do." Trenton softened his tone with the pity radiating from his gaze.

Maybe her goal of finding relatives wasn't a worthy one. "For all I know, this Martie Schrader is a psycho killer, and I should never look for him, her, whatever."

No way would she listen to more of the fed's bullshit. Phasing her body through his grasp on her upper arm, she smiled.

Until he stepped on the unphased portion of her boot. The sole.

"Take it easy, kid. You're going to expose your abilities to Dante. Is that what you want?" Murmured words lacked malice but packed a punch just the same.

With the fed's foot holding her in place, she seethed. "You have no right."

"I have every right. I have the blessing of your family *and* from Clannahan, which makes it both legal and moral. So, how about we both take a calming breath and have a long talk? I'm sure we can come to an agreement. Give me thirty minutes."

"No. Five."

"Not enough. Twenty-five."

"Twenty," Casper countered, aware of Hailey's approach before a calming hand touched her back, further blocking the site line between the verbal combatants and Dante.

"Twenty-five and I'll throw in good food and a surprise you'll like."

"I don't like surprises."

"You'll like this one. It'll give you more control over your life."

Damn if the fed didn't know how to push her buttons. "All right, but I want plenty of chocolate. Like, a year's supply."

"Six months and we'll see how much weight you gain. I understand you have a fairly rigid training schedule. I like the mini dojo Hailey set up in the loft."

"I eat a lot."

"Not a problem. I know you and Hailey will work off the calories with sparring."

There existed no sexual innuendos, and no hint of *slick* in the fed's voice. "Okay. But it better be good food and a great surprise."

"It is. We'll finish here and meet at the loft in the morning."

"Deal." She didn't like compromises but understood them as a part of life. "How'd you know about my vulnerability?" She indicated her boot when he stepped back.

"When I saw you standing *in* a desk last month, I knew something had to anchor you to the floor. Made sense it was the soles of your feet."

"Figures the fed has a brain."

Since her abilities emerged, she'd done her best to keep her life private. Meeting Hailey felt preordained, as did her finding Noah, the classmate who'd thrown his lot in with them.

It wasn't a matter of not trusting Dante and Trenton. The fed had seen her interrogate a prisoner. It was a matter of family. A mantle of approval her people in Pennsylvania granted to Trenton without her knowledge.

It was betrayal of the highest order.

Dante's divulging Noah's status declared his knowledge of the loop. Did that mean Dante was also a psychic or had he and the fed shared information? She eyed both with suspicion, evaluating.

Trenton offered his hand in reconciliation. "Hey, it's not as bad as you're making it out to be, Casper. I've recently met a kid who can phase her body through any solid object. My world's expanded too. For the better."

"Trent, Casper's friends in Pennsylvania, they're not just psychics. They're family, despite lack of blood ties." Hailey steadied a slightly pale Casper. "This *is* a betrayal."

Trenton nodded in agreement. "Maybe, which means you both understand the value of said family. That doesn't mean it can't expand to include us down here."

Dante completed the circle in moving forward and continued with, "Look. We're not gonna ask anyone to divulge secrets any more than we'll question how you come by specific information. We're also not going to poke our noses in your family's business. Olivia, you have family down here, both blooded and non-blooded. You'll meet them in time. Consider this... they're just as concerned with anonymity as your PA group. Okay?"

"You said there's a task force forming? Let me guess, my *legal* guardian is behind setting that up. Sounds like something he'd do." Casper emphasized the word with distaste.

"Yes, on a trial basis," Trenton confirmed. "It was either that or bring some of your family down here for closer support."

"How are we s'posed to keep our talents under wraps from Leigh and Lt. Colson? They're normal."

"I can help there," Hailey spoke up. "Leigh already knows about my visions, so she's kinda tuned into the psychic world. I'll give her a heads up to steer Colson in a different direction when needed."

"We all will," Trenton confirmed.

"And you're gonna explain a high school kid's involvement, how?" Casper shot back, touching her sternum.

"Well, we have options there," Trenton began. "We could confirm you're working undercover at the school. That would be the easiest, most believable, and not expose your talent," Trenton suggested. "Or we could—"

"Stop. Sold on the first try." Just because Casper agreed with the premise didn't mean the scenario would work. It was already fraught with problems when psychics and non-psyches came together in a joint operation.

"What about Leigh and Colson's regular duties? She's a detective, but he's a lieutenant and her supervisor," Hailey asked.

"They'll be assigned to the task force first, then to regular duties when not busy." Trenton's chuckle held no humor. "But I have a feeling you two are going to keep us busy most of the time."

It was a lot to absorb, but the damn men made sense. "There should be a law against you two ganging up on us." Casper still wanted to reach in and yank out vital organs from them both.

"I will share this much." Whether Hailey spoke up to draw attention away from her younger partner or wanted them in on the loop, she offered, "You both know I *see* things from the past through touch. It seems I now see *possibilities* of the future."

"Explain," Trenton demanded.

"I touched the car in the river and saw one version of Yamato's future. He's getting ready to have a child, a daughter, and the family was preparing to move to a farm near Lafayette."

"We hadn't decided that yet. And now it's a future I'll never experience," Yamato declared with regret.

"I'm sorry about that. I really am. But I can promise you this," Hailey looked to where the spirit spoke. "I will check on them and deliver any message you give me."

"Fine, and thank you. Now that we've settled your problems, can we focus on mine?" Yamato said, waiting by the edge of the river.

It was good advice that directed Casper's attention away from the personal problems brewing. One thing she did note, Dante didn't so much as raise a brow, much less question Hailey's short conversation with Yamato.

Normal humans did not hear spirits talk. Did Dante?

Shadows lengthened with the sun's climb in the Eastern sky. The morning was shot.

Casper tweezed her car keys from her jeans pocket as the tow truck pulled to a stop by the road. "Guess that's my cue to scoot. So much for canoeing down the river today."

"Sorry about that. Next time you have plans but get a tip, you can always call. You're part of a team now and don't have to do everything yourself."

Trenton watched Lt. Colson direct the recovery efforts after a short briefing. It wasn't his first operation.

Once read in on Casper's undercover status at the school, the sheriff's deputy relaxed his wary status yet didn't make great effort to develop a rapport. His only concession equaled insisting they call him Waylan.

Leigh, on the other hand, had been all about including her best friend's partner. "Don't forget, Casper. Tomorrow morning we're all meeting at the loft. Nine o'clock."

"Tomorrow's Sunday." She couldn't keep the whine out of her voice. She was tired, hungry, and felt betrayed by those most dear to her heart.

"Which is why it's an unofficial meeting," Trenton replied. "We need to iron out a few details before we dig in—and there'll be food."

"Better be chocolate," Casper muttered before sliding into the driver's seat and shutting the door.

She had family. Living family. Here in Texas. Would they be like Kiera, Ouray, and Nicholai? Or would they mimic the psycho tendencies of Kiera's Uncle Roth, killed by the very spirits he'd attempted to control?

What if coming to Texas had been a life-changing or life-ending kind of mistake? Meeting and befriending Hailey was no error, but what about the rest? Where had she gone wrong?

Chapter Three
Hailey

Gunther raced ahead and down the steps before whining at the exterior door until Hailey opened it. Early mornings were a great time to ponder difficult situations while watching her wolf dog make his rounds and sniff to see what wildlife had visited during the night. She had a lot to consider.

Not only had she taken on a partner, she now worked on a task force, albeit the most unusual ever created.

Maybe this was Major Clannahan's specialty, organizing investigative teams from the background. He'd proven himself an intelligent and shrewd operator, and knew how to manipulate others into specific positions.

Trenton's revelation yesterday had to be the tip of a very large iceberg. From what she'd seen and learned of Casper so far, the major didn't *do* small-scale or haphazard.

Clannahan knew Casper well enough to invade her world in incremental degrees—setting her up in a small mansion capable of housing dozens, enrolling her in her target school in a seamless manner, and gathering information on those around her, all the while selecting those appropriate to accomplish the goal.

Whether the teen knew it or not, Trenton withheld information, even refusing to discuss it with Hailey after a long day by the river. He straddled a dangerous line that could cut him down in her partner's eyes.

This morning, Gunther forewent the rest of his sniff testing in favor of bolting toward the road when a familiar truck turned into the deserted industrial complex. Her partly remodeled warehouse was the only inhabited structure on the street, which made all traffic destined for her doorstep.

It shouldn't have surprised her to see Major Clannahan also exiting Trenton's SUV when she rounded the back corner of her building. Their progressive friendship had seemed natural and befitting two ex-military men. They also shared an undetermined agenda that could create an irreparable rift in the very team they hoped to forge.

Gunther greeted Trenton and sat for an introduction to her other guest. If Clannahan was the surprise referenced yesterday by the river, he'd better have brought *all* of Casper's favorite foods. By the truckload and with a magical, never-ending supply.

"Mornin', Major." Hailey approached and held out her hand in welcome, then understood the early arrival when seeing Trenton lift the tailgate.

"Good morning, Hailey. Hope you're hungry." Instead of accepting the greeting, Clannahan plucked out one of many covered dishes and handed it to her with a warm smile.

Clever man. Casper did warn that he'd avoid my touch.

She'd find another way to delve through his secrets.

Told to expect guests, she'd scrounged folding chairs from her mother's house for their first unofficial task force meeting. She'd also asked Cecile to help prepare a small meal.

Apparently, Trenton had made the same request. She counted a minimum of eight containers and saw more wedged between blankets. It should've bothered her how Trenton and her mom got along so well. No doubt, Major Clannahan was present as well. He was quite the charmer according to her partner.

The picnic table she and Casper had brought in yesterday afternoon was big enough to seat her guests for a meal but couldn't hold all the food too. Looking around for a solution, she frowned.

"Don't worry, Sparkles. We've got it covered," Trenton assured her with a wink and followed her inside.

"Which is why you're early?"

"Yeah. We wanted to set this up right." Trenton set his first two dishes on the picnic bench.

"We've got surprises for you both. *That* is why we're early." Clannahan smiled and turned to Trenton. "Mind if I sit and talk with Hailey for a bit? These old bones aren't as agile as they once were."

Trenton's cheek distorted with his tongue thrust against one side. "Sure. I've got this."

Hailey nipped both teeth between her lips to keep her smile hidden. There was nothing old or slow about her seated guest. "What's on your mind, Major? And why are we talking before Casper arrives?"

"*Hmm*, I wanted to run something by you that concerns, well, pretty much only you."

"I'm listening, but believe me when I say, Casper will hear every word, even if it is secondhand."

"Good. If you'd like to record the conversation," he pointed to her cell phone attached to her belt, "...that'd be fine."

Hailey debated, declined the offer, then nodded for him to continue.

Trenton set two more dishes on the table, his eyes crinkling around the corners with his grin before returning for more food.

"Okay, then. As you know, your task force is up and running. However, it seems you don't have an appropriate meeting place. The police station is too public for the matters you'll be handling. I figured we could do something a little better. Not that anything is set in stone, mind you."

"You want to take over this building? Um, that would be a hard no."

"I've no intention of doing such a thing. You and Casper are partners, and I wholly approve. I thought about making a headquarters at the house where she lives, but then she'd never have complete separation between social and work life. She's young and doesn't realize the importance."

"So..."

"What if we could gussy up the first floor here? You have a ton of space, most of it unused. I was thinking the task force could rent space from you. Along those lines, we'd also set up a proper meeting room, along with a formal training area, since I imagine Casper's Pennsylvania family will become more involved as time goes on."

Trenton deposited more containers then paused before leaving. "Think about it, Sparkles. What he proposes makes sense. You could use the rental income toward purchasing the building. You'll have a solid, dependable salary with no contracts."

Damn if the man didn't know how to pull strings. "You want to rent space from someone who is renting a building? What if I lose the lease before I scrape together a down payment to buy it?" Hailey held her hands wide and gestured to both floors, including the upper level where she lived. "We'd both lose."

"Now that you mention it, that does sound a little shaky. Tell me, how do you like living here?"

"Love it. Wouldn't trade it for the world. I intend to buy the building as soon as I can."

"What if I could facilitate that transaction *and* provide you all with working space? Then you'd not have that burden to carry. Consider it a signing bonus for a job you're already doing. And before you ask, if you ever recuse yourself from the task force, you keep everything we've done."

"Meaning?"

"The board room, a proper dojo, a moderate-sized kitchen for when you have, say, lots of guests. Casper comes from a rather large family." Clannahan held one hand out. "I know she's peeved at me and at them right now, but she'll get over it. She's family."

"You're talking major construction. That takes time, money, and let's not forget permits, which take even more time to get approved."

"All of which I can handle. Along with the construction."

"Ah, I'm more of a hands-on type of gal."

Clannahan smiled. "Just like your partner, and it's a good thing to always be involved in a project starting from the ground up. What do you say?"

"Sounds good, but what you're proposing will take time. We'll probably close the case long before you purchase your first hammer. What then?"

"We move on to the second case. From what I understand, after speaking with Nicholai—"

"Casper's adopted guardian, you're spending a lot of time with him..."

"That's relative. He has a very special talent, too, and advises there will be many more instances where this task force will be needed. Actually, this could take you to different parts of the country if you're amenable to travel. Of course, special provisions would be made for Gunther to accompany you. I understand he saved your life out in the bayou."

The man had just made leaps and bounds ahead before their first meeting. If not for previous discussions with Casper about how he operated and always kept his ducks in line, she'd think him mentally unstable with grandiose ideation.

"Okay, I'm willing to give it a go." With his resources, evidence would never get stuck in the backlog of a lab, red tape wouldn't be a problem, and she wouldn't always have to hide her talent.

She didn't know as much about Colson, except that he'd developed feelings for Leigh, reciprocated by tentative smiles at the riverside yesterday.

Testing the waters with the lieutenant might prove dicey, but if he didn't freak out, maybe he'd provide another corner of their team, fully involved. No doubt the major had vetted him to the nines before approving his participation. Trenton would've provided insight there too.

Clannahan slapped the table with glee. "Wonderful." He looked up as Leigh walked in the front door bearing a tray of plastic spoons, forks, and knives, along with cups and plates. "And just in time for your first meeting. I'll leave you guys to it as I have preparations to make."

Trenton held the door for Casper then followed her in.

A minute later, Colson chocked it open with his foot until helping Dante carry a cooler inside.

Clannahan's exit included a murmured, "Let me know when you're finished," to Trenton before closing the door behind him.

"We've got drinks." Dante handed a cup of iced coffee to Hailey.

She appreciated the strong smell of chicory coming from the cup. "You remembered. Thanks."

The specific reason for his presence remained a mystery Clannahan didn't divulge. The constant friction between him and Casper equaled a prescription designed to keep the group in turmoil. He just didn't fit.

"What shenanigans is Clannahan up to now?" Casper grimaced at the newcomers before removing the top of the nearest covered dish. "Ooh, your mom made bayou brownies with chocolate and pecans. I love these things." She reached in and grabbed two.

Chocolate made everything better.

"Yeah. If she misses a day from the oven, something's wrong." Leigh handed her a plate and napkin, then took one for herself.

"Hails, your mom's cooking is legendary. Shame it's not, like, contagious, or at least passed down through the generations," Casper spoke around a mouthful of chocolate.

Each prepared a plate and sat. Colson claimed a seat by Leigh while Trenton sat beside Hailey, with Casper on the other side. Dante preferred a neutral position beside Colson but kept an eye on everyone.

Hailey marveled over the strange accumulation of personalities, wondering how often and to what extent they'd butt heads. "So, who's leading this shindig?"

"Trenton's got the most experience and training." Colson reached for a napkin and another homemade breakfast sandwich, holding it up to exclaim, "Damn, these are good."

"So does that mean you're no longer a fed?" Casper grinned, her thoughts obviously running into devious territory.

"Waylan's right, and yes, I am. I'm just not assigned to the regional SAIC, or supervisor. This group will serve as its own entity. For now, though, Leigh and Colson will be assigned to us. When we're not busy, they'll work their currently assigned duties."

"Served on many joint operations, have you, Colson?" Casper asked.

"A few. How about you? Since I'm told you're just eighteen, can't have been too many."

Casper snorted but didn't answer.

Trenton chuckled, the latter shaking his head with a, "The major said there'd be growing pains."

"Let's start with what we know about Yamato Takahashi," Hailey suggested.

The earlier conversation with Clannahan still rumbled through Hailey's thoughts. She considered his style as prepared, understated lavish and full steam ahead. What did that mean for her office?

Instead of congregating in a half-circle in folded chairs, they continued their conversation into the investigation at the picnic table.

"Yamato is forty-three, originally from Vermont but moved south when he married." Dante pursed his lips, considering his next words. "His specialty included undercover work, which makes me wonder how anyone could've made him as a spy."

"Who employed him?" Colson asked.

"Classified is all I know," Dante replied without a hitch.

Colson made a disgusted sound in his throat. "Great, the alphabets don't want to play with us. How typical."

"We'll be glad for that eventually," Trenton advised, "...because we're not sharing information with them either. They won't even know we exist most of the time."

Colson started to object but quieted when Trenton continued, "But we'll have access to any information they have."

That tidbit of information instigated a round of chuckles.

"Yamato was investigating the GE school," Dante offered.

"Them again? Do we have another perverted teacher?" Leigh wiped her hands and placed her folded napkin by her plate.

"No, but their vice principal, a guy named Jenkins, has had regular contact with one of the students, Melody Gingham. Not thought to be sexual in nature due to the public meetings." Dante withdrew his phone and checked his notes. A list of dates informed them all of the frequency.

"Oh, she's the one who freaked out at my party. Remember, Hailey?"

"Yeah, her uncle got her admitted to the school and wanted her to do something, although I never got a handle on what. I do know her father was against it."

"What's her specialty?" Trenton asked. "I'll have something to add to that in a minute."

"Numbers and languages," Casper replied. "Did you get much else, Hailey?"

"No. Just that they wanted her to do something underhanded." Hailey closed her eyes briefly in thought. "*Hmm,* didn't get much else."

All gazes turned toward Trenton. "Okay. We've uncovered money transferred from Gingham's uncle to Jenkins. We first thought it was a bribe to get her enrolled. Now, maybe not."

"I'll be sorting through Jenkins' office in the next night or so, and will let you know what I find after I sift through his computer files," Casper's addition received nods from all.

"Good. We'll go through it at our next meeting." Trenton closed the folder in front of him.

"What's your connection with Yamato, Dante?" Lt. Colson asked, clearly unsettled with hints of Hailey's abilities.

"He was a friend. Contacted me when he moved to Texas a few months ago."

"Okay. One more question no one has answered. How'd we find out his body was in the drink?" Colson shot back.

"Anonymous tip," Casper replied without missing a beat. "The same one who told us there're more bodies dumped in the bayous."

"Tell us something we don't know." Colson finished his breakfast sandwich and grabbed a brownie. "Interesting menu. Love it." It was the first time he appeared to loosen up when on duty.

To Hailey's knowledge, he wasn't the stuffed shirt type yet maintained clear boundaries between work and play. Previous interactions had proven him likable, competent, and extremely focused.

"Look at it this way. We'll always have work," Trenton said after swallowing the last of his Creole mini quiche.

"Back to the vice principal," Leigh redirected the conversation. "It seems Casper has the best opportunity of making loose contact. The problem is, we should work in teams, and we don't have anyone else who would fit."

"Actually," Casper smiled, "...we have exactly what we need."

"Noah? Is his family on board with him helping?" Hailey asked, not wanting to rile her unsettled partner, but cognizant of the other student's desire for anonymity.

"Yeah. He's helped us before, and he's already approaching the problem from his own angle." Casper paused in contemplation, her gaze sliding toward Colson. "Makes sense to join our efforts."

"Might not be in *his* best interest. There *is* a risk." Trenton's jaw tightened. He'd made every effort to keep students out of any investigative fire, until learning about psychics.

"We weren't a team then, fed. We are now," Casper said as if it were the simplest explanation known through expectation. "'Sides, it's just a little snoop here and there."

Hailey chuckled.

Each of the others groaned.

"So why don't you approach him, see if he's okay working with the rest of us?" Hailey suggested.

"Ah, I believe *this* is why there's usually a designated leader in any task force," Colson prompted.

"I'll clear it with Clannahan," Trenton said, then detailed what information he'd learned through his search the previous afternoon. Retrieving his phone from his jacket, he sent a text.

Dante added what he knew from an informal perspective.

When they'd concluded the meeting, Trenton briefly took Hailey's hand. "Now, for your surprise."

With his touch came a flood of images of him and Clannahan, late at night, poring over a poster-sized paper with lots of blue lines.

So that's what he'd been hiding.

He and the major had more in common than originally suspected.

"What?" Casper asked. "What's Clannahan doing now?"

"Some construction. Not sure where," Hailey replied.

"I suggest we clean up, and Colson, if you could help me take this table outside where it belongs, I'd appreciate it." Trenton collected the mostly empty plastic containers and headed for the door.

Gunther hopped up from where he'd been lying beside Hailey's chair when she stood. "Why do I get the feeling my life is getting ready to take a drastic left turn?"

"Because Clannahan's involved," Casper grumbled. "Whenever you say yes to the major, count on it. Also, it'll be in ways you don't expect and never would've seen coming."

Her young partner was still reeling, either from the news about having family or from the addition of others to form a new, Texas-based extension, Hailey wasn't sure. Either way, the teen had a wariness about her not seen in months.

By the time they'd cleaned up, two ladder trucks rolled to a stop out front. Gunther beat her to the door and barked as two more pickups parked behind them.

In all, a dozen men poured out, none recognized as local but each bearing the movements of military precision. Unlike the laid-back demeanor of local building contractors, each man wasted no time in grabbing whatever tools needed and heading for the door.

It shouldn't have surprised her when Clannahan strode in and introduced another man wearing jeans and a denim work shirt. He carried a rolled-up sheath of papers resembling blueprints.

"Oh, hell. He does move fast. Doesn't he?" Hailey wondered what she'd gotten herself into.

"Yeah," Casper said beside her. "You just made a deal with the devil before reading the fine print."

Clannahan greeted them both with a wide smile and gestured to the picnic bench outside. "Ah, good. You're both still here. Just the two I need a word with. I'd like you to meet my architect, Jason Caldwell, a damn fine builder." Agile and confident, Clannahan's gait bore no evidence of middle age as he continued with small talk.

"Um, Major, I didn't know you meant to move so fast on this. We need permits…"

Clannahan waved away her concern as if brushing off a minor annoyance. "Told you, taken care of. How 'bout we four sit outside where I can spread these out and you can see what we're talking about? We need to discuss what you'd like to happen and can offer a few ideas for you to consider."

At the door leading out, Hailey looked over her shoulder to see Dante rolling up his sleeves. It was the first time she'd seen him in jeans and t-shirt instead of the suits he always favored.

"Might as well go with it, partner. You'll like the outcome if not the means." Casper sighed heavily behind her then addressed her guardian. "I'm guessing I should invite Noah for this?"

"Splendid idea. I'd love a chance to get to know my ward's boyfriend."

Clannahan's warm smile didn't fool either woman. He'd begin his friendly interrogation the minute Noah set foot on the premises. They'd spoken casually a few times prior, but the major was nothing if not thorough.

Casper would be the first to recognize that and give her friend a heads-up and option to decline, not that he would. Noah embodied the confidence his aura projected.

"You want me to consider options but already have blueprints in hand?" Hailey nodded toward the light blue paper rolls in Jason's hand. "Looks like you've already made decisions." The first edge of uncertainty crept in until realizing, *Damn, that's why Trenton's been quizzing me about construction lately.*

"Nonsense, young lady. You have final say over any and all construction." Ever the gentleman, Clannahan waited until she and Casper were seated before sitting across from them both. "These are just preliminary and will change to your liking."

"You've been planning this for weeks?" Hailey mused, glancing at the blueprints of her building.

"Probably months, Hailey. He doesn't *do* impulsive, and is always in it for the long haul." Casper shook her head but studied the prints. "Nice. Is this a training area?"

"It will be, if you want. I figured it'd be appropriate to have it next to the tactical room, you know, for convenience."

"Training area? Tactical room, like, for weapons?" Hailey parroted, dollar signs running through her thoughts.

"Don't sweat the small stuff, partner." Casper pointed to the back wall. "I know it might present a minor security issue until everything's reinforced, but it'll be safe, and not look like a fortress, although a safe room might be in order..."

"What specifics are on your mind, young'n?" Clannahan studied the print as if to see its fault. "I think a safe room is a good idea. Are you thinking underground?"

"Possibly, maybe in part. The rest of the back wall, well, it might be nice to have more natural light, as in multiple sliding glass doors, like along here." Tapping indicated an area between a large board room and the area designated for training.

"*Hmm,* not a bad idea. What do you think, Hailey?" Clannahan side-glanced the architect, who nodded.

"I think that's a load-bearing wall and would be a huge pain in the butt to accomplish," Hailey replied.

"*Aw,* I doubt that." Clannahan gestured to Jason, wearing khakis and a white button-down shirt. His high and tight haircut suggested he'd also served in the military.

"Not a problem at all," the architect confirmed. "Matter of fact, it might be good to have more than one entrance... maybe bump out the wall here," said as he tapped the paper.

Specific, precise details of how to accomplish the objective took less than sixty minutes and included questions about desired style, finishes, and colors.

It was a lot to take in. A throbbing began behind Hailey's left eye as she listened to and considered each option presented, amazed at the thought behind the various possibilities.

By the time she'd made the decisions and they went inside, workers had condensed the receptionist area and prepared to begin construction.

Jeez, they don't mess around.

"Do we have a plan?" Trenton asked.

"We do, with a few nice additions. It always pays to have a woman or two help in making decisions." Clannahan handed the prints back to Jason who signaled his men to gather around a folding table.

Hailey and Casper were given the option to help with construction, as was the rest of the team. It seemed appropriate to do so, if for no other reason than as a team-building exercise.

And exercise they did. Clannahan's men worked as a cohesive unit, each confident and competent. Casper proved she could swing a hammer with the best of them, earning a lowered brow from Dante.

Hailey spent time making selections of furniture and deciding details on placements, colors, and surfaces for a kitchen capable of feeding dozens.

Noah's arrival stirred as much interest in her team as with the major. The student had spent summer vacations with a construction crew, most often with framing, but proved willing and able to help with anything asked of him.

Casper's obvious hesitancy seemed to keep her classmate wary at first, but he loosened up with time, even cracking a few jokes with Trenton.

Lunch came in dozens of containers, supplied by Clannahan's forethought. By the time shadows crawled across the floor, all were exhausted.

Chapter Four

Casper

Changes in configuration to Hailey's building took place not in slow degrees, walls erected one at a time, but in multiples, due to the number and organizational prowess of the construction team.

In fairness to Clannahan and much to Casper's surprise, he'd bowed to Hailey's suggestions while he and the architect provided structural insights.

Not only that, but the crew had worked well into the evening, long after the others called it a night. Regardless of the hours they kept, they were well-fed.

Today, Casper was glad to be back on the investigative track and leave construction behind. An open-ended mystery set her teeth on edge.

While Colson and Leigh followed the evidence, first with Yamato's autopsy at the coroner's office, then with forensics from the submerged vehicle, she and Hailey drove to the victim's temporary rental house. Dante rode with Noah, following in the teen's Trans Am.

Tight smiles and stiff postures continued the prior day's animosity between Dante and Noah, seemingly straining the limits of all, yet it was Dante who'd suggested today's pairing. A fly in the vehicle would probably suffocate from the excess testosterone present.

Yamato's pregnant wife had been relocated to a safe house via Major Clannahan, with Trenton's accompaniment, giving the two men time to compare notes after getting the widow settled. Not an ideal situation from the PI's perspective, but bound to happen at regular intervals.

"*Turn left ahead on Mahoney Road,*" Yamato grumbled from the back seat of Hailey's truck. The spirit had sulked since she'd started the engine.

"*I don't know why you want to go in my house. It's not where I was shot, and I've not invited anyone inside. It's just temporary housing during the assignment. You ladies are wasting time while warm leads are cooling.*"

"You haven't divulged the name of your employer, and we've no idea what other information you're keeping under wraps," Hailey replied. "Casper and I like to be thorough."

"*I didn't know you were going to get all sneaky and finagle a way to work with Dante. That's underhanded.*"

"What's done is done. Let's focus on finding your killer. Since you and Dante both have withheld important details, we're working the case as if he weren't part of it, except for taking the occasional tidbit he offers with a grain of salt." Casper gave a mental nudge to Simon, riding her shoulder and looking for all intents and purposes to be king of everything he surveyed.

He responded by leaping over the headrest into the back. Yamato's low growl morphed into a, "*hmm,*" moments later.

She'd noticed the capuchin monkey's penchant and ability to calm agitated spirits, especially the newly deceased. The one in the back seat had not just lost his life, but also his wife and unborn child.

"*I sent my wife a picture of this house since she's a fan of Frank Lloyd Wright's style, but I think the owner added the garage with an eye for a more modern taste.*"

"Oh, I forgot you're from the New England area. Is that fairly popular there?" Hailey asked, turning off State Highway 73 to a more remote section of the county.

"*Where we lived, yeah. She fell in love with all the glass walls and simplistic interior design. She would've loved this house.*"

Casper's thoughts revolved around her expanding family versus her Pennsylvania group. Ouray had traveled via portal south to heal Trenton's mortal wound obtained while protecting Hailey before Thanksgiving. Hence his inclusion into her southern circle.

Noah had been present at the time and earned his spot. Her partner knew the area and the locals, making Hailey's psychic talent and experience invaluable. Which left Dante as the odd man out.

The Italian held key data over her head like a carrot, knowing how much she wanted to connect with family. Regardless of his motivation, it'd become clear when he'd saved Hailey's life that he meant them no harm. That did nothing to declare his goals. He barely tolerated either teen.

Noah, on the other hand, appeared to have transparent motivation. He liked the school, and he liked her. He'd helped them during previous sneak-and-peek operations and proved he could think on his feet.

The attraction to be near him had grown disproportionate to the time they'd known each other. He enjoyed a good sense of humor and was both kind and intelligent. They were the same age and shared common interests. If Dante thought that made for a good spy, he might have a point, but she trusted the shifter.

"Hails, I was thinking. Now that you'll have a proper dojo, do you mind if Noah joins us for training? He doesn't have as much experience, but he's fast, has good instincts, and usually has a short learning curve."

"It'd be great if he'd join us. I already consider him part of our team. If and when we fully induct Colson, it'd make it easier to bring in Noah. Especially when they see what he can do with a computer and torque wrench. His car runs damn smooth."

"He's gonna teach me how to fly too."

"He's got a pilot's license?"

"He's not exactly legit, but he's been flying for five years, like everywhere. His family is close-knit, but everyone there is self-sufficient. I think there's some red tape or special hoop he needs to navigate. Can't remember the specifics."

"No doubt the major will smooth that out once he proves himself capable. I don't think there's much he can't accomplish. Did you see the plans for the paintball course?" Hailey turned into the short driveway and cut the engine. "They're gonna take down a few more trees out back."

"I think that's his nod to Colson, Trenton, and Leigh, the non-psychics," Casper agreed. "He's good at organizing a team into a cohesive unit. Clannahan's shared information with my family and said Kiera and Nicholai are gonna meet with Noah's folks. Wish I could be there for that."

"So, you're looking to meet your beau's parents? That serious, are you?"

"What? No, it's not like that. They're all psychics, some with multiple talents, you know, other than shifting. I'm curious, is all." Whatever fascination shown to her new almost-boyfriend, Major Clannahan and Dante carried it to the next level.

Though Clannahan was in favor of accepting Noah as part of the team, Noah's status as a high school senior would make that problematic for Leigh and Colson. For the time being, he'd help from the sidelines, joining the task force at a later date.

"Hails, should we expect fireworks from Noah's car? That's about as unlikely a pairing as I'll ever see. What is Dante's point, unless he's spewing poison about me? I wouldn't put *that* past him."

"I haven't figured Dante out yet." Hailey made the turn and slowed down for three deer crossing the road. "I thought a couple times yesterday they were going to have at it. Of all the places for intervention to come from, I didn't think it would be Trenton."

"Yeah, your fed is a bit hard to read at times, but he seemed to get along with Noah just fine." Casper snickered. "I did catch him scowling once in a while, probably because Noah proved a little stronger than his size and mass would dictate. Shifter blood and all that."

Hailey chuckled. "Looks like Trenton is becoming our guide as well as middle child, settling disputes and soothing ruffled feathers."

The neighborhood they'd entered was quiet with residents either at work or busy inside. A mix of architectural styles reflected the general trend of preferences over time.

"*Third house on the right. There's a key—oh, wait. You don't need one.*" The spiritual growl drifting from the back seat communicated more sentiment than the wispy words spoken to date.

The cottage encompassed one part quaint and two parts quirky personality, an older structure with mixed architecture located in an expanding neighborhood where owners showed pride in well-maintained homes.

Hailey slid out and held her hand out to stop Gunther from hopping over the seat and out. "Sorry, fella. You have to stay here for now. The windows are down, and you can keep Simon company."

Casper noticed Noah's blank expression when she exited the truck. Noah wore it most of the prior day when around Dante. Considering she'd mostly settled her differences with Trenton and accepted him as the thorn necessary in her world, perhaps Noah and Dante could also find a common middle ground.

Two constants existed to lend an old-town feel to the street. Christmas decorations adorned every yard, including giant glowing Santas, elves, and strings of colorful lights. Each side of the street also boasted an abundance of interlocking shade trees, some minus many of their leaves.

"There's a fence around back. How about we enter from the rear? Less chance of nosy neighbors watching us go in." Casper led the way and opened the gate of the wood-slat privacy fence. Its squeak reminded her of a previous mission that hadn't turned out as well. She remained wary.

Wide brick steps led to a landing where a sliding glass door offered a clear view of the interior. Dual sets of footfalls indicated the men's approach behind her.

"Shall we? Everybody grab on. Dante, you're new to the experience, so if you need to puke, please step outside." Casper held out both hands.

"No problem phasing three of us?" Hailey asked, accepting her partner's hand.

"Huh," Casper chuckled, "...not for this short period of time. I once phased three others underground in the middle of an Everglades wildfire."

Noah took her other hand and then linked with Dante, whose mouth formed a straight line of displeasure.

Noah grinned. It seemed he liked needling Dante as much as Casper liked irritating Trenton.

Inside, the air was stale but clear of the rotten food odor expected from a man living alone. Gleaming hardwoods extended to the tiled kitchen floor where wood wainscoting contrasted eggshell-colored walls.

Each spread out to look around. It was doubtful the victim secreted anything vital in the rental house, but it was a stone they couldn't leave unturned. Sometimes the smallest clue unraveled a case.

Dante circled the small living room then stopped. His manner was all business.

"Hey, you all smell that?" Noah sniffed the air with his eyes closed.

"I smell mildewed laundry." Casper wrinkled her nose, standing just in the bedroom doorway. "Jeez, Yamato, really? I saw a stacked washer and dryer in the hallway alcove."

"Hey, I'm dead. It's not like I care about laundry that didn't dry all the way."

Dante ambled down the hallway and faced Casper. "Why are you speaking to a dead person who's not here?"

So used to talking to spirits directly, Casper realized she'd forgotten to *think* her comments to the victim. She and Hailey were the only ones who could converse with them.

"Sorry. I'm a kid. If I think it, I say it. You know, lack of brain filters and all that." It didn't bear thinking what type of excuse she'd use when older.

The frown creasing the Italian's forehead was worthy of a world-class chess player. He and Noah didn't know they were getting noncorporeal help, regardless of how belligerent the victim became.

"Nuh-uh." Noah's voice grew louder as he approached the second door, his feet shuffling on wooden floors. "It's something else. More like... someone else."

"No. I've had no one else here. It must be old." Yamato floated away from her to hover beside the shifter.

Casper followed. "Do you recognize the scent, Noah?"

"No, but I will if I find him."

"Him?" Dante asked, a measure of respect raising one brow.

"Yeah, and he's a shifter." Noah moved forward cautiously until entering the master bedroom. Slow steps circled to the wall side of the bed where he pointed. "There. He marked his territory."

"Damn." Hailey knelt to study the slash marks on the side of the mattress. Pieces of foam and a wire spring poked through a long gash. "You're right. Do you know what kind?"

"Tiger."

"Well, hell. All my adult life I've investigated crime, and I have to die to learn a bigger truth."

"Were you a cop of some kind?" Casper made the mental request, hoping for a careless tidbit tossed out.

Yamato floated to hover within inches of her face but remained mute.

"You might as well tell me, I'm gonna find out anyway."

"Casper? You wanna ask your friend to come and take a look?" Hailey met her partner's gaze, unwilling to expound.

"Yeah." Casper nodded when Dante crossed both arms over his chest. He stood directly behind Yamato, the dual image more disturbing than it should've been.

"Why the secrecy? We all know about shifters." Dante uttered the last word like he'd tasted something foul.

"Because," Casper said with all the patience she could muster, "...as much as you protect your anonymity, Dante, others do too." Snagging her cell from its case, she sent a text to Kiera, whose sister Silver, a shifter and investigator, preferred to work alone.

"Speaking of shifters, Casper, did you give Noah the good news?"

Noah looked from Hailey to Casper. "What news?"

"Oh, yeah. So much has happened, I forgot. You're soon gonna have free run of a local preserve. Clannahan's searching for a place where you and any visitors you entertain can stretch their legs without worrying about hikers or hunters."

Noah's mouth formed a perfect O. "Why would he do that?" Said before he tilted his head and dawning registered in his gaze. "Probably be a hundred cameras."

"If so, it'll be to ensure no poachers wander through without detection. That's a big deal in some parts," Hailey warned. "You can always get around that by telling others to shift before entering the safe zone. That'll protect their anonymity and give them freedom."

"He's trying to make you and your family feel welcome here in Texas. Anyone who's important to the team is important to him." Casper noted Dante's eyes narrowing. It was time to address the elephant in the room, hence, she faced off with him.

"I didn't say a word, Olivia."

Glare met glare, equally stubborn, equally determined.

"You didn't have to," Casper retorted. "I have eyes, and I want to know what your beef is with Noah. As in right now."

"Fine." Dante stretched his head to one side as if preparing a speech. "Your acceptance of him might be premature. Did you think about that? How long have you known him? And... you met him at school, the same school you're investigating."

"Listen, bub." Casper poked him in the chest. "You're not my father, uncle, brother, or guardian. You have no say in what I do, where I go, or who I see."

"You," Dante made a swipe to grab the offending digit and failed when she pulled back, "...are a part of this team, same as me. *He* is not. Team members look out for each other, even when they don't like each other and have their head up their ass."

Casper had several choices, none of them good. She could phase through his manhandling, which would serve to increase his determination.

Drop-kicking him into next week would be counterproductive in promoting a working relationship between a current team member and one expected to join them in the future.

In the end, she settled for a smile and slight chuckle. "*Simon? I could use a hand in here.*" A slight weight on her shoulder announced his presence. "*Help yourself to this dipshit.*"

The arrogant Italian may not know spirits exist, but he'd feel their effects long after they parted for the day.

"Damn. That smile makes even me a little nervous." Hailey proved the peacekeeper in the end. "Hey, Dante, we get it. Noah's new, and you don't like anybody on the task force. Why don't we all take a step back and slow things down a bit?"

Dante pulled in a deep breath and tilted his head to the side. "Fine. Noah, I'm sorry to offend you. However, I think—"

"I knew it. You don't know how to back down, Dante," Casper snarled. "Everything is your way. Well, not this time, buddy. If you don't like the current team, leave."

Hailey ducked her shoulders when Simon squealed.

Dante swiped at the back of his head, then his left ear. "What the hell is this?"

"Wait, Cass. It's okay. You're both right. I can wait and earn his trust. All right?" Noah stepped between them, bumping Dante a step back. A triumphant smile back over his shoulder elicited a growl from the Italian.

"Yeah." Casper accepted Noah's arm around her shoulders before he led her away. "I'm not sure if it's you or the fact you're a shifter that ruffles his panties."

"Ya know," Hailey began, nibbling on her lower lip as if deep in thought, "...Yamato was investigating ties at the GE school, so was Donald Fitzpatrick several months ago."

"True, which is kind of odd," Casper agreed then turned to face Dante. "And another thing they *both* had in common was an Italian... whatever you are."

"I'm the Italian trying to keep two teenage misfits out of harm's way." Dante's steady voice rose in volume when stepping forward to face off with the teens.

Noah took a protective stance beside Casper, again bumping Dante's shoulder to step between them. "Yeah? That is interesting."

"Spill it, if you want us to all remain *amici*." Friends didn't come close to the actual description when considering the newly formed task force. It was more of a work in progress. Casper hardened her resolve. She didn't understand his animosity toward her or Noah.

"Fine, yes. We all knew each other. We worked the same investigation from different angles." Dante exhaled slowly, a measure of pain crossing his features. "And now, I'm the last one standing. If I could have been there to help either, I would have done so."

"He's telling the truth, guys. The three of us have been friends for years. This is hard on him too. Give him a break. Okay?"

Dante closed his eyes briefly. "Yamato was supposed to meet me. We were going to pool our information and decide on our approach. One that didn't include putting teenagers in danger."

"Does this have something to do with the fact you know a relative of mine? Are they involved in this somehow?" Casper thought back to their previous interactions and the memory of her best friend's uncle trying to kill them all. "Is my relative a psycho under investigation?"

That would explain a lot.

"This does involve a family member. One I will not divulge until I've cleared out the lowlifes infecting your school. As to your other question, yes, your relative has been called many things. Nuts might not top the list, but it sure comes close."

Yamato snickered.

Casper fisted both hands at her sides. She'd faced men like Dante before. Stubborn as hell and difficult to break. Use of force wasn't an acceptable option any more than scaring the crap out of him, not that she thought she could.

Hailey circled her waist, saying, "I think we've learned all we can here. Let's go back and see what progress the others have made. We now have picnic tables behind the loft where we can sit and talk."

"Plenty of room to bury a body too," Casper murmured over her shoulder.

"Knowing your guardian and how he works, we'll have a fully functional outdoor kitchen by the end of the week. His crew isn't messing around," Noah added.

"I have another question." Casper flicked her gaze from Noah to Dante. "Can the two of you ride back in the same car without gunfire or claws erupting?"

Noah relented first. "Yeah. Don't worry, Cass. We'll be fine. If not, I'll dump him out at fifty miles per hour. No claws needed."

His smile neglected to allay Casper's agitation.

* * * *

Dante

Smoothing the material of his slacks after sitting in the passenger seat occupied Dante's hands, a better option than strangling the kid who acted too familiar with Olivia. He still couldn't accept the idea of calling anyone Casper, a foul-mouthed teen in desperate need of a muzzle and hobbling.

Mutual fascination and raging teenage hormones did not make a good combination during any investigation, especially with a complete unknown.

"It seems yesterday's truce was short-lived," Dante tossed out hoping to elicit something other than hostility. They needed to find common ground to work together.

He couldn't imagine what hell Olivia's mother survived before succumbing to the long sweep of evil that took her life. The kid was destined for the same fate if she didn't change her ways.

"Yeah. I guess we both need to try harder, but I'll tell ya what, old man. Let's both concentrate on solving this case and see where we stand afterward. Deal?"

The cocky kid backed out of the driveway and headed toward Tempest Street. From there, he threaded his way back to the highway and eventually through Hamchet's version of rush hour. Two cars waited ahead at the stoplight near the residence remodeled for courthouse usage.

"Agreed. Seeing us at each other's throats is a distraction for the team and hard on us all."

"Why do you dislike her so much? What has she or her family done to you?" Noah eased down on the accelerator with the traffic light's change.

Colorful swags of garland and lights formed an enclosed passageway through town. Hamchet was nothing if not festive. He remembered a time long ago when his entire family would ride around just to see the Christmas decorations.

"I once knew a relative of hers."

"As in now dead?"

"Yes." Dante fiddled with the bracelet around his wrist, a memento of his own family. Received in the mail at a pivotal time in life, it had a meaning he one day hoped to share. Until then, he'd guard it with every fiber of his being.

"That doesn't explain why you obviously hate shifters. It's not just me who sees it."

Dante looked out the window at the festive window displays. Several moments passed before he could speak.

"It was a shifter who killed one of Olivia's relatives. It stamped mistrust on all things shifter-related."

"Oh, damn. Okay. I get it, and I'm sorry, but it wasn't me or mine. My pack is from Connecticut, as in, all of us. We've remained isolated until this generation, so again, it wasn't anyone related to me. I take it she doesn't know about this?" Noah asked.

"No. And I'd appreciate it if you didn't tell her. She's quite talented and capable of focus. She's also vulnerable where family is concerned. I will tell her when she is no longer in danger. And believe me when I tell you that as long as you are at the school, you are a target."

"More than the other students?"

"Probably. Yes, because of your psychic status." Dante shook his head before Noah could interrupt. "I've spoken with Clannahan, the fool. He won't pull her out. After an in-depth discussion, I had to agree. If he did pull her out, she'd find another way to go about solving the problem."

"Crap."

"For that matter, you're also a target because of your determination to be with her. If you'd like to become a day student instead of a boarder, I—"

"No. Full-time status gives me better access to the admin offices and other students." Noah headed out of town and turned toward Hailey's office. "'Sides, we don't hang out together at school."

"Smart. It's almost as though you've done this kind of thing before."

"Yeah, well, we hashed that part out in one of our first meetings. Does my family know of the danger, you think?"

"I hardly doubt it. As far as I can tell, they are not involved in anything illegal."

"Which you've checked out," Noah replied with irritation.

"Of course. As soon as Olivia's interest in you became apparent."

"You call her that, but that was the name her adopted parents gave her."

"Is it?" Dante monotoned.

"They betrayed her."

"Which doesn't reflect on her name, or her, for that matter."

"I know you have psychic talent. I feel the same hum around you as other psychics when they're experiencing high emotion."

"You can feel the presence of psychic ability?"

Noah shrugged. "Only when they're really tense, angry, whatever. Pretty much your usual state."

"Remember, you're not the only one sensitive to others' abilities. Your aura will mark you. You may not get approached, just slated for elimination."

"Sounds clinical, like the asshat organization that tried to eliminate psychics in one fell swoop. Casper described it as a worldwide effort, which would've succeeded if not for the combined efforts of various psychic groups. Keep that in mind... various psychic groups *worked together*."

Dante leveled a stare on the young upstart. "Yes. And they had a traitor among them, which is one reason she has a difficult time trusting anyone."

"That and the fact one set of foster parents spied on her for the enemy."

"Yes, psychic talent has all kinds of ramifications which should be carefully considered before making decisions. You should also know this. The forces she and her family faced in Pennsylvania were not the only ones who tried to kill or enslave talented individuals. There are others, some more sophisticated, some less. All dangerous."

"Others, as in still out there, still organizing? This isn't something you should keep to yourself. If we're in danger, we have a right to know from which direction it's coming." Noah shot a glare over his shoulder.

"I'm not sure of who or what. We're still trying to gather information, and you see where that landed Yamato."

"Fine. Hold your cards close, but if Casper gets hurt because of it, there's no rock you can hide under that I won't find you. And understand something else, I trust Casper, and she trusts me."

"That status is non-transferable to others. Trust is earned, not given, Noah."

"Yeah, I get it. So, let's earn some. Why don't you tell me about your talent? What is it?"

Working alongside an unknown could cost lives if someone failed to anticipate a likely response to a situation. They all understood it yet were unwilling to fully trust at face value.

Dante had seen the effects of a team not fully melded years ago. On the flip side, Olivia's mother had relied on the wrong person, and paid for it with her life.

"C'mon, Dante. We need to work this out for all our sakes."

As an unofficial part of the team, Noah deserved an answer. Eventually. Now wasn't the time. Not until he ensured the kid wasn't an indirect threat by association.

"Do we? I suggest we give it more time and see."

Chapter Five
Casper

Communicating with the dead was difficult at times. Inability to understand a spirit unable to speak amplified their agitation to epic proportions with no relief on the horizon.

Simon's intermittent edginess manifested in constant fidgeting and resettling on her shoulder. The next time her family visited, she'd ask Kiera to connect with the capuchin monkey and figure out the problem.

She'd waited until dark to sneak through the woods backing the school property to phase through the rear wall of Noah's room and surprise him.

When he and Dante exited his car earlier, she'd seen no blood, bruises, or evidence of the expected physical confrontation. In fact, they seemed to have called a truce.

What happened?

What could Noah have possibly said to placate Dante and diminish the obvious mistrust? Whatever it was, it had to be good and worth repeating.

They'd finished sparring in Hailey's loft, an open space with decent mats but no equipment yet. Clannahan's upgrades would include a fully stocked armory.

Due to her guardian's oversight and insistence, the loft now boasted an enclosed conference room with a table capable of seating two dozen comfortably. Clannahan didn't know how to do anything half-assed.

After the workout, Noah left, declaring the need to study for final exams. She should have been studying, too, but was curious about his sudden change in behavior.

She'd recently found through sparring with Colson and Leigh that purely human reflexes, if properly honed, rivaled that of most psychics she'd fought. She'd also earned a measure of respect from each of the sheriff's deputies.

As a side benefit, the norms gave insight into criminal behavior and activity she hadn't considered. Though purely human, the pair were intelligent, quick-witted, and experienced. In other words, useful to the team. It was likely the reason Clannahan included them in the task force.

They'd planned a nice dinner for the team, then some frank psychic conversation after Leigh and Colson left. That alone should have guaranteed his participation.

She'd taken her time strolling through the woods and considered the day's strange turn of events. The cool evening held a definite nip, reminding her of Pennsylvania winters. Snowboarding, snowball fights, and watching the dogs romp as the sky released its white burden equaled her idea of winter.

That was true until the people she cared about most went behind her back and rearranged her life without so much as a consult.

In cahoots with Clannahan, they'd formed an entire working group to look into *her* case. Well, her and Hailey's investigation.

Then, they created ongoing jobs for each team member. Where would they draw the line? In retrospect, she didn't agree with the *how* of the group's coming together, but each member had skills and were proving useful. She wondered if Nicholai went through a similar process in assembling the Pennsylvania team.

She'd ignored repeated calls from Kiera, Wyatt, and Ouray, not ready to forgive their betrayal. In a final effort to maintain a bridge of sorts, Kiera called Trenton with an update on the unknown shifter who'd entered Yamato's house. Silver stated with certainty that the intruder was no one she'd crossed in the past.

The runaround didn't mean they couldn't be professional. They still had a job to do, but she didn't have to endure the hatchet in her back without recognizing it for what it was. Lack of trust and confidence.

It wasn't the same as when her adoptive parents spied on her every move and reported to her enemy, but it was a betrayal just the same.

At times, it seemed the only one she could count on was Simon, and even he was spending more time away lately.

Lord knows where.

After Noah had blown off dinner with the team, she figured their favorite snack and a movie would provide time to talk. Maybe his ride with Dante stirred up animosity he couldn't abide. She hoped to help him iron out the wrinkles.

Other than handholding and a few stolen kisses, she and Noah kept their budding relationship low-key. She told herself the doubts cropping up stemmed from multiple betrayals of those considered close friends.

Her one previous romantic relationship ended before it had a chance to take off. New situations in life required caution, but that had gone out the window after meeting Noah. They'd just clicked. Was it authentic or had she been manipulated into feeling so much so soon?

His room's overhead light was off, as was the lamp on his desk. Clearly, he had motivations to return to campus other than studying. Unless he was cramming with a classmate.

As long as he isn't cramming into another classmate.

He hadn't struck her as a player. *That* was something Hailey would've pointed out at their first meeting.

Maybe shifters need more sleep?

Phasing the anterior portion of her face, she peeked inside his room. It took a minute to adjust to the lower light level. No sound of music or movement caught her attention. No lumpy presence broke the smooth plane of his nature-laden bedspread.

Climbing up to floor level didn't tax her energy, but seeing the room empty depleted the remnants of her hopeful mood. The bed was made, his open closet and desk neat as always.

Noah wasn't there.

That left several options. Since she was already on campus and all seemed quiet, she might as well make good use of her time and move up her snooping itinerary. Jenkins' office and computer wouldn't search themselves.

The campus was quiet as students were studying for exams or preparing to go home for the holidays. Noah had said he wouldn't return home until Christmas Day.

Looking at the empty room weighted her shoulders. Had she misplaced her trust again?

The vote to bring Noah and Dante fully into her family's circle wasn't unanimous. Neither was the timing. For once, Casper had applied the brakes in favor of clear heads during the middle of an investigation.

Is Dante's obvious suspicion of Noah based on more than speculation?

Outside again, she skimmed along the brick exterior to the end of the boys' dorm and scanned the lawn and parking lot ahead. No one dallied outside. Perhaps fate and hormones combined to intervene to help her since the girls' dorm lay on the opposite side of campus.

Casper strolled across seventy-five yards of perfectly maintained lawn before quietly crossing the side parking lot. She remained wary and expected to cross someone's path since it seemed to be her lot in life.

Despite her anger, she fired off a quick text to Wyatt to get Noah's location. It bugged the hell out of her that she lacked tech skills. Noah was willing to teach, but time was short, and learning a skill known by others on her team took low priority.

When the answer came back with a puppy dog emoji, she had to smile. He was the most difficult person to stay mad at.

Damn. I've got to learn how to navigate this security system.

To date, other concerns had taken precedence.

Noah was off-grid according to Wyatt. Not only had he turned off his phone, he'd dismantled it. Her first thought included the little redhead who usually hung on his every word at lunchtime, sucking up to him then inviting him to visit with her family over the holidays.

Earlier, they'd agreed to search the VP's office after tomorrow, once the students vacated for the holidays.

Is he meeting with someone?

The soft buzz of her phone in her jacket pocket startled her. Whatever Wyatt suspected she was up to, he knew she'd be up to her eyeballs in it and wouldn't pry now.

All cameras are offline. Can't see if someone's inside Jenkins' office. Approach with caution.

Huh, guess he figured out where I'm headed.

It stood to reason Jenkins wouldn't hide his presence in his own office, unless maybe for a particular rendezvous. If she hurried, she'd either catch a student intent on mischief or someone else checking up on the VP's activities. It didn't bear thinking Noah was an intended visitor.

Again, she checked the blueprints on her phone. The target office took up a sizable portion of the southeast corner of the building and joined with the headmaster's suite. Both were on the second floor. Whether to insulate them from the student body and staff or for more nefarious reasons remained to be seen.

They hadn't learned a lot about the administrative personnel other than what looked good on paper to prospective students. A few suspicious emails weren't conclusive evidence. She'd had few dealings with Jenkins and little cause for contact.

His secretary provided a world-class buffer according to Noah. No one got in to see the man unless vital to the school's operation. It wouldn't be hard to concoct a reason to meet, but they needed evidence for leverage.

She phased through the north side wall which put her in the student affairs department. A direct path through filing cabinets and secretaries' desks led to a hallway. On her return trip, she'd take a peek at specific records, something she would've already done if there'd been time.

Two stairways, one on either end of the building, led to the second floor.

A curved and carpeted flight of steps took her deeper into the shadows. Unlike shifters, she didn't see well in the dark and used a small penlight. She kept her body phased, then remembered to don the balaclava kept in her ever-present backpack. Anonymity numbered high in her priceless commodities.

Distractions get you killed.

Before leaving Pennsylvania, Nicholai, who'd taken her in and trained her to survive, ingrained in each lesson that lack of focus led to death. Experience had driven that fact home on a regular basis.

The mask was uncomfortably snug over her ponytail, but the holes were perfect for sight and breathing. It also covered her neck, thereby further disguising her gender. Not that she considered herself feminine. The few attempts at using makeup likened her to a child playing dress up.

At the top landing, she studied the layout ahead. A few select classrooms preceded administration offices lining the rest of the wide hallway.

Curiosity led her into the first room on the right. Initial tours through the building didn't include these rooms, nor had she suffered a burning interest to explore. Noah said they were devoid of anything significant.

A well-equipped chemistry lab with fume hoods, incubators, and coolers took up one wall. A spoked wheel on the six-by-ten safe-like structure in the back reminded her of a latched door separating submarine compartments.

What would they keep in there?

If she weren't pressed for time, she'd stick her head through the door for a peek. In passing, she noted five islands containing a variety of Bunsen burners, scales, and centrifuges waiting for prodigious minds to concoct the next lethal virus.

No wonder outside influencers wanted a piece of these kids.

Jesus. How is this room not noteworthy?

An isolated existence created a world's difference between her and these kids. Without attending a normal high school with normal kids and classroom instruction, she had no basis for comparison.

The sight raised doubts as to Noah's prior education and knowledge. He had to be on this level to attend. She sure as hell wasn't. Her specialty included spying and fighting, not concocting lethal biochemical agents or the next great computer virus.

Had Noah even been inside this room? He didn't take chemistry, which didn't make him ignorant. The possibility existed that he far exceeded the instructor's ability to teach, nullifying the need to attend.

What good was snooping without collecting evidence? Her Pennsylvania anatomy and physiology instructor could fathom the equipment from the photos taken with her phone. She looked forward to either a long and boring explanation or one that stirred excitement from myriad possibilities.

It appeared the building's architect wanted distance between these students and the ones geared toward literary pursuits. The second floor contained a limited number of classrooms, all containing desks, fewer in each room. It raised the question, *which students attend classes up here? Super geniuses?*

The other classrooms were smaller and contained less than a dozen desks. Each included space for its own tower beside it. A few of the classes she'd attended also had computers, even though each student received a laptop upon entrance. How were these machines different?

A considerable number of students here attended via scholarship aid. Now she wondered who provided said assistance, and what they required in return. Servitude could take many forms.

Jenkins' office shared a wall with his secretary's space, where Casper waited and listened for stealthy movement. It didn't warrant wasting time to scour through these files until finishing in the next room.

Simon's help granted advance warning of trouble brewing on more than one occasion. Tonight would be no exception. She'd like to know if, and how many, people were in the room ahead before entering. The spirit could hover over a shoulder unobserved and report back.

Leaning against the wall adjoining the VP's office, she touched the amulet at her neck and called him, "*Hey, buddy. How about a little help here?*"

A heartbeat later, she felt his weight and his tiny hands on her cheek and head. He fidgeted and shuffled from one shoulder to the other before settling down.

She pointed to the room ahead, knowing he'd get the message. "*Can you go and see who's there?*"

He vanished in the blink of an eye.

The capuchin monkey so often by her side, was smarter than she'd originally suspected. Perhaps spirit form changed more than the physical body. Despite lack of speech, he communicated just fine.

In less than three minutes, he returned with a squeal only she could hear. Both arms raised high and wide communicated his excitement, but little else.

In his former life, he'd resided and trained with circus performers. While he delighted the public with antics and tomfoolery, he picked their pockets clean, having learned stealth as well as caution.

More often than not, he rode her shoulder during the days when classes, other than computer science, bored her to death. Even that one hazed her vision when talk went over her head and Wyatt had taken control of her computer. Though a necessary skill she wanted and needed to learn, coding numbed her mind.

"*Am I clear on this side of the room, buddy? Tell me what's going on.*"

Extending one finger on his right hand, he slipped tiny fingers of the opposite hand under the base of her mask and lifted it slightly.

"*There's one intruder wearing a mask? Alrighty then, my kind of sneak thief.*"

Simon's tap on her head equaled a *go* sign.

With a nod to caution, she phased a portion of her face through the wallboard to note the position and activity of the intruder. This talent earned her the lead position in many missions with her Pennsylvania family.

Jenkins' office was dark, except for the masked person using a penlight to take pictures of papers spread out on the desktop. A broad back presented a perfect target for which she'd take full advantage. Size and shape suggested she'd face a male.

He wore a balaclava and dark clothing with a backpack, which obscured better definition of his form.

Time to find out.

On quiet footsteps, she phased through the wall and stopped behind her target. Her right arm slid *into* his back and up to the elbow, reaching to where she estimated the location of his lung's right lower lobe.

Experience taught her the hard way never to go to the left side. Setting off an accidental run of ventricular fibrillation induced more than pain. Some humans, especially those older, proved more sensitive to someone tweaking their heart muscle. Death was not tonight's intended outcome.

Gasping from instant agony provided various sounds with silence terminating any attempt at speech. Her prey swiveled his head to the side. Through the bottom hole of the mask, a mouth opened to reveal perfect white teeth.

"Don't move." Keeping her voice a harsh whisper helped conceal her identity while stepping around to grip his mask and rip it off.

Black hair brushed to the side with eyes impossibly wide from pain, shocked her more than the first time she'd phased her body.

"Noah? What are you doing here?" Startled, she almost unphased her hand before removing it from his chest.

"Wh-what...?" Further words failed to erupt with his explosive gasp for breath.

"I asked, what do you think you're doing?"

Instead of answering, he leaned over and braced both hands on arms locked for support. Slow in and out respiration signaled his fight for control.

"Damn. I've wondered what that felt like since you first told me you could do it."

"And now you know the rest of the story. So, what's up? Why'd you skip our meeting tonight for this?"

He squeezed his eyes shut while regulating his breathing. When he opened them, his gaze remained on the desk. "Wanted to see what Jenkins is up to. We know he's communicating with someone but haven't got the gist of what's going on. I'm tired of waiting."

"Did you find something during recent hacks?"

"Not exactly."

Casper considered his words and the circumstances. "Okay. Explain." Removing her mask granted a deep, unrestricted breath. Her bunched-up ponytail settled halfway down her back.

"We all know this guy's in cahoots with someone. It's time to figure out exactly who, how, and his objective. I intend to put an end to this."

Since she was here, she might as well continue the night's unplanned exercise. Retrieving her phone, she nudged him aside and took her own photos, sending them to Wyatt for a deep dive.

"What is all this stuff?" She didn't recognize the names on the letterhead, or the addresses. "Have you been in his computer?"

Computers were his specialty, although she wasn't yet sure how he'd stack up against Wyatt. She watched as he booted up the tower.

"I was just getting ready to look when someone shoved their hand in my chest." Noah gestured to one of the papers with four names at the top. "This, however, comes from a law firm. Look. ESQ is after each name. I don't know what the firm's area of expertise is since they're not local. We can figure that out later."

Soft light accompanied the hum of the tower as the monitor came to life and revealed an aquarium scene with piranha.

"Odd choice but somehow fitting here, I'd say." Casper watched Noah sit, sliding papers out of his way before his fingers flew over the wireless keyboard built into the desktop.

A small black and white window appeared on the screen.

"What's that?" Casper leaned in for a closer look. "I've seen Wyatt open them frequently. Then he writes a whole bunch of jumbled mess that means absolutely nothing."

"Um, remember when companies like Proton offered services with TOR anonymity?"

"The only proton I know about is a unit of electricity, or something like that."

Noah chuckled. "This is kinda similar to Proton, minus the company. Meaning, its communication developed just for him and those he communicates with through TOR."

"TOR as in the onion router, dark web stuff?"

"Exactly." Noah smiled, his face reflecting the muted glow from the monitor.

"Jeez. Hold on. Let me plug in a flash and send it to Wyatt."

"Not yet. Not until I make sure the intrusion won't shut down the system. I don't know if this guy developed the system himself or he's riding piggyback."

"Crap, I have so much to learn. You guys have got to start teaching me this stuff."

Screen after screen of weird scribble popped into view. None of it made sense until she saw what resembled an email program. "Ah, let's see who he's been talking to and what he's been saying. I'm surprised Wyatt hasn't been into this before now."

"Unlike the email clients we use on the light web, or the internet you're used to seeing, this program can only be hacked at the point of initiation or receipt. Interception along the way requires specific code, none of which we have."

Noah proved he'd earned his confidence the hard way. He truly belonged at the school by right of intelligence.

"Damn, boy. Way to go. Tell me, what do you want to be when you grow up?" Sarcasm frequently erupted during periods of insecurity. At that moment, she felt the gulf between them widen, a rift she could never breach. She wasn't a genius on any level.

"Ah, it's not that big a deal. I'll teach you. Once you get the hang of it, it all just kind of comes together at once. Don't get me wrong, I still have a lot to learn, but I've got the tools to work with. As far as what I want to do, I need time to figure out what I want my life to be, which direction to take. My family wants me home, but I'm thinking of taking a different track."

"Let me guess, your folks are increasing the pressure to return home after graduation and stay with the pack?"

"Yeah. They believe in keeping everything low-key. Hell, they'll blow a gasket when I tell them I'm staying in Texas, at least for a while."

Moonlight weaved its threads across his face. His smile, genuine and hinting at deeper feelings, drained a portion of the uncertainty and self-doubt welling in her chest.

"Oh, here we go. We have an email to—"

"*You're not supposed to be in here!*" The voice roaring through the office reverberated off the walls.

So caught up in Noah's revelation and her own worries, Casper failed to notice the approach from behind.

She grabbed Noah's shoulder and whirled to face the threat, only then realizing it was Yamato's spirit who accosted them.

Letting go of Noah, she grumbled, "Damn it, Yamato, you startled the shit out of me." Blowing out a breath and shaking her head, she realized she'd experienced too many missions to act like a newbie.

"Why are you speaking to someone who's no longer living like they're standing right next to you? I think—" Noah leaned back in his chair but kept his eyes on the screen.

Casper grinned and gripped his shoulder, tapping him on the head with her other hand and pointing to the side.

"Holy shit." Noah shoved back in his chair with a force that broke their connection and would've dented wallboard.

The chair creaked when slamming into the exterior cinderblock wall. The noise equaled a mini explosion.

"What was that? Where'd he go?"

The stance adopted proved the shifter a fighter prepared to meet any threat.

"I spoke to him because the idiot startled me, and, of course, he is standing right here." Casper stepped forward and laid her hand on Noah's forearm. "See? Noah, meet Yamato Takahashi. Yamato, meet Noah."

Noah retracted his arm, then returned to take her fingers.

"Ouch, Noah. Pull your claws in, will you?" It felt like she'd tried to make friends with a demon cat intent on maiming anyone within reach.

"Ah, sorry. I usually have better control." Noah withdrew claws erupting during his response.

"Thanks. Much better." She took his hand and squeezed. "Welcome to my world. I may not be a genius, but like yourself, there's more to me than meets the eye."

"And both of you foolish idiots are going to end up like me if you don't get the hell out of here. You should leave this to Dante, like I've been telling you all along."

"O-kay. This is new. And very cool. Hi." Undaunted by the reprimand, Noah held his hand out to touch the spirit. "I take it I can only see you if I'm touching Casper. Does this mean I can feel you too?"

"Yes." To prove his point, Yamato smacked Noah along the side of his head. *"Feel that? It's nothing compared to what Jenkins will do if he catches either of you here."*

"Yeah, yeah." Noah reseated himself and glided his chair back into position but didn't break contact with Casper. "I'm into his dark web emails. Did you get that far?" Noah challenged the spirit.

Casper giggled.

"No. obviously not. I'm not a foolish kid."

"No," Noah retorted. "You're a dead investigator."

Casper squeezed her friend's shoulder in caution. "Look, Yamato. We're here, and we're going to finish this. Might as well help us."

"Like Burke and the others? You've sent them on their way so I can't communicate with them."

"No, I didn't send them anywhere. It seems you have a lot of misconceptions about me. Why don't we have an earnest chat later on and iron out a few details?" Casper corrected.

"I'll think about it."

"Look, Yamato, I have no control over what happens after a spirit completes their unfinished business. I don't know where they go or what they do. When I can't call them, I assume they've moved on to whatever the next phase is. Wish some of you would give a few deets."

"Casper, does Trenton or the others know about spirits?"

"Just that Hailey talks with them. He knows I can phase through objects, and Ouray can heal injuries. I haven't told him much else. You'd know all this if you hadn't bailed on dinner and a frank discussion. The others aren't in the loop where I'm concerned. I want to wait until I'm sure before I tell them. Dante—"

"Is a concern. Yeah, he's really got a briar up his ass when it comes to you and me. I hope he works through whatever it is."

"Makes group meetings difficult when we have to parse our words so carefully. We should bring everybody up to speed." Casper realized the difference it would make in team dynamics.

"We'll get there eventually, but I've learned caution through experience. I'm not ready for full disclosure. Neither is my pack."

"Speaking of full disclosure, why'd you ditch us for something we were supposed to do together?"

"Because Dante is concerned we're both targets. I don't want you at risk."

"What? Damn that Italian prick. I'll rip off his little boy parts and feed them to Gunther!"

"Hold on, Casper." Noah reached up to cup the hand on his shoulder. "He didn't know I planned on doing this tonight. This was my idea."

"Then, you're an idiot. Solo missions shouldn't happen."

"You mean like the first time you entered my room?"

He had her dead to rights on that count. "Fine. From now on we stick together. Agreed?"

"Okay." Noah nodded then smiled at Yamato. "Damn, that's cool."

"*How about you two copy the emails and get the hell out of here? Work on your communication skills tomorrow.*"

"Yeah, I can decipher these later. But believe me when I say we need to have some in-depth conversations, Cass." Noah kept working, his face a mask of concentration despite the incredible revelation. He grinned every few minutes with obvious internal thoughts.

She had to hand it to him. He took things that would blow most people's minds without missing more than a few beats.

"What are you seeing so far?" Casper retrieved the cell from her jacket when it vibrated. One swipe opened the message.

I've got control of the video feeds. You need to get out. Jenkins just entered the building. Heading up south stairs. Classroom below you. Teacher's desk.

"Shit. Jenkins is coming. We gotta scoot. I'll phase us through the floor, but we might have an awkward landing on a teacher's desk." Casper motioned to Yamato. "How 'bout trying to slow him down?"

"He must've picked up his office security going down." Noah retrieved the flash used to copy files, then shut down the computer.

Fast-approaching thumps outside in the hall signaled Jenkins' rush to catch them.

"Here, grab hold. Express route down." She held her hand out expectantly.

Instead, Noah scooped her up in his arms. "No. Easier this way. I always land on my feet. Less chance of injury."

The outer door cracked open as Casper's head passed through the floor behind the desk. The knob's forceful thump against the rear wall should've broken the glass inset.

True to his nature, Noah dropped the distance to land on the desk with a quiet thud. Six inches to the right and he would've landed in a waste basket and made a lot of noise.

He dropped one arm down to set her on her feet. "Shall we?" Indicating the exterior wall, he took one step before she squeezed his hand.

"No. If he looks out the window, he'll see us running. Let's exit the way I came in." She led them north and phased them through each wall until finally exiting into cool fresh air.

"C'mon. Let's get back to my room where we can talk." Noah kept hold of her hand and urged her onward.

"How about we go to my car instead? Have you swept your room for electronic devices?"

"No... and you have a good point. I know we've kept our conversations devoid of real purpose, but there's no need to take chances."

Not only did she want to pass the obtained information directly to Wyatt, she wanted more details about Noah's conversation with Dante.

She'd learned the hard way how lone wolf behavior proved more dangerous and stretched the limits of trust. Noah belonged to a close-knit pack. It hadn't occurred he might have equal reservations concerning exposure.

Chapter Six
Casper

Last night's mission ticked off several boxes on Casper's to-do list yet initiated several more. If Noah excluded her for her own protection, he'd soon learn the error of his ways. He had a solid fifty pounds on her, but she had strong fighting tactics, having trained with the best while utilizing her abilities.

Her last exam equaled a milestone. She'd completed her first semester of school without a major incident. That marked a good reason to celebrate. She hoped nothing dampened her enthusiasm, such as finding out her boyfriend was a double-crossing, low-down, dirty spy.

Winter break officially began the moment she walked out the door and inhaled the rich scents of pine and fir trees. She'd not finished Christmas shopping yet, either for her northeastern family or the new one developing here in Texas. On second thought, she should consider it one family, expanding and suffering growing pains.

Frank conversation with Hailey's sister offered ideas on what to get for her partner. Trenton was easy enough. The others, not so much.

A shame they hadn't wrapped up the current investigation already. She wanted to concentrate on life, not death.

Both Wyatt and Noah would continue decrypting Jenkins' files and unraveling the intricate web of communications. A geek-type tenuous bond developed stronger between them each day.

School closed early with the conclusion of final exams. Students had fled the building and emptied the parking lot faster than shoppers looking for their best deal on Black Friday. She didn't mind being one of the last to leave since she hated crowds.

They'd planned on spending the rest of the day working at Hailey's loft. Side benefits of good food and a fully functional training area made the decision a no-brainer.

She paused at the top of the steps when someone cleared their throat behind her.

"Hey, Casper. Wait up a minute." Melody Gingham offered a tenuous smile.

They hadn't spoken much since Casper's party weeks prior. It was unfortunate her partner's gift resulted in freaking out the copper-haired senior. Hailey had helped with entertainment, regaling each student with a "psychic reading" that included some anecdotal tidbit from their past.

Melody excelled at anything related to linguistics and numbers, an unusual combination in their world. Rumor had it that she also held incredible talent with patterns. Her presence in computer science seemed a little off, but maybe she wanted to branch out.

"Hi. What's up?"

The fact Melody's uncle recently applied for a position on the school board perked the investigative team's interest. Technically not a loner, she didn't go out of her way to make friends.

Casper had yet to find the appropriate subject to draw the rail-thin junior into a meaningful conversation.

"I was checking my email, and I think I got something by mistake. It's from my uncle. When I opened it up, there's this whole list of numbers, letters, and well, it's a bunch of gibberish I don't understand. Could you take a look before Winters makes a sweep and sees what an incompetent mess I am?"

Crap, now?

On second thought, it was the perfect opportunity to get closer. "Sure. Let's take a look. No need to get called on the carpet for a minor setback."

In her jacket pocket, she flipped open her phone and pressed the power button twice, her signal to Wyatt for help needed. From there, he'd alert Hailey, Trenton, and the others if necessary.

"Thanks a million. My dad is so uptight about me being here. If I get in the least bit of trouble, he's gonna yank me out."

"Why? Talented as you are, you certainly belong here. What's the problem?"

Melody looked around before opening the big double-door entrance. "He and my uncle had a big argument before I came. Dad doesn't want me here, but my uncle insisted it was the best place for me, even arranged for a scholarship."

"Sounds weird. What's their beef? First time away from home for an extended period?" Casper followed her classmate down the hall and to the first-floor computer science lab.

Damn shame I didn't have time last night for further exploration.

"I-I don't know. Dad wouldn't say. But he did tell me if I didn't like it here, I could come home. Any time. So far, all the teachers have been really nice and everything's great. I want to stay."

"You'll be able to get any job you want after graduation. I'd think that would ease any father's fears." Casper wondered if Melody's father had caught wind of underhanded dealings between his brother and school administrators.

"That's what I said. He's always been practical and level-headed. It's this school he doesn't like. Says it's not a good fit for me but won't explain why."

Finding money flowing between his brother and Jenkins would definitely raise a red flag. It all warranted another look.

Casper trailed Melody to her desk and then sat. Known for not liking shoulder-surfers, she arched a brow.

"Oh, right. Yeah, sorry. I just wanted to figure out what's going on." A slight quaver in the girl's voice defied explanation.

"I'll explain in a minute." Casper's first touch of the keyboard woke the monitor. On-screen, she saw two windows. One was a black screen with so much meaningless crap. From her backpack, she withdrew a flash drive and plugged it in, thinking, *Okay, Wyatt, I hope you're on board and ready.*

She figured he'd have it fixed in less than a minute, allowing her to open a frank conversation. When Melody looked away for a split second, she turned the keyboard off and started typing at random. She'd watched Noah enough to pull off the charade.

The sudden appearance of a skull and cross bones wouldn't be Wyatt's idea of a joke. Still, she leaned in to get a closer look at the small lettering underneath.

The unexpected puff of air directed at her face from the camera on top of the monitor caused rapid eye blinking. The gas was hazy and smelled strange.

"What the hell?" Waving a hand in front of her face didn't dispel the fuzziness creeping in from the periphery of her vision.

"Sorry. Babar said I had to do it or something bad would happen to my dad."

"Your uncle's name is Babar?" She now understood why Melody's voice shook. A small hand supported her weight and prevented her face-plant on the keyboard.

Her spine turned to jelly, and acid ate at her stomach. She didn't have enough focus to phase her body, not that it mattered. She'd been knocked unconscious before and knew what approached. She didn't have the strength or coordination to escape.

In training, Nicholai always warned how distractions led to death. She'd been thinking of the day ahead and things she wanted to do. Now, she'd accomplish none of them.

Dipping her hand in her pocket, she again tapped the power button twice before a wave of nausea led to her vision narrowing to a fine point. Then, nothing.

Blackness closed in with Melody's continued whispers of, "Sorry."

****

Hailey

"This is exactly why you shouldn't send kids to investigate that damn school. Trouble comes from the least expected angle. Always." Dante swore again as he tucked his S&W SD9 at his back waist. "She's too young for this kind of assignment."

"And what makes you her boss? Hell, we don't even know how you finagled a spot on this team," Noah countered as he entered the board room.

"We'll get her back. Wyatt's getting a position on her phone as we speak." Hailey panicked inside, wondering how anyone could get the drop on her partner.

"Like they won't know to toss her cell?" Dante shouted to the room at large.

A grinding noise outside signaled Trenton's SUV skidding to a halt in front of the loft, their new headquarters.

Noah opened his computer bag on the conference table and lifted the lid. "It's only been a few minutes."

"And how long do you suppose it takes to snap a neck? Here's the video Wyatt got from the computer lab. She's unconscious at best." Dante held his phone's screen up amid a flurry of epithets.

"I saw her walking down the steps when I pulled off the lot. The only other student lagging behind was, ah, Melody Gingham. I'll ping her cell."

Dante growled. "If Jenkins knew you were in his office, they're probably using her to get to you, Noah."

"They couldn't have seen me. I wore a mask... um, most of the time."

"*Most* of the time?" Trenton asked with hands fisted on his hips as he entered the room. "Did you at least wear gloves?"

"Shit." Noah pinched the bridge of his nose between thumb and forefinger. "They got my prints and matched them to the ones taken when I arrived at school, didn't they?"

"Probably, but we can deal with that later," Trenton relented with a huff.

"I'll find her." Noah opened his laptop and then his tracking program.

"How long have you been tracking her movements?" Dante narrowed his gaze and leaned over to look at the screen, a mixture of relief and fury intertwining his features.

"For the same length of time I've been able to find all of you. We exchanged phone numbers, remember?" Noah gave Dante a one-handed shove back. "We're a team. We all take risks. We need the ability to locate each individual in case of emergency."

"I, for one, am thankful." Hailey checked her weapon and addressed Trenton. "What about Leigh and Colson?"

"I'll text them before we arrive at her location. Hopefully we'll find her without their involvement. Classes are out now, so there should only be a skeleton crew if she's still at school, yes?"

Noah nodded his agreement. "I've checked security feeds, and they're all up and running except for the cafeteria and the rear of the administration building."

"Great. This Melody and whoever she's working with have Casper, but stopped for lunch before leaving?" Hailey studied the multi-quadrant video feed on Noah's laptop.

"We know Melody's uncle is the newest to apply to the school board," Noah replied, still focused on his keyboard. "What I can't figure out is how he connected me to Casper. We've played it pretty cool on campus."

"Then they made the connection off campus. They could've been watching you since her party." Hailey thought back to when the students left. "Noah, you were the only student who stayed behind. That could've been their first lead."

"Regardless," Dante growled out. "We need to find her now."

"Double damn. Maybe they put her in a cabinet or closet for temporary storage. Her last class was in the building in front of the student center." Dante stepped closer to view Noah's screen. "Show us the rest of what Wyatt sent you."

Hailey pointed to the screen showing each structure on the campus. "Here's the student center which houses the cafeteria." Indicating the building in front, she said, "This is where she has her last class."

"Someone drugged her and took her out the back door to the student center." Trenton watched the split screen. "She hasn't been taken out of there?"

On the right played the video of Casper, her bangs blown to the side as she scrutinized the screen. She blinked several times before slumping forward, her words muffled. Though she clearly spoke to someone, that person remained out of video range.

"Who is Babar? I've never heard that name before." Hailey checked her phone when it pinged. Two sets of numbers flashed across her screen before a map of the GE campus appeared.

"Doesn't matter right now." Noah closed his lid and stuffed his laptop back in its bag. "I've sent each of you coordinates. Let's go find my girl."

"Jesus, what a cluster fuck." Dante retrieved his keys. "Kid, you're with me. At least I can keep one of you idiots safe."

Trenton nudged Hailey toward the door. "Sparkles, you're with me."

Hailey led Gunther out and opened the passenger door to Trenton's SUV. Her K9 partner bolted up, then bounded between the bucket seats to the back.

The vehicle shot into motion before she'd clicked her seatbelt closed.

"Trenton, um..."

"Spill it, Sparkles. Now's not the time to hold back." They took the turn out of the industrial park on two wheels.

"Okay. I can speak with spirits. You know... ghosts."

Trenton's hands tightened on the wheel as he thought through her revelation. "The recently dead?"

"And the older dead too."

His gaze shot to Hailey, his pallor evident. "Are you saying we're too late?"

"No. Not at all. Just that I can talk to them. I haven't heard Casper, or anyone who knows her."

"So, there's this whole other world I can't see or communicate with and, what, you think she's *going* to be there?"

"I-I don't know. It's just that Casper and I have been talking about our group's dynamics. The more secrets we keep from each other, the less effective we'll be. That's all."

The federal agent nodded, then shook his head. "All right. We'll hash that out later. Okay?"

"Yeah."

Silence held sway for long minutes, each lost in their own thoughts before Trenton cleared his throat. "Does Casper communicate with spirits also?"

"It's not my place to—"

"Damn it, Hailey! I need to know. Her life could be on the line."

"Yes. Yes, she does. You already know she can phase through any object."

"Only if she's conscious, but would anyone else know that?"

"Don't know. I wouldn't see how Melody *could* know." Behind her, Gunther whined. "I know, boy. We'll get her back."

Her dog always responded to an emotionally charged situation. His instincts were good, his nose better. The problem was, Casper's scent would be all over the school.

Back roads blurred into meaningless barren scenery interspersed with older tracts of timber and thinning vegetation while her mind raced for answers. "What if more of these kids have psychic abilities? It wouldn't be the first time a group has gone after their own kind."

"Clannahan said Wyatt found two hidden accounts in Jenkins' name. The weird thing is, both are pretty much empty." Trenton swerved to go around a slow-moving compact.

"That doesn't make sense if he's taking bribes to admit kids into the school." Hailey laid a steadying hand on Gunther's shoulder.

The wolf dog whined and licked her fingers, his weight shifting with each of Trenton's turns.

"He's got to be wrapped in this mess up to his neck. I just don't understand the workings." Trenton's abrupt deceleration slid them into the lawn making the turn onto the school property.

"Casper has tried to get closer to Melody. Said she's aloof. But why would Melody work with Jenkins? Because of her uncle?" Hailey tried to think through the motives. "Melody's good with numbers and linguistics. Maybe she's psychic too?"

"One of the first questions I'll ask." Trenton swerved in the twisting driveway straddled by ornamental kale and cabbage, along with other winter-time bloomers.

No other vehicles dotted the lot other than Casper's Camaro. Most students had packed their vehicles before starting the final half-day of class, for a speedy exit afterward.

Noah's Trans Am slid to a stop beside Trenton's SUV. Whatever he and Dante had discussed during the drive intensified their demeanors exponentially.

Hailey had no doubt they'd agreed to kill whatever threat they encountered. Though one held a ten-year advantage, they each embodied the same aura, that of a predator on the prowl.

Trenton voiced no objection when Dante palmed his gun. Anyone found on the premises equaled at most a target, at least, a suspect in kidnapping.

"Any change in location?" Trenton directed his focus to Noah, who'd gripped his phone tight enough to crack the plastic.

"No. Looks like her phone is still in the student center." Noah held up his screen to show the agent. "We have three exit points from the cafeteria. One from the front. Two on the back, both within sight of the other."

"Dante, I assume either you or Noah can pick a lock?" Hailey knew how Trenton would divide the team.

Both nodded.

"Hailey, you and I will go in the front. Dante, take Noah and come in through the back. Watch out for crossfire, but don't hesitate. Questions?" Trenton waited a beat then pivoted when the others turned to go.

Across the lot and around the administration building, Hailey and Gunther kept pace with Trenton. If presented the opportunity, she wouldn't hesitate to shoot to protect her partners.

She'd been inside the student center once and remembered its layout. A grand foyer with white marble flooring stretched the entire width of the building where the student affairs office occupied one side and the bookstore claimed the other.

Ahead, the cafeteria spanned the rear half of the building with the kitchen on the right. They had no cover or concealment.

"I'll take the office, Trent. You take the bookstore."

"No." Trenton's touch of her shoulder redirected her course. "You wait at the door while I go in and clear each. Keep your eyes open and watch our six."

They hadn't started group training, which would make those dynamics interesting. Casper held equal experience in deadly fights, equivalent to Trenton's military and FBI assignments. She also held the edge when working with psychics.

On the other hand, Trenton had accumulated life experience and weaved his insight concerning human behavior into the mix. Dante was a wild card, along with Noah. Ironic that the other two members of their task force, Leigh and Colson, had less combat experience than the teenager whose presence had brought them together.

Hailey waited by the student affairs' office, scanning the interior through half-glass walls before ensuring the open space behind them held no threat.

Trenton moved with a stealth perfected in the military, but he'd not faced psychics, at least not to their knowledge. At least he'd suspect what he was up against.

The office was spacious, a long counter with a computer monitor on one end and two silk houseplants adding a rare hint of color. The counter separated a seating area from a desk and the filing cabinets beyond. Light from above the cabinets carried tiny dust particles in beams cutting the counter into oblong segments of dappled granite.

Trenton opened each of two doors, both lacking depth, judging by his quick scan and nod. On return, he gestured to the opposite side.

A multi-faceted crystal chandelier held dominion over the wide lobby designed to impress those who entered. The designer left no detail in the realm of the mundane.

The bookstore maintained the same level of elegance. In addition to school supplies, boarding students could enter the shop taking up half the space and find everything from designer shampoo to computer workstations where they could order the latest fashions.

Three stacks containing shelves running two-thirds the length of the store held books arranged by call number. The main counter ran perpendicular and remained bare except for a ceramic nativity scene.

They'd spared no expense during construction.

Trenton's footfalls made little sound. His scowl upon return betrayed the direction of his thoughts. He shook his head and signaled for her to follow him.

Distance seemed to grow with nothing but their quiet breaths and soft tread to mark their passage. Security cameras in each corner failed to show the tiny red dots indicating recorded movement.

Entrance to the cafeteria entailed one of three sets of double doors, all chocked open as if waiting for ravenous students to pour in. Instead of long rows of tables, the room contained dozens of round wooden tables, each with silk flower centerpieces.

Tinted glass windows lined the entire back wall of the building.

Ducking down, Trenton scanned the space below the tables then stood with a grimace.

"Main room's clear." Noah appeared at the entrance to the kitchen and waved them over.

Even from thirty yards, his pale face and pinched expression took Hailey's breath away. She bolted over and through the door before Trenton could stop her, shoving Noah aside in the process.

She passed the combination ovens and counter with veg prep machines to the open door of the walk-in refrigerator.

Metal rack shelving lined three walls and held an assortment of meats and ready-to-prepare dishes. Against the far unit, she saw jean-clad legs sprawled beyond where Dante crouched.

"No!" Breath froze in her lungs which refused to expand. Bile rose from her stomach to the back of her mouth.

Streaks of blood splatter contrasted brown cartons of eggs and plastic containers of cheese beside bags of local fresh vegetables. The crime scene reminded her of Clarence Burke's murder. They'd caught the shifter responsible, but not his partner, a person he couldn't identify.

The Italian stood and whirled, grabbing her shoulders before she could get around him. "It's not Olivia."

Hailey peered around his torso to see locks of copper-colored hair partially obscuring the green gaze staring into oblivion. Slumped against a stack of cartons, Melody's shirt bore the slash marks of her killer.

On her chest rested a piece of white paper stained red and held in place by a familiar phone. Casper's phone. The message conveyed in a hasty scrawl read:

Send Noah to the rear of the movie at 9 PM, alone, if you want the troublesome whore back. He and I have matters to discuss.

Duncan

"Why would they kill Melody? She obviously worked for them." Hailey knelt close to the body but was careful not to disturb blood pooled around her. "The killer was left-handed. Blood spatter is all to the right side."

The teenager had hardly begun her life, only to have it taken in senseless violence.

"This doesn't make sense. In the video, she said they threatened her father. Who? Her uncle or VP Jenkins?" Noah urged Hailey to stand and take a step back.

Trenton studied the scene. "We don't have enough details to make sense of this. For instance, is there enough bad blood between her father and uncle to induce murder? Did Jenkins order this or did Melody somehow throw a monkey wrench in the plan to get Noah?" He shook his head before meeting Noah's gaze. "And why do they want *you*? Have they caught you shifting?"

"If they know he's like them," Hailey cut into the thread of conversation, "...they might want you to join their cause, whatever that is. Or maybe they figured it was you in Jenkins' office last night. Either way, it's not good."

"They'd want to know who else has the information I retrieved last night. Who I'm working for and with," Noah replied.

Trenton retrieved his phone. "The rest of you go back to the loft. We'll devise a plan for tonight. I've got to call this in and figure out how to handle it. There's no way this can be done by the book."

"Yeah, I can't see Leigh and Colson explaining how a large cat got into a locked building, coerced a student who shouldn't be on campus into a walk-in fridge, then killed her before closing up behind him." Dante waved his hand in the general direction of the body. "Just another murder." His expression dictated it anything but normal.

"I'll call Clannahan and enlist his help. Timing is crucial." Hailey dreaded relaying the situation but knew they'd have backup. "He can sweat the details while we find Casper."

Chapter Seven
Noah

The night's plan was solid-ish. In a strange and deceptive environment where Noah could take nothing at face value, anything could happen. And usually did.

Night lowered its cloak after shopkeepers figuratively rolled up their sidewalks. To say he went out on a limb with this assignment equaled the understatement of the year.

He didn't question his current action, only the intended outcome. Both sides of the town's main street were devoid of traffic, auto and foot.

Back home, his pack prioritized anonymity and self-reliance, knowing one day he'd face the world on his own terms. He hadn't expected to fall for a black-haired spitfire who'd turn his world upside down.

He'd incorporated Casper into his life without thinking about it. She was as necessary as his next breath. By all appearances, she'd done the same; though, she didn't understand her role in his life yet.

His parents often warned him of how each shifter found their soul mate but that humans didn't always reciprocate. He hadn't wanted to scare her away by moving too fast.

She'd been suspicious when catching him snooping by himself, but his motivation to protect her rose above all else. It'd taken long moments before he could speak, not because of pain, but because she took his breath away, with her grip on his lung.

She didn't wear makeup, preferred to corral her long raven locks in a ponytail, and cared little what other people thought about her, marching to the beat of her own drum.

Now, he wondered if he'd gone too slow. If he'd kept her close, she wouldn't be in this situation.

Tones in the key of G broadcast the hour for any revelers leaving the bar down the street. The church's announcement hurt his shifter ears, though he tried not to cringe.

A nonchalant stroll carried him through the street's shadows between pools of light from streetlamps. He listened for quiet breathing or the rustle of leafy debris underfoot before entering the designated alleyway.

Short eruptions of claws from his right fingertips would extend with a thought, ready to defend in a heartbeat. His pack was small, but they exercised and trained daily. He felt comfortable in defending himself against another mountain lion or similar-sized predator.

He'd never known a like-sized cat to survive an encounter with a tiger or other large predator. It didn't matter what he faced. The bastards held Casper.

He had backup. His job entailed keeping his cool and stalling until Clannahan and Trenton could move men into position.

Tonight's pre-mission meeting didn't include Colson and Leigh since they existed outside the loop of shifters and other psychics in their midst. The latter two would remain on the fringes until fully immersed in the psychic world.

A slice of pain on his thigh warned his claws had extended.

Various odors assaulted his nose within feet of entering the four-foot passageway. None of them included Casper's scent.

"Guys, I'm getting a whiff of... something. Not sure what. Heading down the alley now." He kept his voice to a low murmur.

"Movement at the tree line behind the rear entrances."

The voice belonged to Kiera, Casper's friend. He didn't fully understand his girlfriend's family yet, but they'd been making progress—until this happened.

It stood to reason the kidnappers would keep her hidden until he satisfied whatever conditions they demanded. Hence, he needed to take this contact alive. Hailey could ferret out Casper's location with a touch and a few questions.

His first fight against a non-pack member carried the responsibility of his girlfriend's life. *Jesus. What a mess.*

He could think of two reasons she hadn't phased her way to freedom or torn out their hearts. The only viable option included drugs in her system. The other didn't bear consideration.

At the end of the passageway and before stepping out, he tapped his mic twice. Clannahan's team monitored his position with micro drones both in the trees and interspersed among the rooftops. Support wasn't close enough to assist within a reasonable time. Not in a shifter's time frame.

Never had he felt so unsure of himself.

"Your contact is waiting ahead just behind a trio of oaks. I've spotted more figures deeper in the woods." Trenton's voice radiated a calm confidence, obviously used to directing covert operations.

He listened for the click of a weapon or stealthy draw of metal against leather yet heard none. Perhaps he faced merely one man who kept his backup hidden.

Which doesn't make sense. Not with what's at risk.

A darker shadow stepped from the woods, larger than expected. In Noah's experience, the bigger the human, the bigger the animal. Power coincided with size in the shifter world.

"Who are you?" Noah sized up his opponent and steadied his nerves. Massive was the only term coming to mind. Initial assessment declared him a tiger.

Six-foot-three with red hair cut high and tight spoke volumes before the stranger opened his mouth. Massive arms crossed over his chest declared he didn't feel the need to prepare any defense.

"First things first. Give me the photos and flash drive from Jenkins' office."

Micro-currents brought the stranger's scent to his nose. Realization struck.

He's the tiger who marked Yamato's mattress.

If he were part of a pack, he might not have killed Yamato.

"At least three others are lurking close by in the woods. More are beyond our cameras."

Noah stepped from the shadows with his best attempt at a confident stride. He'd come prepared, taking a small flash drive from his pocket and tossing it to his opponent.

"Where's Casper?"

"Who else has copies? And by the way, hats off to your hacking skills."

"I'm prepared to topple the whole enchilada. Where's Casper?" He wouldn't stand a chance against four shifters, but if he could locate Casper's position, Clannahan would see to her rescue.

"We could put your skills to good use, even if you are just a panther."

"We prefer the term mountain lion."

"You're still in a different subfamily, kitty cat. But don't worry, us tigers look out for our own."

"Like you did Frank Thompson? He's rotting away in black-site seclusion as we speak." Muffled shuffling and light leaf crunching indicated others approaching from the shadowed tree line.

"Frank went off-script. That was on him. Besides, he had no other talent, unlike you."

"How do you know about me?"

"Resources. Vast resources we'd be willing to share, along with a very healthy bank account, if you swing over to our side. We'd even be willing to bring your little plaything, although as tiny as she is, well, that's your decision. All cats love to play."

"How do I know Casper's still alive?" Shifting air currents inside the tree line denied Noah the opportunity to accurately define the other scents.

"Check your phone."

On cue, his phone pinged with an incoming message. Noah fished his cell out and opened the app. On screen, he saw a still shot of Casper lying on a bunk, unconscious. An IV needle inserted at her left elbow delivered some type of drug keeping her unconscious.

"She's fine. But since we didn't know *what* she is, we decided to keep her sedated."

Noah pocketed his phone. "What's your goal here at the school?"

"Well, like my colleagues back there, my interest is purely professional. I like money."

Noah tried a different tack, hoping to circumvent, or at least delay, the coming fight. The photo he received populated the entire team's phones by now, but didn't divulge a location. "What is it you do for your boss Jenkins?"

"Hardly met the man. But we pretty much do what we're told, sans a bit of discretion." The smile playing about Duncan's lips indicated the type of play he preferred.

"Like today in the cafeteria?"

"Hey, that was necessary. The little bitch was gonna tell her daddy."

"So what? Her uncle is one of your bosses. What's the big deal?" His stomach churned with acid at the callous words he used for cover.

"He's an investor, not a boss. They exist on a lower tier but still incur a slight risk." Obviously tired of talking, Duncan said, "Listen. It's like this. You can join us and keep your girl. Or you can die, along with her. Of course, you'll take the blame for Melody's death too."

"What? I had nothing to do with her."

Duncan continued nonplussed. "Don't worry, Casper will outlive you either way. She'll be entertaining my boys. They seldom enjoy such a prize."

Noah shifted without conscious effort. The loud, *"No,"* in his ear proved an annoyance left behind with his change in shape.

He felt his tendons pop, his bones crack and reshape. The hazy glow surrounding him formed and dissipated faster than ever before. His sweatpants puddled at his feet.

Before he'd completed the arc from his leap, Duncan shifted to meet him in midair.

His opponent's change occurred faster than Noah had ever achieved, the combination of power and self-control indicative of vast experience.

He faced no novice.

Fights, in Noah's limited experience, seemed to last longer than reality dictated. His backup would arrive, but not in time.

He didn't care that he'd challenged a tiger with greater speed and strength. The image of Casper, sedated and helpless, had fried his mental wiring.

Training tactics and strategic maneuvers evaporated in the face of his rage. Casper remained forefront in his mind when he collided with the enormous cat who used his greater mass to knock him down.

Noah landed on his feet and staggered aside fast enough to avoid the deadly swipe aimed at his throat.

He was well aware of his opponent's attempt to latch onto his head and neck with his front paws then use his back claws to rip through his abdomen. In lieu of strength, Noah had speed and experience with his pack.

He swatted Duncan's face to the side before the tiger could clamp down and crush his windpipe.

Shots fired in the distance flagged another battle underway within the tree line. Shuffling and moving vegetation registered in the back of his mind. The distinctive roars declared Duncan's companions either tigers, leopards, lions, or jaguars. Over thirty species of cats existed, but only four of them could roar.

The appearance of a second tiger in his peripheral vision necessitated Noah change his position. His move wasn't fast enough to avoid the long scrape of nails along his flank.

Again, he dodged a fatal swipe before turning to face two enemies.

The wound over his right hip proved deeper than anticipated when his leg dragged behind him. Strength of will relegated the soul-searing pain to a lower level in favor of maintaining focus.

Duncan's repetitive exhalations announced his superiority and impending victory in a combination chuffing wheeze, the sound universal in any species.

Acting prematurely and without thought would not only cost him his own life, but maybe Casper's too. All the training in the world couldn't save him now.

The second cat circled and charged from the side as Noah faced off with Duncan.

Noah's position equated to the center of a circle since he'd failed to keep his back to a wall. Casper's warning about distractions haunted his thoughts. How many times had she faced a like scenario?

He felt the cat leap from behind and dragged his leg to the side to avoid the greater weight crushing him to the ground.

The cat never landed, either on him or nearby.

Duncan roared but didn't bolt forward. Instead, he cupped a small rock in his massive paw and tossed it in Noah's direction.

It, too, failed to make contact. Its disappearance created a pregnant pause in his enemy. An enemy who learned fast.

Duncan shook with rage, his next roar reverberating in the quiet night. Instead of charging into an unknown situation, the tiger pivoted and bolted for the woods.

There bore no evidence as to what or who protected him from the quick death intended, but he prayed they didn't kill the one who'd taken Casper hostage. Either in spirit, human, or cat form, Noah would dispense justice.

Noah dropped to the ground, unable to stand, much less give chase. When he'd figured his last breath was nigh, his only thoughts were for a black-haired girl who'd stolen his heart.

Shouting and shots continued to grow more distant. Noah waited, the pain in his back and hip growing exponentially before fading with his life's blood soaking the ground. Cool air bit deeper into his bones, his body languid.

A young woman with a long blonde braid approached from his right. "Hey, Noah. Remember me? I'm Kiera. We met at Casper's party before Thanksgiving."

Yeah, now he placed the voice in his ear. Noah tried to keep his eyes open, failing to comprehend much of what the blonde said.

"Looks like you could use a hand. Sorry I didn't get here sooner."

Noah waited, watching, barely keeping his eyes open.

"We've got to get you out of here. Colson and Leigh can hold others off for a bit. I understand you can heal a lot of wounds by shifting, but that's not gonna happen with this one."

He tried to lift his head but couldn't manage it.

"Hey." Hailey knelt beside him, her hand on his head. "Don't try to move, you'll just increase the bleeding."

He wanted to ask about Casper, but he didn't have the strength to shift, much less heal himself, not even to save his life.

Chapter Eight
Hailey

"Don't pick him up yet, Trenton. I need a word with him, so he doesn't struggle and cause more damage." Kiera brushed her fingers over Noah's shoulder. "Hey, fella. You're gonna be okay. Give us a bit, and you'll be right as rain."

Hailey watched the blonde psychic close the distance until kneeling eye to eye with the mountain lion.

Kiera kept one hand on the cat's head. "I can relay a message to him through our link. He's foggy, but still with us."

Hailey met the other woman's gaze with a question in her own. "Will Ouray help?"

"He'll meet us at the loft."

Kiera bent to rest her forehead against the cat, closing her eyes. "We're gonna put you in the back of Trenton's SUV. Can you handle a short ride?"

A long moment passed when no one spoke.

"Wish I could do that," Hailey commented with her hand on Noah's shoulder. "What's he saying?"

Trenton paused in sliding his hands under the shifter's body. A gaze shifting to scan the perimeter revealed his only outward sign of restlessness. "Saying?" His gaze bounced between Noah, Kiera, and Hailey. "I have a lot of catching up to do."

Kiera stood. "In time, Trenton. All in good time. I'll get Ouray and meet you two at the loft." Kiera turned and made her way toward the woods.

"Ah, Kiera, you're going the wrong way," Trenton said over his shoulder as he carefully picked Noah up. There existed a sense of wonder in the agent's expression. He'd seen Noah shift after Casper's party, but now obviously realized every advantage had consequences.

"Don't worry, Trent. We've got this. You may not remember Ouray, but you would've died without his help." Hailey guided them behind the row of buildings to his SUV where Clannahan waited.

The distance seemed to stretch exponentially with sporadic clouds creating shadows that tried to swallow them whole.

Two men with military bearing secured the entrance to the side street, quiet despite the eruption of gunfire. Curtains to apartments over shops slid to the side, but their windows remained closed. No doubt, Wyatt monitored 911 calls.

Beside the vehicle, Clannahan stood with his phone to his ear, assessing the situation and issuing orders. On seeing the trio approach, he nodded and moved to open the rear hatch.

"Where's Dante?" Trenton asked.

"Trying to chase down their leader." Clannahan arranged several blankets in a makeshift bed. "He's damn motivated, that's for sure."

Hailey knew the others weren't aware of Kiera's *other* travel arrangements. It wasn't the time for the revelation, but prior knowledge would've expedited the operation. Now, more than ever, the entire team needed to be on a level playing field.

If they could heal Noah before Leigh and Colson arrived, Noah's secret could remain hidden a little longer. Hailey had found it easier to induct others into the psychic world in small increments, unlike Trenton's introduction to the shifter world.

"Kinda jumped the gun on us, young man, but we'll discuss that later." Clannahan half-closed the hatch after Hailey slipped in and applied pressure to the worst of Noah's wounds.

A moment of silence didn't settle her racing heart. She'd watched the scene of horror unfold from the drone cameras. The plan of drawing out information until Clannahan's men could get in place went sideways when Noah shifted. He was young, inexperienced, and under hormonal influence.

"Dante and the others okay?" Hailey asked quietly.

Soft glow from Clannahan's screen cast half his face in shadow when he pivoted to speak. "All fine. It seems our opponent brought quite a few of his friends. So far, we've captured none alive. My men are clearing them out and providing local authorities with an appropriate cover story."

Trenton wasted no time nor spared an apparent thought for speed limits. They reached the town's outskirts with Clannahan in the passenger seat directing cleanup operations from his phone. Clipped commands and abbreviations, only some of which Hailey understood, ended with a low growl.

"What's the situation?" Trenton turned onto Hailey's Street and skidded into the parking lot behind her building.

"We've got three live shifters, soon to be two. The one calling himself Duncan slipped through our net. We've not recovered one damn phone. We have nothing to trace back to Casper."

"Major, I can help there. Take me to one of those bastards and we'll find the location of their base and how many are involved. I may not get current facials if they'd already shifted, and I don't know how well they communicate in animal form…" Hailey let the statement hang in hopes he or Trenton could add something.

Clannahan jerked around in his seat. "Why, yes, that just might be the ticket. Thank you, young lady. As far as their communication, I don't know if each pack is different, so I really can't answer to that, but it's something we all should know for future reference. Let's remember to ask."

Security light from the rear of her building illuminated two people approaching. If not for recognition, she'd have retrieved her gun due to the sheer size of the man.

Kiera strode beside Ouray, her blonde heritage contrasting the Native American beside her. If Trenton asked how she arrived sooner, or for the location of her vehicle, would Kiera reveal the fact she could open portals to any place she'd visited or seen?

Yet another instance where they didn't have time to play catch up.

Hailey shoved at the SUV's tailgate the minute it started to open. Her foot caught on the blanket when she tried to scoot out while keeping one hand on Noah's makeshift bandage.

Ouray steadied her with a hand on her arm. "Easy there, we'll fix this."

Hailey breathed a sigh of relief at Native American's confidence. "He got clawed down his flank. Bleeding pretty bad. Thanks for helping us out." He'd never understand the depth of her gratitude.

She'd seen the way Casper's eyes lit up when Noah walked into the room. It was the same way she felt about Trenton. Nearly losing him the prior month tested her ability to cope.

The Native American merely grunted. "We are family." He sat beside Noah. "If this one is to join us, he needs proper training. At least you'll have an appropriate facility. We can work on the rest."

"Need some help getting him inside?" Hailey asked.

"Not yet. I'll work right here. Healing while seated is less taxing." Removing the bloodied cloth exposed the deep gashes along the animal's side.

Noah's breath issued in small pants with an occasional hiss declaring his pain. His eyes remained closed.

Holding his hands over the open wound, Ouray closed his eyes in concentration. Tilting his head to the side, he murmured something low, something about kidneys and intestines.

Hailey had watched the psychic heal Trenton's wound after a bullet meant for her almost ended the agent's life. She'd never thought of her ability as truly remarkable, but this gentle giant was different. Reported to be a fierce warrior in battle, he restored the gift of life.

A soft glow streamed through the open spaces between fingers spread wide. He nodded intermittently as if putting together puzzle pieces in his mind. "He will be stiff for a while, but the damage isn't as catastrophic as I thought."

Clannahan and Trenton's low murmurs relegated to white noise before the older man was again on his phone issuing orders.

"*Hmm*, I wish I could say I remembered what he's experiencing," Trenton offered, moving closer to observe the healing process. "But I don't."

When Ouray leaned back against the interior side panel, he heaved a slow, deep breath. Perspiration dappled his forehead. "He will be fine and able to shift in a few minutes. When he does, his wounds should be healed, except, I do believe he might have a scar."

"Good." Clannahan nodded, always the commander. "We all need reminders of our vulnerability now and then. This might be the catalyst that steps up his training."

"Major, I'm gonna take Ouray home. We'll be back in a few, with reinforcements." Kiera kept an eye on the weary psychic healer as he exited the SUV's back.

"Let me know if Nicholai has any suggestions," Clannahan replied.

Nicholai, the psychic who'd helped rescue Casper off the street, shared his visions of the future when he deemed necessary. Casper had described him as cagey, always knowing more than stated, but always fair.

Hailey again sat beside Noah and rested her hand on his shoulder. She knew when his eyes opened and his head cleared, just what he'd feel. Ouray had healed her wrist months prior after a cougar crushed the small bones and left her hand useless.

The cat's respiratory rate picked up and became irregular. Memories assaulting his mind brought him to consciousness.

Guilt for not maintaining a level head. The weight of Casper's life on his shoulders. The agony of failure. He'd worn his feelings on his sleeve, so obvious to all. That fact would keep his emotions churning and fog his insight and deductive reasoning.

Sure enough, the pain-induced shriek filling the night when his eyes first opened had nothing to do with the flank wound now healed.

She felt the rumble of his pain through the vibrations under her palm. Maintaining contact took all her willpower, the urge to withdraw from a wounded animal instinctive.

"Noah. Listen. I hope you can understand me. She's not lost to us. Please, shift so that we can find her and finish this." Hailey waited, understanding the rage shaking his body.

"Son. Hear me." Clannahan had placed a pair of BDUs in the back, retrieved for Noah. "We have two prisoners who'll lead us to her, but we'll need all hands on deck. So, shift and help us out."

Unfolding the blanket, she used a part not soaked with blood to cover him. "Go ahead, shift. I'll lower the hatch most of the way to give you privacy."

They didn't wait long.

Noah emerged, shirtless, shoeless, and full of rage. "I heard shooting. How many are still alive?"

Trenton edged Hailey to the side. "They're bringing in two for interrogation." His smile held no warmth when two black vans pulled to a stop behind them. "Looks like we have company."

Three men exited each van, carrying a fourth. Neither prisoner appeared to be conscious.

"How long until the drug wears off?" Noah unfisted his hands at his sides while stalking his prey. Claws emerged from his fingertips.

"Hold on now, son. They'll stay under until given an injection." Clannahan directed his men to take the prisoners to where three metal chairs waited.

Hailey side-glanced their unofficial benefactor and asked, "How'd you know to set this up? That we'd be successful."

"It *was* our plan B objective."

Two of Clannahan's stout soldiers secured each prisoner to a chair while the third prepared a syringe from the pack strapped to his waist. After a nod from the major, the medic injected the first prisoner.

"Now is where it gets interesting." Clannahan indicated Hailey. "I'm not clear on the specifics of how this should go. Do you need anything?"

"Nope. I got this." Hailey had no compunction about using her ability or requesting help from spirits present.

Unfortunately, they couldn't possess shifters. She remembered that when listening to the exchange between Noah and Duncan, wanting to provide immediate backup if needed.

Both prisoners dwarfed the chairs to which they were tied. The first blinked several times when he lifted his head. Confusion engulfed his aura until he shook himself and fought against his restraints. "Bitch, we've heard rumors about you. You won't get anything from us."

"I wouldn't be so sure about that." Hailey squared her shoulders. She'd never hit a defenseless person before, but then again, this man was *always* armed, or clawed.

"Major, if you'd like, it might save time if you ask questions, starting with the most pertinent. We can circle back and visit the answers later for more detail." Hailey rolled up her right sleeve, but instead of touching the red-haired shifter, she balled her hand into a fist and slammed it into his jaw.

"Not to understate the obvious, young lady, and I fully understand your anger," Clannahan murmured with a frown, "...but doesn't a broken jaw hamper his ability to answer?"

Hailey grinned wide, shaking out her fist. "Nah, it'll actually help a little if he can't talk. Less distracting that way. You ask, I'll answer for him."

"Well, then." Clannahan chuckled. "Let's get this ball rolling."

Though she couldn't direct the shifter's specific thoughts, she could pick through them. Remnants of drugs diminished his ability to block her from sifting through myriad images until finding what she wanted. Pain also clouded his focus, each a bonus for her.

When she'd laid her hand against the shifter's cheek, he jerked his head and tried to bite, so she resorted to ripping his shirt open and connecting with his massive bicep.

He continued to struggle, secure in his bonds and the two soldiers on either side of him.

"Listen, asshole. You're not going anywhere. Neither am I until I get some answers. You might as well settle down."

Fur erupted along the prisoner's jawline until a gun pressed into one temple. The soldier looked to Callahan for the order to shoot.

"Not gonna happen, moron. You are well and truly caught." Hailey looked to Trenton for a solution and security. She needed the man alive and conscious, able to think.

Trenton suggested a small dose of sedative.

The prisoner continued to fight until the drug took effect, and he slumped in his bonds. His gaze rambled from one face to another, his heavy lids struggling to stay up.

"There, good kitty-kitty," she borrowed from Casper, who'd addressed Noah the same on their initial meeting. "Shall we proceed?"

Trenton now directed the questions, prioritizing what he wanted to know.

The prisoner slobbered, unable to control much of his reactions. Several attempts to shift failed. All the while, he glared his hatred after his head bobbed up. He mangled each threat posed toward his captors.

When she stepped back and held both hands up, Clannahan moved to stand beside her. "Everything okay?"

"Yep. Just need a minute to sort this stuff out." Hailey waved off the major's supportive hand at her elbow. What she wanted was to use the prisoner's head as a punching bag.

Closing her eyes, she reordered the images received through touch, taking note and memorizing each face. Her photographer's eye would come in handy when it came time to sketch each likeness.

She nodded to herself when it appeared the events lined up in chronological order. Reviewing the information out loud further helped define specific details.

Noah's obvious desire to kill reflected back at him through the prisoner. He'd stood in silent rage, his body so wound up he shook with the need to kill. "So, this piece of trash doesn't know where Duncan's keeping Casper? Does he know who hired them?"

"No, but hopefully we'll get more out of this second guy. He's higher up in the pack." Hailey waited while the medic sedated the first prisoner to keep him ignorant of what his partner divulged.

The second prisoner was smaller and came out of his haze a little slower. Visual scan of his circumstances ended with a groan. His head bobbed twice with repeated blinking of his eyes. "You all will die for this. You've no idea who we are or what's waiting for you."

"Well, then, let's figure it out," Hailey suggested with a nod to Trenton.

Slower slurred speech, head shakes, and the inability to hold his gaze straight negated the second shifter's need for a slight bump in sedation.

To Hailey's right, Clannahan clamped a hand on Noah's shoulder when he started to move forward. "Not now, son. Patience. Watch Hailey and see how it's done. You know damn well she'd rather kill him right now, but she's focused. Always keep your objective forefront in your thoughts. It'll help with the distractions they throw out."

"Where's Casper?" Trenton asked in a calm, controlled voice.

"Fuck you, idiots and psychics. You're nothing."

Hailey inhaled slowly to maintain concentration. Images flashed through her mind. Sorting them required time and thought. Some appeared to be of an older man, an older version of the prisoner.

A relative?

No, it was a version of his future, but it faded then disappeared. Other scenes arose, replaced by the same man in a jail cell.

It took a few minutes to align the sequence in its proper order. Once done, she saw him aging in a prison cell while the other video clips of him running through a forest vanished.

It finally congealed into a linear progression of his timeline.

"Okay, interesting. I know where you are heading, but I want to know where you're keeping my partner." This time, she slapped her open palm against his chest and left it there.

A low growl rumbled his warning when his gaze appeared less foggy. Her distraction worked.

Another flurry of pictures revealed him and one other carrying Casper from the school. She followed their progress west until they loaded into a van. It was like watching a horror show, the way they all sneered at their captive.

No one touched her despite the myriad suggestions dictating their black thoughts.

This shifter was second to Duncan and watched over Casper as the van wound its way through the countryside until finally pulling to a stop in front of a secluded farmhouse.

"Gotcha." She stepped back, her gait unsteady until Trenton's strong arms wrapped around her waist. "Explosives. The house has explosives."

"Care to fill in the rest of the class?" Trenton guided her to the picnic bench to sit.

The roar of another vehicle's approach interrupted her spiel of Casper's location and the best approach for rescue. Skidding tires and slewing stones announced Dante's arrival.

No sooner had the engine stopped than he popped out and rounded his hood. Never in the time Hailey had known him had he appeared unhinged. LED security lights publicized his fury if not his intended target.

His path led him directly to Noah.

"What the fuck was that all about? We lost our only lead to Olivia because you couldn't think with your big head?"

The two males clashed, one with a roar, one on a low growl.

Noah's self-directed anger turned outward to meet Dante's first punch, catching it easily in one hand. Between the Italian's rage and the shifter's strength, the brawl that began appeared an even match.

They grappled and exchanged punches in a flurry.

Shifter strength combined with frustration won the tide when Noah knocked Dante back, who twisted to maintain his balance.

Greater experience leveled the playing field when Dante attacked for the second time.

Trenton, Clannahan, and six soldiers rushed to break up the combatants, but Noah was faster.

Whether from fury or instinct, he shifted his arm from the elbow down. Fur covered his wrist and his hand morphed into a giant paw. He rushed to meet Dante halfway, using his weight and momentum to take his opponent to the ground.

Noah shrugged off Trenton and two soldiers' weight before lifting one paw with claws extended. His downswing came fast, his claws reflecting the building's rear security lights.

Upon contact, Dante grunted and shouted his fury, his body rolling instinctively to throw off the weight. He maneuvered to all fours before standing.

Clannahan's men and Trenton separated the two forces and formed a barrier between them. It took all of them, with success granted due only to their positions.

"Enough!" Clannahan shouted. "Both of you cool down before opening your mouths."

Hailey didn't need to touch either man to know the instigating factor for the brawl. Dante didn't like to lose, and Noah felt guilty for blowing the op.

"He's not wounded," Trenton said, checking the Italian's chest for wounds.

Five circular red spots marked the Italian's chest.

Hailey reached out to touch Dante's shirt, but no evidence of puncture wounds existed. "Can you phase your body? Are you like Casper?"

Dante straightened his clothes. "I am nothing like Olivia." No blood welled up to mar the smooth expanse of skin. No slash marks marred his shirt.

"What the hell is this?" Noah choked out from behind.

Hailey whirled to see Noah shaking his hand.

The fact he no longer had tawny claws was a bonus. To see each nail replaced with a black rubber-like substance came as a shock.

The shifter pulled at each digit and held his hand up to the light.

"That is what happens when you go off half-cocked, young man." Clannahan chuckled from the sidelines.

Hailey's gaze bounced from Dante's chest to the shifter, whose lower arm still held the shape of a large cat, but with black rubber in place of claws. "What just happened?" She didn't know which question to ask first, so she started with, "I didn't think shifters could just change one part of their body."

"We can't," Noah said, then turned his wide-eyed gaze toward the PI.

Clannahan chuckled. "Looks like you can now, son. Care to change it back?"

"Um, yeah." Noah complied. Fur receded and fingers lengthened before the black substances fell to the grass. He scooped some up to examine it closer. "They were stuck on the ends of my fingers."

"That shit happens when you're unprepared. You get sidelined. I exchanged your claws for rubber. When you act like a child, you're treated like one," Dante grumbled. "Stupid kid. Had no business being out there in the first place."

"Rubber? You replaced his claws with rubber?" Trenton fingered one of the fallen pieces.

Hailey blocked Dante's path when he would've stepped around her. "Ah, no. Not yet. First of all, Noah had to go. He's the one they're after. Secondly, how'd you do that?" She looked around at the gathering, noting that the major's men didn't appear shocked.

"We all have our talents. Now, you know mine." Dante crossed both arms over his chest in a clear move to refuse further questions.

"You... that's your ability? You can change matter, change things from one substance to another?" Hailey moved closer to Noah and selected a rubber replica that had fallen away.

"Will his claws be normal when he shifts again?" Concern for the teen tightened her grip on his hand. "Shift that again and let's see."

Noah twisted his lips to the side and made a low noise in his throat. Claws, as seen earlier in the back of the SUV erupted from his fingertips.

The teen exhaled a pent-up breath then growled low in his chest. "Why didn't you intervene with Duncan? We could have Casper back by now."

"Because I have to see something to affect it, like, up close and personal."

Clannahan strode forward, having watched the entire scene play out. He slapped Dante on the back. "Good move on your part. Solid thinking. I knew you'd make a good addition to the team."

"I meant to teach him a lesson, not hurt the boy."

"All this time, you've held psychic talent but didn't share?" Hailey asked, offended. "Why?"

"We all share when and as much as we're comfortable with," Dante replied brushing off his jeans.

"That's why the major accepted you." Trenton turned to Clannahan. "How come you didn't tell us?"

"It wasn't my secret to share. Now that we're all on the same page, or at least most of us," Clannahan waved a hand in dismissal, "...how about we get this operation underway?"

Ouray and Kiera exited the loft's back door, their prior arrival unchallenged by anyone. Ouray's earlier pallor after healing Noah was gone. He was all business with no sign of weakness.

"Okay, folks. Can you catch us up to speed? The others are waiting in the meeting room to plan the rescue." Kiera used her phone to take pictures of the prisoners. "I'll send these to Wyatt and see what he can dig up." The blonde had strolled out like she'd done this every day, nothing out of the ordinary.

Trenton held one hand out then shook his head. "Yeah, I know. Later."

His thoughts about Kiera's arrival would stew on the back burner until an appropriate time. He'd done the same with Hailey for months, not pushing for full disclosure.

Kiera smiled. "Yep. Priorities."

Hailey gave a brief recap of what they'd learned about Casper's location, Duncan, and his pack of shifters. "Duncan didn't lie. He wanted to be the one to kill her, which is why they've kept her under heavy sedation."

"Then we don't need these pricks around anymore." Noah bolted toward the closest prisoner.

It dawned in the next instant that Hailey should've kept the knowledge to herself. She spun and whipped her arm out to catch Noah but failed when he dodged.

Instead of making contact with his objective, Noah vanished a foot from the chair.

"Where'd you send him, Kiera?" Clannahan asked in a mild tone of disapproval.

"What the hell? What do you mean where'd she send him? How'd he vanish like that?" Trenton moved to stand where the teen had been moments prior.

"To the end of the road. He'll have time to cool off while running back." Kiera waved off other questions with one hand. "Later, Trenton. Hailey, where's Casper?"

Before she could answer, both Colson and Leigh pulled into the back lot. Each held tight expressions, but Leigh was the first out and to speak. "Where is she?"

Hailey described the location with as much detail as possible, ending with the street's name as Noah rejoined the group.

"I don't know who did that, but not cool. Not cool *at all*." Noah scanned the faces, not lighting on one in particular.

Kiera smirked. No one spoke.

"Fine. We'll table it for later. But I *will* want answers."

"Let's go inside. We can pull this up on a map and devise a plan," Kiera suggested with a slight grin.

With tension high and tempers short, they'd walk a tightrope during meetings until the last two of the task force were up to speed concerning psychic abilities.

As Kiera had said, all in good time.

Chapter Nine
Noah

Each muscle in Noah's body proclaimed it a fool's errand to move when he stood and stretched at the table. He hadn't noticed the residual stiffness earlier in the grip of high emotion. Now it bit him in the ass.

Transformation in front of others occurred as a natural event in a pack of shifters. Altering only one part of his body had never happened, except for extending his claws.

"Thanks. And sorry for blowing the op." His first time out of the gate and he'd acted like a kid. Dante had a good point, which didn't mean he liked the man.

Shame over lack of self-discipline would haunt his nights forever. His pack would label him an embarrassment. Would his rash action cost Casper her life?

"We'll find her." Clannahan led the group to the loft while his men took the prisoners away.

"What will happen with them?" Dante asked hesitating at the door and hooking a thumb over his shoulder.

"They're heading to a site with no freedom outside a secure six-by-ten cell where light enters from a tube located sixty feet above them." Clannahan waited until everyone was inside, then followed.

"So, they'll be underground and climbing the walls," Dante suggested.

"Only if they can survive better than a hundred milliamps passing through their bodies while climbing smooth block walls. Of course, that's the minimum standard for prisoners. Each cell is designed specifically for the ability contained within." Clannahan smiled knowingly. "Don't worry. They'll never escape and never discuss what they know with another living soul."

"It's not the first time we've dealt with that type of ilk," Kiera cut into the conversation as they all entered the meeting room.

"Experience is a good thing." Hailey nodded to Kiera before taking a seat beside Trenton.

She reiterated what she'd learned through touch, minus the future vision. Each took note of the location on the map Clannahan mirrored from his laptop to the large screen on the wall.

Expressions remained tight around the table, expectant, and lacking the informality of recent pre-op briefings. Each member contributed what they knew or suspected.

They still didn't have full disclosure amid their team, which bred mistrust. The revelation of Dante's talent at least confirmed his rightful place on the task force.

In the center of their new conference table sat a cube shaped microphone. Knowing Clannahan, it probably housed a miniature nuclear arsenal.

"Good evening, ladies and gentlemen. My name is Nicholai Semenov. I am Casper's adopted father."

"Seems she has quite a few," Leigh murmured as she sat beside Colson.

"Yes, well, be that as it may, we should concentrate on retrieving her."

"Hold on. Why should we trust you?" Noah demanded. He'd sat apart from the others, leaving at least two chairs between himself and anyone else.

Hailey realized she had the best chance of getting through to the wary teen. "Noah, I haven't met Nicholai yet, but I know enough through many conversations with Casper, that I'd trust whatever he said. I'd trust him with my life."

"The question is, do you trust him with Casper's life?" Noah challenged.

"Yes, I would. I do," Hailey replied, hoping the matter was settled.

"Kid, you participated tonight only because the kidnappers demanded it. Remaining here now is an option we haven't discussed." Colson met the younger man's glare with one of his own.

"He will see this through to the end, then decide for himself what his next step will be." Nicholai's words and tone closed the matter of debate.

"Yes, now that we have *that* matter settled, shall we continue?" Clannahan arched a brow in Noah's direction.

"First, one more thing." Colson held up one finger, his gaze locked with Clannahan. "You are here because...?"

"I am the official head of this task force. I don't generally get involved with the day-to-day situations. Think of me as support." Clannahan rapped the table with his knuckles and said, "Okay, Nicholai, you were saying?"

"Yes, I've studied the map. Satellite isn't giving us much more to go on, but we all know there could still be any number of others present at that location."

"And the teams?" Kiera asked.

"Major, you'll provide support after Kiera, Hailey, Trenton, and Noah go into the house."

"Let me get this straight. You'd send in *one* badge, one kid, a female PI, and," Colson gestured toward Kiera, "...whatever you are, to rescue a hostage?"

"Yes. Lieutenant Colson, you and Leigh will provide overwatch from the van at the end of the street. But stay on guard as you will likely encounter hostiles. The major's men will fill out your team."

"Got it," Leigh said before her counterpart could interrupt.

"Major, you and Dante will wait at the north end of the street after dropping off the others. Part of my group will provide backup as you will encounter talented hostiles. Kiera and her team will take care of their return transportation."

"If you think I'm gonna leave them at that house and drive away, you're nuts, whoever you are." Colson crossed his arms over his chest, clearly unwilling to budge.

"I'll have alternate transportation available," Clannahan assured them all.

Clannahan flicked a button on his computer and brought up an image on the screen taking up the majority of the side wall. Using a laser pointer, he noted the target objective and items Nicholai described. "I assume Wyatt will have security systems down?"

"Yes. And the rest of us will be ready to support however necessary. If they have... talented mercenaries we haven't yet uncovered, we'll handle them."

"Talented how?" Colson demanded. "I know you've kept Leigh and me on the fringes of this operation, yet we're two of the three most qualified."

"Hailey, may I?" Nicholai asked, his voice lacking the tinny sounds of lower-quality devices.

"Uh, yes. Go right ahead." Hailey visibly paled, as if unsure how much of her abilities Nicholai would divulge.

"As you all know, Hailey receives visions through touch, a talent that has led us to know where the kidnappers are holding Casper. This is neither the time nor the place to take the lid off, as it were. You also know we are all more than the sum of our parts. Lieutenant Colson, I'm asking you to trust your teammates and know that each has much to contribute."

"Are you saying that everyone here is some kind of psychic?" Colson studied each person at the table as if in a new light. His eyes narrowed on Noah. "That would explain Noah and Dante's presence. Hell, I don't know a damn thing about either except one has an Italian accent, and the other is attached to Casper."

"Waylan." Nicholai's use of Colson's given name received immediate attention. *"You are right on that count, but this is not the proper time for enlightenment. One of our own is in great peril. She must be rescued before 11:14 PM tonight,"* Nicholai stated with certainty.

"Well, that's oddly specific. I look forward to explanations. Does this have to do with Hailey's prediction of explosives present?" Colson relented.

"Yes," Nicholai replied.

Drone surveillance footage accompanied details of what little they knew about the upcoming mission, except that there'd be more resistance than expected.

"That information came through joint effort. Hailey can explain later." Nicholai didn't expound on the PI's psychic talent with touch. Each knew enough.

Increasing wind scrubbed the overhead branches together for an eerie accompaniment to the filtered moonlight crawling along sidewalks.

Noah tilted his head back slightly for a deep breath. Covering his mic so Colson and Leigh wouldn't hear him, he said, "I can smell others upwind. Some are shifters." He stood beside the van, and scanned the street, unable to see Clannahan's other contingent with Lieutenant Colson and Leigh.

"Where?" Clannahan checked his tablet's screen showing thermal imaging. "I see five figures inside the house other than Casper. Two downstairs. Three up, one of which is sitting in a chair beside her bed."

Noah indicated first the hedgerow, then the area beside the house. "Coming from back that way best as I can tell. I can't pick up what's downwind from us."

"*Hmm,* a factor I need to keep in mind in the future." Clannahan tapped his ear mic, "Unsubs present outside and not picked up by thermals. Stay alert. The team's heading in now."

The plan was plausible with Clannahan's contingent ready to move from the north end of the street, tracking the group's progress with tiny stationary drones hidden in the trees.

From the south, Leigh and Colson maintained surveillance on the other side, joined by a select team of Clannahan's handpicked soldiers.

"If they've taken reptile form," Noah grimaced and shook his head, "...I won't pick them up since everything pretty much smells of water in this area."

"So, gators and snakes crawling the grounds this far south. Eyes open, everyone." Clannahan made notes on his digital pad.

Noah knew little about Kiera, other than she was psychic, could communicate with animals as she'd done when he was wounded, and could somehow teleport others to locations unseen. None of that told him how she would react in a pinch, which way her instincts would direct her.

Kiera urged each of the advancing team in a closed circle beside the van for a final briefing. She removed the mic from her ear and pointed to the others.

Each followed suit.

"Okay, Noah, Trenton, and Hailey. We're the rescue team. Remember, I've got us protected from the front and sides. My portals are one-way deals. We can shoot through it to the other side and nail our target. However, anything that enters *from that side* will not reach us."

"Which means when you switch it to go inside, we'll be vulnerable and anything approaching can kill us," Noah finished.

Kiera nodded then added, "Move quickly because as soon as we're in, I'll switch to protection mode, but there'll be a split-second gap between."

"We'll stay tight," Trenton confirmed with confidence.

Kiera leveled her gaze on Hailey. "You help Trenton watch our backs, and whatever you do, don't hesitate. We know Casper's not in this mix, so shoot first and forget about questions."

Casper's family included a clairvoyant who predicted the future with unerring results. It wasn't the first time she'd put her life in someone else's hands.

Still, there'd be a brief window between portal switching when they'd be vulnerable to attack. That's where Nicholai's prediction came in. Judging the time when the shooter reloaded.

The blonde psychic had declared it a small risk and given each a chance to back out without judgment.

"When you spot a merc, tap me on the shoulder and point. Trenton and Hailey, you two will watch our six and take out anything that approaches from behind. They won't be friendlies or nosy neighbors."

"Done, and just curious. You know this how?" Trenton asked.

"Consider it a fact and act accordingly," Hailey replied, smiling.

"Oh, hell. You've seen the future here?" The agent's voice drifted off to a whisper.

"Later. For now, if you trust anything, trust me with this." Hailey touched his arm to reinforce her point.

"I do. And for the record, this is gonna be one hell of a conversation. I've stored a thousand questions." Trenton chuckled.

Noah slapped him on the back. "You'll get used to it." Casper had claimed complete confidence in her mentor, which was great, but it didn't make up for lack of training together or working with an unknown. Kiera.

They all knew there'd be risk, if not the specific type. Hence, trial by fire and on-the-job training. They all knew other unique abilities existed even if they hadn't seen them in action.

Trenton had been healed by a psychic. Casper and Hailey had shared their experiences with spirits and phasing.

Noah cleared his throat. Maybe Kiera was blonder than he thought. "If you want, instead of a portal, how 'bout I shift and—"

"No need. We'll waltz right through the front door. I doubt we'll come out the same way, but we'll work that out when the time comes. For now, I'm asking for your trust."

Noah tilted his head in thought. "We know she's been drugged. We know the house is rigged to blow. Seems to me we should take out the IV so she could phase us through the explosion." Noah's reasoning received questioning glances from Trenton and Hailey.

Kiera hummed low in her throat as if considering alternatives. "One possibility, yes. However, we don't know what drug they've used or its half-life. Yes, Ouray can clear her system of drugs, but that takes time, just like it took time for you to heal, Noah. They could blow us up while we're figuring it out. Hence, we get her out then clear her system."

"And you can get all of us out of there? Like, when you sent me down the street earlier? That was kind of freaky by the way. One second, I was preparing to rip into Dante's chest, the next, I was at the end of the street slashing at empty air."

"As long as I'm conscious, I can open a portal. That's where you and Trenton come in. He won't hesitate to shoot, and your keen senses will pick up the mercs before they get to us. At least, that's our working theory."

"According to Nicholai, a man I've never met but should trust with my life."

"Yes. See, I told you all he was a quick learner." Hailey patted Noah on the shoulder.

"Fine. Let's get in there. Why not take Dante, and let him convert any bombs we find to boxes of playdough?" Noah questioned, still unsure of the plan, which didn't seem to be a plan at all.

"That's still an option, but plan B since he has to see an object to affect it, and the explosives are probably planted all around the house. That would take too much time even if we knew where to look," Kiera replied taking Noah by the hand. "Now, smile, we're supposed to look like a couple walking down the street."

"This time, you're the cougar." Noah shook his head but let himself be tugged along the sidewalk of an upper-scale neighborhood. If this house belonged to Duncan, the killer-for-hire business paid well.

Lot sizes fulfilled the requirement for privacy without losing the cozy feeling of a suburb. Ornamental trees he couldn't name anchored flowerbeds bearing colorful blooms of pansies and sweet Alyssum, according to Casper's informative floral spiel during a prior hike.

She would've avoided all this if he'd just escorted her from her last class to her car. No one else blamed him for that, except Colson and Dante, who now observed from vans parked at opposite ends of the street. Each claimed students had no business in the night's venture.

To date, it all equaled a jumbled mess laid at his feet.

Some boyfriend material I'm turning out to be.

If he couldn't protect his mate, what good was he?

The two-story colonial shed no light from any window, either upstairs or down, nor were there security lights, not that the inhabitants would need them. Even a new moon catching Earth's reflected glow and returning it was enough for shifters to navigate outdoors.

Prickling down the back of Noah's spine suggested more than one pair of eyes watched their progression down the street.

"I hear movement," Noah murmured just loud enough for his companions to hear then touched his ear mic to make sure it stayed in place. He'd never worn hi-tech equipment. It felt strange, and he wondered how long it took Casper to become accustomed to it.

Kiera offered a light squeeze in acknowledgment.

He paced his partner for the night up the brick basket-weave sidewalk lined on both sides with a sweet-smelling low hedge.

Landscape lights shaped like miniature Santa sleighs stood sentinel at intervals to illuminate the path. It seemed so wrong to see flowers in bloom amid colored reindeer when a foot of snow blanketed his hometown in Connecticut.

Blue, green, and red lights decorated each of the yards with flashing reminders of the season amongst giant blow-up figures depicting various scenes.

"I promised her we'd do something special on Christmas Day." Noah climbed the brick steps thinking if Casper were here, they'd simply walk through the front door.

"I think we should all get together at Hailey's place..." Kiera let the last drag out as if in question.

"Great idea. My mom would love to cook again for us all. Just give me a head count." Hailey paused before mounting the steps with Trenton.

During many hours in conversation talking about the mundane, family had become a favorite topic. The men and women in Pennsylvania who'd adopted Casper were such a cohesive unit he figured she'd want children of her own yet hadn't wanted to touch on a potentially sore subject.

She hadn't fully forgiven them for setting up the task force without her knowledge or involvement.

Does she see herself with toddlers tugging on her shirt sleeve one day?

At the top of the steps, Kiera paused to let Trenton and Hailey move closer. "Remember, guys. Tight grouping."

Noah's shifter hearing picked up the sound of a shell being shucked on the other side of the door. "Shotgun."

Instinct yanked Kiera in his direction, his feet already in motion. He wasn't prepared for her to withstand his strength and hold him in place.

The slug punched a hole in the door two feet in front of his chest, yet nothing struck his body. No pain knocked him down, nor did the deafening blast push him back.

"You've got one figure on the other side of your door, Kiera. Three feet clearance," Clannahan informed the group through their mics.

"Might've been nice to remember that *before* the shot was fired." Noah looked at his chest, then at the couple behind him, then to Kiera.

Multiple shots fired in quick succession.

Noah watched the force of each throwing wood shards from the door into Kiera's portal. It was the strangest thing he'd ever encountered since failing to bite an intruder's leg in his dorm room.

"Damn strange to stand here while he's shooting," Trenton murmured from behind, still holding his Glock.

"Yeah, this is cool," Noah agreed with a sheepish grin at Kiera. "You all wanna join me and Casper for a trip to visit my family?" He couldn't prevent his mind from wandering despite the circumstances.

"Focus, Noah," Kiera reprimanded. "As soon as he stops to reload, that starts our window of time to enter."

"Movement on the south side. Rounding the corner. Coming fast." Leigh's succinct details alerted Trenton to pivot with his Glock, modified with a suppressor.

The agent fired twice when the target appeared, with Hailey taking an instinctive half-step back to provide backup.

A groan, a thud, and Trenton's target dropped to the ground. Soft light reflected off the gun barrel by the man's side. Crimson seeped from the small hole in the resident's forehead.

Contrary to popular belief, suppressed fire wasn't noiseless. Since the shot through the front door announced their presence, it didn't matter.

Noah had warned them they wouldn't be able to sneak up on Duncan or another shifter. Kiera held prior experience. Hailey and Trenton did not yet understand the power and fighting prowess of large cats. Though they'd begun training in earnest, until full disclosure occurred with Leigh and Colson, they were limited to non-psychic fighting tactics.

Through the door, sudden silence reigned.

"Kiera, your other outside man just went in the back door. I see no movement around the house." In the van, Colson tapped on a keyboard in the background, his voice distracted.

The blonde psychic briefly closed her eyes and with her extended finger, drew a six-foot diameter ring. A faint glow represented the boundaries which contained thick gray fog.

"It's time to party, guys. This is our portal. We step through and stay together. Simple. Got it?"

"Got it," Noah replied, wondering if the shifters on the second floor would go after Casper.

"Remember to keep your hands and feet inside the rim at all times." Whether intended as sincerity or a joke, Kiera moved forward and tugged Noah's hand.

He picked up his foot and moved forward, figuring the worst that could happen included kicking the front door with his tennis shoe. Into the mist he moved, feeling its coolness but not the dampness expected.

Chapter Ten
Noah

Noah set his foot down inside a wide foyer. Unlike earlier when he charged Dante and a portal sent him to the end of Hailey's Street, this time he tightened every muscle in his body in preparation.

A slight tingling invaded every cell as he moved through the gray mist of Kiera's unique transportation. He couldn't prevent the full-body shudder.

With his first step, light had flooded the room from the chandelier overhead. If they thought to blind intruders wearing night-vision goggles, they'd be sorely disappointed.

He felt as much as heard Hailey and Trenton step in behind him.

"Switching portal polarity," Kiera announced with a smile, letting go of his hand.

They faced a broad-chested man dressed in tactical gear holding an automatic shotgun. Its barrel was inches from Noah's chest and held steady. The strong odor of burnt powder filled the air.

Red hair and brown eyes declared the shooter held much in common with Duncan. Size and facial similarity dictated him part of the tiger's pack and probably a relative.

He fired three more times.

Noah's knees almost buckled. He thought of all the witty crap Casper would spew at this point and smiled.

Each shot went into Kiera's portal to parts unknown.

"That was right damn stupid, I'd say." Kiera stood her ground, unflinching when the mini giant tossed his gun and charged. She'd retrieved the gun from her back waist but made no move to fire.

Before contact, the advancing redhead vanished, the same way Noah had several hours prior. He wondered where the idiot landed.

What he could see of the downstairs consisted of a large living room with two leather sofas and three wing chairs creating a circular conversational area. A broad set of stairs with storage underneath led to the upper floor. No lights or holiday swags adorned the banister. No Christmas decorations gave note of the season.

"Huh, didn't think shifters were scrooges. I'll have to check with my sister on that one. Maybe it's a local thing." Kiera's gaze scanned the room.

"Maybe his pack gets confused with the decorations, you know, climbing the tree and batting the ornaments around," Hailey suggested from behind them.

Glimpses of a dining table defined the next room when the door swung open on quiet hinges. A second clone of Duncan stepped forward and smiled.

A third kidnapper dressed in BDUs entered at the same time the distinctive metal-on-metal sound of a bullet being chambered drew Noah's attention to the top of the stairs. Shots left Kiera and Trenton's barrels before the dining room door closed.

Both of his teammates hit their mark. Kiera's thug fell against the door, its swing close prevented by the torso across the threshold.

Trenton's unsub tumbled down the steps to land in a heap lying broken at the base. Blood formed a crimson circle on his chest, his breathing wet and ragged.

Will he return as a ghost? Noah knew from conversations with Casper that spirits couldn't possess shifters. They could play hell with his teammates, however. He wouldn't be a threat until losing his pulse.

Hailey reached out to touch the gasping form. "There's one more outside. One upstairs," she whispered, listening for movement and tightening the grip on her gun handle.

It came from behind when the door opened on a soft squeak. Hailey didn't hesitate, her aim true.

The gun he carried hit the floor before he did.

"It's 11:07," Colson's voice warned in Noah's ear.
We don't have much time.

"Let's go, guys. Times a wastin'," Noah said as he tugged Kiera up the steps. He knew from the pre-op meeting and Hailey's gathered info that Casper lay in the bedroom to his right. "Portal?"

"Up and ready. When I say, 'switch,' be ready to move fast, Noah. This next part is all you, so stay focused." Kiera opened the door to the sound of multiple shots fired at point-blank range.

Again, the shots sailed harmlessly into Kiera's portal.

Unsure of what to do, the kidnapper threw his weapon, where it, too, traveled to some distant point. "Figures you'd find other ilk, shifter." Wide-set eyes with white showing clear around each pupil betrayed Duncan's disgust. "They thought you could be turned since you're from the northeast. Tried to tell him you had the hots for this bitch."

Duncan backed up and drew a knife. Holding it inches from Casper's neck, he smiled. "Now you get to watch the consequences of your actions."

Casper lay on her back with an IV in her right antecubital vein. Her face bore no sign of the strain he'd seen when facing a threat, only peace and contentment.

A bag hung from the tapered end of the four-poster bed post and delivered their drug of choice. He heard the steady sound of drops landing in its drip chamber and the soft breath moving in and out of her lungs.

Her eyes were closed, and she appeared unmolested. A thought which brought bile to the back of his throat. Any harm she incurred would lie at Noah's feet.

The scene would've stopped him in his tracks if not for Kiera squeezing his hand. Hard. Damn if the girl wasn't strong.

"Now, Noah," Kiera yelled and released her grip. "Shove him hard."

Noah leaped just as the blade of Duncan's knife dipped down, but not into Casper's neck.

The end of the sharp steel disappeared into Kiera's portal.

"Switching sides," Kiera shouted.

He didn't see the portal but knew its one-way passage would take Duncan from the room, probably to a secure site of Clannahan's designation.

The tiger shifter's reflexes were equally fast. He planted his feet and braced to meet his enemy. Whether he knew not to approach was uncertain. He'd seen the effect of Kiera's portal even if he didn't understand it.

He avoided the full brunt of Noah's momentum by twisting his body. His knife clattered to the floor.

Noah had latched onto his target's upper arms, shifting his hands to claws for purchase into softer muscle. His theory was sound and simple.

Unfortunately, Duncan's mass and strength proved greater. He twisted loose to free himself regardless of the flesh and blood left behind. Bunching his muscles and crouching, he turned his body and leaped through the window, shifting in the process.

Glass shards rained down and left trails of blood on the sill and floor.

Noah stepped closer to see the shifter land two stories down with a soft thud.

Shaking his body, the tiger looked over his shoulder and roared. A swish of his tail and he vanished into the night.

"Shit. I lost him again." Noah started his shift. This time, he'd keep his head on straight and not let himself get distracted.

Kiera's firm hand on his shoulder halted his progress. "No. We need help getting Casper out. It's twelve minutes after. We've got two minutes more or less before the big boom."

"More or less? Which is it?"

"Hard to tell, these things are not an exact science."

Hailey was yanking the IV out of Casper's arm and shaking her shoulder. "Hey, kiddo. Wakey, wakey."

"No time," Trenton said, scooping the unconscious teen into his arms. "Let's get out of here." He headed toward the door, stopped with Kiera's command.

"Hold on. We'll take my portal. Even the thick-headed shifters." Kiera closed her eyes briefly. "Opening a gateway you all can see."

Noah saw in an instant how training could make a unit's operations seamless. The agent's first thoughts went to escape, but not through supernatural means.

A silver ring six feet in diameter appeared in front of Trenton. Thick mist filled the center to make it opaque like something out of a movie.

"Go, Trenton. I'll close the portal as soon as we're through. Hurry."

Noah watched the blonde psychic hustle Hailey through the gateway after the FBI agent. Not leaving anything to chance, she grabbed Noah's hand and shoved him through on their heels.

The atmosphere morphed from scents of animal and stale cigarette smoke to fresh air and familiar trees in stepping to the side of the loft's backyard. The welcome change felt like home.

A not-so-gentle shove knocked him sideways and to the ground the minute his second step touched grass. Unprepared, he landed on his hands and knees with a glare over his shoulder. "Ah... Oh. Thanks."

Shock muffled his outrage when he saw Kiera had gone the opposite direction as force from the blast jettisoned deadly debris into the night. The muted explosion lost volume as her portal disappeared, but not before shards of wood shot through it—wooden spikes that would have impaled him.

"First, thank you. Second, damn it. Duncan got away," Noah complained looking around and realizing Trenton and Hailey stood by the picnic table with slack jaws.

"How'd you know to shove Noah?" Trenton asked, shifting Casper to a better position.

"Nicholai," was all she said.

"Where's the rest of the team?" Hailey asked, moving to offer Kiera a hand up.

"My sister's bringing them here. Colson and Leigh are riding with Clannahan's men. They'll arrive soon after." Kiera headed to the back door and gestured them to follow. "We'll use the conference room for Casper. Ouray's coming."

They'd heard over their mics indications of another firefight beginning down the street.

The major's voice rang clear and strong in Noah's ear despite the device's modification in consideration of his shifter status. *"We've engaged their support. We'll return as soon as we've cleared the area. Leigh and Colson, report but hold your position and keep your eyes open."*

"Where's Ouray?" Noah tuned everything else out in favor of following Trenton and Casper into the loft, shedding his jacket to provide her a pillow after the agent laid her gently on the conference table.

"He and the others provided backup for Clannahan," Kiera advised.

"And you know this how? I haven't heard anything over our coms."

"Because it was the plan, and someone would've hollered if they needed help."

Trenton grinned, his obvious attempt to elicit information drawing a deep sigh from Kiera. "I can't tell you how much I look forward to meeting your Nicholai. Quite a handy fellow who can predict flying wood shards, time rescue efforts per subtle moves, and with specific knowledge of how to select a team."

"Then, why didn't he warn us about Casper's kidnapping?" Noah challenged.

"He doesn't have the power to select specific visions. He doesn't always even share them. They are subject to interpretation, like with your talent, right, Hailey?" Kiera asked.

Hailey nodded. "And sometimes I get them wrong, but I have little experience with my talent, and none with battle. I look forward to learning."

Dante was the first of their team inside, making a beeline for Casper. "How is she?" Raising first one eyelid, then the other, he made a disgruntled noise in his chest. "This shouldn't have happened, Clannahan. This is why you don't send children in to do an adult's job."

Behind him, Clannahan and Ouray strode in with the Native American taking a seat by Casper's head.

When Dante refused to stop his triage, Ouray took a deep breath. "I can't work on anyone who's in physical contact with another. It's too confusing."

Dante relented with a glare.

The air was solemn and somber with the others taking a seat, none of the normal post-mission congratulations voiced in lieu of watching over the silent teen.

Noah sat on her other side, noting her diminutive size compared to his own. He vowed to keep a better eye on her. After all, keeping his distance on campus hadn't protected her. So, screw it and anyone who objected.

A soft hum vibrated from Ouray's chest as he hovered his hands beside each of her temples. A minute later, he paused. "I've not experienced this one before. I don't think it's on the open market. Kiera, get a tube of blood for my wife to study." Ouray tilted his head to the side, deep in concentration.

Noah waited for the blonde to retrieve a first-aid kit from the other room then extract the required specimen with confident movements. The same fluid consistency existed between his pack members.

Experience and training.

This new team in its infant stages could attain that status—one day, and with a lot of work. Until then, they had many revelations to share and growing pains to endure before they melded into the assemblage Kiera and her family represented.

Did Nicholai see this event as a catalyst of some sort?

Noah spent the night by Casper's bed, watching as she slept off the remnants of her mishap and reliving every mistake he'd made along the way.

When peach and cream hues arrived on the horizon, he'd come to few conclusions and had obtained little sleep.

Casper opened her eyes with the first shafts of light spearing them. He finally released the built-up tension with a sigh.

"Hey, Cass. How d'you feel?"

"Good, except for a splitting headache."

Despite knowing the others who waited in Hailey's living room would want to see her the minute she woke, he took her hand in his. He needed this moment in time. "I'm sorry I wasn't there for you, and that I screwed up with Duncan. Twice."

"What? How could you know they were after me?"

"Doesn't matter. I'll do better. I swear it. I'm gonna go tell the others you're awake, now. Be right back."

He didn't have to say anything when he stepped into the waiting accumulation of misfits. The smile on his face said it all.

They'd waited through the night, quiet and steadfast. His team.

Sprawled on the couch were Dante and Trenton with his sister Leigh. Hailey paced between the kitchen and front window, no doubt rehashing her refusal to touch Casper and learn of her ordeal.

Colson sat at the window seat overlooking the street below. In the kitchen, Clannahan kept busy making coffee.

It was Trenton who reacted first, on his feet and moving toward the spare bedroom before the others could stand. "Good. I need to see her." As their team leader, he felt responsible for everyone.

The others followed suit, piling through the door to surround the bed. What greeted them wasn't the calm young woman full of sass. No, this was someone he didn't recognize, gripped in a panic he'd never witnessed.

"Simon?" Casper's frantic scramble included repeated grasps at her neck and then checking her jeans pockets. Failure to find that for which she searched led to tossing the bedcovers back and scrambling out of bed. Top sheet followed bedspread, each searched before being thrown to the side.

"Casper, what's wrong?" Noah asked, his senses instantly alert.

"My amulet. They took my amulet."

"Oh, hell." Hailey's pallor matched her partner's.

Noah understood the ramifications, having recently witnessed her connection with spirits through the artifact worn around her neck. "We'll get it back."

Casper shook her head. "They knew you all would come. They intended to blow us all up. Did they know about my amulet too? Did they take it or just leave it behind?"

Kiera laid a calming hand on Casper's shoulder. "Hold on, kiddo. I'll talk with Nicholai and let you know if he's *seen* anything."

When finished and assured she hadn't overlooked her treasure, Casper sat, her hands loose at her sides, tears forming in her eyes. "Simon?"

Chapter Eleven
Hailey

Hailey had spent most of the night in silent conversation with Addy while resting against Trenton's shoulder. The spirit realm still baffled her, what with her sister not providing much insight, but the sense of comradery between siblings deepened her appreciation for family.

After Casper's tragic discovery and the following discussion, she needed a brief nap. She emerged from her bedroom with Gunther at her side.

"C'mon, Gunther. We've got to figure a way to find Casper's link to the spirit realm. It's a part of her just like talking with Addy has become part of me."

Her furry protector bounded out the door and *whoofed* after hearing someone in her kitchen. His paws lost traction on the tile in rounding the corner of the hallway and up to Noah, the pacer. She hadn't expected the others to stay after seeing Casper physically recovered, but instinctively knew Noah wouldn't leave her side.

Casper sat on one of the two sofas, her face devoid of all expression. She'd lost her best friend Simon all over again. Without the artifact, she could no longer communicate with the spirit realm.

Maybe I can help a little.

Before stepping into the living room, she paused and closed her eyes. *"Addy? You still here?"*

"Yeah, sis. What's up?"

"Can you find Simon? Casper would know he's here with one touch even if she can't talk with him."

"I've no idea where to look. I can try, but I'll let her feel my presence first, so she doesn't feel so alone."

"Good thinking. Thanks."

Hailey made no effort to soften her steps to the kitchen. "Mornin', everyone. Are we meeting up here now?" Accepting the coffee from Noah, she nodded to Dante and Leigh.

Both offered a subdued greeting, their gazes flicking to Casper when a slight gasp reached her ears.

"Oh, Simon? Is that you? I can't see you, but I feel your touch on my hair." Casper turned her tear-stained cheeks toward Hailey. "Is it him?"

Hailey choked on her coffee and took an extra minute to compose her answer. In the end, the truth mattered.

"No, it's Addy. She doesn't know where to find Simon." It broke her heart to see the teen visibly deflate then offer a grim attempt at a smile.

"Thanks, Addy. I wish I could tell you where to look, but I just don't know where he's been spending his time."

Noah sat beside her and took her hand in his, squeezing lightly. "Don't worry, Cass. We'll get it back."

"It may not even exist now. It could've been destroyed in the explosion for all we know. I never woke up during my time there."

Dante rounded the kitchen island with a coffee cup in one hand, tweezing his phone from his pocket with the other to view a text message. "Ah, breakfast is ready downstairs. The others have arrived for our meeting. Shall we continue down there? We'll figure this out." Ever the gentleman, he opened the door, each filing out in turn.

"I'm gonna take Gunther out back then meet you all in a few." Hailey sipped her coffee as Gunther bounded downstairs.

Her wolf dog slipped out and sniffed a few bushes around the backyard. He didn't dally, not with his ears twitching from the number of voices emanating from her office.

The prior night's conversation with Addy surfed through Hailey's thoughts. She searched for the best place to pick up their investigation.

By the time she took her seat between Casper and Trenton, the meeting was underway. Due to Clannahan's forethought, the table held takeout bags and platters of breakfast sandwiches and pastries.

"Um, not to jump the gun or coerce those who aren't ready, but I came to the conclusion last night that I think we should all consider." Hailey directed her gaze to Leigh, then narrowed her eyes on Colson. "It's time I bring you a little further into the fold."

"What does that mean?" Colson asked.

"First, let me ask you this. Do you believe in spirits?" Hailey smiled sweetly, knowing just the way she'd introduce the detective and one of three norms on their task force.

"What... like ghosts? Jesus. I think we're far enough into the crazy dimension and have enough on our plates for now. Are you sure you belong here?"

A round of guffaws erupted from each, except for Casper.

"There's someone who wants to meet you, Waylan. Say hello to Addy."

"Addy?" Colson glanced at the conference room door as if waiting for someone to walk in and join them. "We've got another person joining our task force? Please, tell me it's someone with a badge and experience."

Even Casper snickered this time. "Boy do you have a long way to go."

"Not going anywhere until someone starts explaining what's happening here." Colson swatted the right side of his neck. "Damn. It's a little late for mosquitos, isn't it?"

"Dunno about that since it's my first winter here, but I am pretty sure about this. You're meeting Addy as we speak. Yes?" Casper looked to Hailey for confirmation.

"Yep, and I didn't think you were the type to cut off your nose to spite your face, Waylan," Hailey emphasized the lieutenant's first name.

Colson rubbed the end of his nose and said, "Ow. What's going on?"

"You're pissing off my sister."

"Sister? Hailey, you don't have a sister." Colson looked to Leigh for confirmation, who just giggled.

Clannahan chortled then cleared his throat. "I think we could speed this along the good old-fashioned way. Lieutenant, how about you put both hands behind your back and hold out a few fingers."

Colson scrunched his face up but did as directed. "I think insanity is contagious around here."

"*Addy?*" Hailey asked silently, then nodded when her sister answered.

"*This guy's a douche, sis. How about I possess him?*"

"No! Don't do that." The last thing they needed was for the straight arrow to run screaming from the building.

"Don't do what?" Colson asked.

The rest of the group watched in rapt attention. No one spoke, their gazes swinging between the two facing off.

"Never mind. She says you're holding out six fingers. No, two. Now eight. Will you please make up your freaking mind?" Hailey huffed out a breath then said, "Keep it up and I'll let her possess you."

Colson sat utterly still. "Oh, fuck."

It was the kind of quiet one experienced before a great revelation.

Clannahan's shoulders trembled. Trenton shook his head.

Casper bared her teeth. "Wait till I get my amulet back. You'll be singing a different tune, old man."

"You too? You talk to ghosts?" Colson jerked sideways, ramming Leigh's shoulder. "Ow. Stop it. That's not nice."

"She says you haven't treated my partner very nice from the beginning." Hailey offered her hand up for Casper's high-five.

"Wh-what about Trenton?" Colson searched the group's faces, then pointed to the federal agent. "He gave her more guff than I did."

"Addy says she's come to terms with Trent," Hailey replied and studied her best friend since grade school. "Leigh, you're taking this well in stride. So is Dante."

"I'm not new to the world of psychics," Dante said but offered nothing further.

"Explain," Colson demanded.

"No," Dante returned with a little more vehemence than necessary.

Leigh grinned at her best friend. "I grew up with you, Hails. I've listened to everything your mom said about Vodou and the spirit world for years. With the strange things you've gotten into—and out of—I figured you've had help. From the other-worldly variety."

"Damn. All this time. You've had insider information." Colson rubbed his head where a lock of sandy blond hair suddenly stood straight up. "Tell her to stop it."

"If you want her to leave you alone, I suggest you choose your words with care and speak in a civil manner." Hailey took another sip of her coffee, trying to keep a straight face.

"Young man," Clannahan rapped his knuckles on the table in front of Colson, "...I know this is a lot to absorb, but save your questions for later. We have work to do. Oh, and I would strongly suggest a sincere apology to both members of H&C Investigations."

"Hailey and Casper." Colson frowned. "But, Hailey, you opened up shop before Casper came to Texas. How'd you know about her?"

"I just did. Sometimes you have to take things on faith." Hailey shrugged but noted Casper's slight smile. It was one of the few positive reactions visible since her awakening.

"Major, any word from Nicholai?" Casper asked, her objective obvious.

"Yes. He says the amulet still exists, but he's not sure where, and that you should retrieve it before long."

"Anything else?" Hailey understood Nicholai only shared visions when necessary. According to Casper, it drove them all nuts.

"Yes. Now that we're nearly on the same page, Ouray is going to spend some time down here to help with training. Since work on your dojo is finished, you can set up a regular schedule."

"Finally, something normal," Casper muttered.

"Normal?" Colson parroted. "Damn if I'm not behind the eight ball again. Who's Ouray? Another ghost?" Colson asked, clearly discombobulated while rubbing his left ear.

"No. He's the one who trained me, well, mostly. He helped out last night, although he didn't stick around for a proper meet and greet." Casper sat straighter in her chair, a semblance of her old self. "We call him Mountain. Don't worry, Waylan, you'll see why."

"Jesus. There's this whole other world..."

Noah pushed his chair back and stood. "If you think that's cool, and in the vein of full disclosure, then I've got something to show you."

Trenton erupted with a guffaw, obviously remembering his own induction into that aspect of the psychic world. In rapt attention, he leaned forward in his chair.

"Whoa, kid. I don't think this is the time or—" Colson held his hand up as Noah removed his shirt. "Oh, shit."

Noah rolled both shoulders as fur began sprouting on his arms. Taking several steps back from the table, he smiled. Crouching down, he bent over and coiled his body to spring. With one leap, he flew free of his jeans and landed on top of the table in front of Colson, and growled.

In the form of a mountain lion.

"Guess that answers one of *my* questions." Casper smiled. "Commando style."

"Fuck me sideways." Colson shoved back in his chair so hard it toppled to the floor, thumping his head on painted concrete. "Ow."

Noah hopped from the table and stood over the downed man. The sound rising from his chest resembled a cross of chuffing and laughing, if, in fact, great cats could do so.

"Alright. Now that we have that out of the way, I think we should continue." Clannahan stood to retrieve Noah's jeans and held them out, releasing when the animal took them between his teeth.

When Noah returned, fully dressed, Colson kept a wary eye on the teen shifter.

"Okay. Now I see why this team consists of everyone here. What I don't get, why Leigh and me?" Colson side-glanced the detective. "Please don't tell me you change into an animal or see ghosts?"

Leigh shook her head. "No. I'm like Trenton, just a normal human."

Clannahan made a low noise in his throat. "On the contrary. Each person on this team has been hand-selected for your expertise."

"Now I know why you've had Leigh and me working on the fringes. If I'd seen—oh, hell, is Duncan an animal too?" Colson rubbed his temples as if trying to ward off a monstrous headache.

"He's a tiger, and yes," Clannahan confirmed. "Until you're fully vested and have trained with psychics, you and Leigh will be liabilities. We'll work on that as we go. We're facing more than we first suspected."

"What else can there be? Oh, damn, I shouldn't ask that. I know it." Colson selected a pastry, as if that would make him look more casual in everyone's eyes. A slight shake in his hands reflected his mental status.

"Yeah, we've learned a lot over the past week. This is much bigger than just Casper and me. These guys are after psychics as well as the GE school kids." Hailey explained what she'd learned during the prior night's mission after touching the fallen shifter.

"Maybe they think a percentage of the students are psychic and figured they'd start their search for recruits there," Casper supplied, finally selecting a breakfast sandwich and soda from the table's center.

"Sounds plausible." Clannahan nodded. "Either way, this student, Melody Gingham, is involved. I think it's prudent to start there. My men will comb through the remains of the explosion and search for clues and the amulet while you concentrate on Melody and the school. Also, I—"

Hailey jerked sideways and slammed her hands over her ears with the sudden screeching that filled the room. Simon's audio reappearance came with the understanding his best friend had lost the means to communicate.

"Hailey?" Trenton grabbed her by the shoulders and pulled her close. "What is it?"

"Simon's here and he is *totally* pissed off." Hailey pulled back and sat straight. "Simon, please. Let me explain what's happened." Cursory details of the prior twenty-four hours ended with Casper's stolen amulet.

Background conversation between Clannahan and the others included Simon's history with Casper.

"Oh..." Casper tilted her head to the side and closed her eyes. The grin overtaking her face declared admission of something extraordinary. "Simon. I've missed you. We'll be able to talk soon, buddy. I won't stop until I find that amulet. Promise."

"Uh, Simon?" Colson asked.

"Is a capuchin monkey. Her friend," Hailey replied as if the most normal thing in the world.

"Right, then," Clannahan said in a way to move things along. "Trenton, I suggest you take it from here."

"Okay, let's see how we can divide and conquer," Trenton suggested with a nod to the retreating Major Clannahan.

"I think we should have at least one... paranormal in each group. Agreed?" Colson asked the room at large.

"Yes. It'd make sense if Hailey, Trenton, Casper, and I revisit the school where Melody was killed. If I understand it right, her spirit might still be there and Hailey can interview her," Noah offered.

"I understand Melody is from Montana?" asked Leigh, nodding her agreement.

"Yes, we have her uncle and father under surveillance and can fly up to interview them. Also, her body will be *found* as a result of an auto accident," Trenton stated with obvious distaste.

"She had a boyfriend at school who lives an hour north of here," Colson advised. "Dante, Leigh, and I can drive up for an interview." Pausing, he added, "How 'bout we wait and take Hailey with us? It would help to have specific details of their relationship that only Melody would know. We'll wait till you're back, Hailey. You can be the go-between."

"Wyatt uncovered bank transfers from Melody's uncle to the vice principal. For what purpose, we don't know. Something to ask the girl when you talk to her," Trenton suggested.

"What about Duncan?" Noah asked. "How do we find him?"

"He was contacted via email and phone texts." Hailey wiped her mouth after finishing her pastry. "Unless we define another access to him, we won't. But, according to what you and Casper found in his office, Jenkins is the link for students and whoever he's talking to on the dark web. That should lead us to Duncan."

"So, why don't we just go straight to Jenkins and let Hailey do her thing?" Noah asked.

"Because." Clannahan sighed. "We don't know if he's psychic, and I don't want to blow our connection to the money trail until we know more about him. We'll get to him eventually."

"Sounds like you're putting us off, Clannahan," Noah accused.

"No, he's not." Casper slapped the table in front of her. "We have a lot of experience in fighting psychics. You could walk in there, and maybe he'd throw a lightning bolt straight to your heart, killing you on the spot and making it look like a *normal* cardiac incident."

"Oh, shit. Okay. I get it. I may be a shifter, but I have a lot to learn." Noah held both hands up in surrender.

Hailey flinched when Addy murmured in her ear. *"Sis, we have a problem."*

"What?" It wasn't until everyone stopped talking and stared at her that she realized she'd spoken out loud. With a vague wave of her hand, she said, "It's Addy. Says we have a problem."

"Sis. There's some kind of disturbance going on. I'm, like, blinking in and out."

"How so? I can't see you."

"I don't know how to explain it. But I feel different."

Hailey translated the conversation to the non-psychics despite their inexperience. "Could this have something to do with the amulet? Can someone else use it?"

"Damn. It's happened before. Kiera's uncle tried to kill us all, coercing the spirits to end all psychics. They can't possess shifters and others who have a natural mental shield, but the rest of us are fair game." Casper paled, her eyes closing as if in pain. "This is bad. This is very, very bad."

"Possession? We're dealing with possession? How do you fight that?" Colson asked.

"You don't," Casper replied. "You. Just. Can't."

Chapter Twelve
Hailey

"Does anyone else find it weird and creepy that we're visiting a murder scene at school? In a refrigerator no less?" Noah climbed the marble steps to the student center, closed for the holidays but decorated to the nines nonetheless.

"I've been to worse scenes." Casper's gaze scanned the area behind them before she rolled one shoulder.

"At least it's not underwater." The more psychics Hailey interacted with, the more she understood they existed as a culture unto themselves.

Noah and Casper seemed to have ridden the same wavelength concerning worldviews since their first meeting. With the school closed until the new semester, he resided at Casper's home. By outward appearances, they hadn't taken their relationship to the next level.

Casper's guardian per school records, maintained the day-to-day operations and oversaw the home's security. Sarah hadn't mentioned issues over the new arrangement, which meant they'd accepted the shifter on some level.

In part, she credited Casper's wary status to the number and severity of upheavals in her young life. Another factor included lack of leisure time to develop relationships.

While Hailey's own life also suffered drastic changes, it was balanced by a stable and nurturing relationship with her mother and friends.

"This is the place I'd thought to make my mark in the world, or at least start. Not as a shifter, but as a person, an individual. Instead, it's changed me in ways I never could have imagined. Not that I regret meeting you all, just that people had to die to bring us together."

"Creepy or not, this is my best chance of connecting with Melody since this is where she died." Hailey watched Casper phase through the heavy glass and wood door then open it from the inside. Each filed in behind Trenton.

Casper's mood had improved with the relay of Nicholai's message that Duncan hadn't destroyed the amulet. At least she had hope.

Melody Gingham had nothing.

Through the open expanse to the cafeteria, they remained on alert. An atmosphere of death hung in the air and contrasted the abundance of Christmas decorations mocking all good things in life.

The kitchen appeared as if nothing tragic had taken place. According to Clannahan, and in concurrence with everything she now saw, his men had moved the student's body and staged the accident scene down to the last detail.

Hailey heard sobs as soon as the fridge's thick insulated metal door opened. She couldn't see the spirit, but felt the student's despair with each choking breath.

"Melody? Melody Gingham? Can we talk to you for a few moments?" It wasn't the first spirit Hailey interviewed, but it was the first kid. A fact which somehow turned everything upside down in her head.

"*You can see me?*"

"No, but I can hear you. My associates and I want to bring your killer to justice, but we need your help."

"*I didn't know. I swear I didn't.*"

"Didn't know what, hon? That they intended to kill Casper?" She hoped the spirit saw her hand motion and would come out into the kitchen proper.

Spirits didn't feel changes in heat, cold, or pain. Yet they appeared to run the gamut of emotions with little difference after they ceased to affect the world.

Hailey and her teammates weren't on level footing for the interview, so to speak. Trenton had more experience with interrogations, and she needed his input to coax out details that could further the investigation.

When Casper shut the door, they gathered around the nearest food prep area. The stainless-steel counter reflected light from the bank of windows.

"*They said they just wanted her to sit still for a full conversation, that if they approached her without drugging her first, she'd walk away and they'd lose their chance, especially if she went to the authorities.*"

"Chance for what? Did they say?" Hailey relayed the spirit's words and waited.

"Not exactly. They said they wanted some of the kids to join a special group but didn't explain its purpose."

"And after she was unconscious?" Hailey pushed, hoping Melody would be forthcoming and not give in to the emotional upheaval.

"I was told to leave. But I didn't. When I saw them carrying her out the back, I knew something was wrong. I asked Duncan what he was doing, and he dragged me in here then hit me. I don't know what with. It happened so fast, I didn't see. Then, I got cold. I woke up with a headache and... and there was this animal standing over me."

Hailey knew Duncan's talons strafed her neck and upper chest. She'd bled out in seconds. "You said something to Casper just before she lost consciousness..."

"I-I'm not exactly sure. I said I was sorry, and that they just wanted to talk to her. My uncle said I had to or something bad would happen to my father."

"Your uncle sent money to VP Jenkins, over fifty grand. Do you know anything about that?" Casper asked the question, probably realizing it could have been her on the other side of the earthly plane.

"No. Nothing. I just wanted to graduate from this school. I was doing well. Are you saying my uncle paid to get me in here?" The spirit's voice rose in disbelief.

"No, we know you earned your acceptance through merit." Hailey held her hands out in surrender. "We don't know what the money was for. I believe it had something to do with one or the other wanting to find other psychics. It looks like Jenkins pointed out specific students who were special."

"How would he know?"

Hailey relayed the question but had no clue to the answer.

Her young partner did. "If he has access to medical records, there's a blood test a geneticist can perform, well not any geneticist. The person has to know exactly what they're looking for, and there aren't many that do."

Both Trenton and Noah did a double take.

"What? One of my family is a prodigy among geneticists."

"That would mean they'd need blood from each student," Trenton suggested.

"They did ask for student volunteers to donate to the Red Cross since the news hit the air after the Florida disaster." Noah made a note on his phone. "I can check out the validity of that claim and snoop through the nurse's office records."

"And we have our own group hacker right here in Texas." Casper elbowed Noah in the side. "Kudos to us."

"Casper, you're a psychic? Why haven't you spoken to me before now?"

"Melody wants to know if you're a psychic, Casper, and why you haven't spoken to her before now," Hailey interpreted, knowing how it felt to be on the outside of a conversation.

There was nothing normal about the current situation.

Casper toyed with several of the pots hanging above her head in a rack before answering. "Psychic, yes. I haven't talked with you before now because first, I didn't know if you were aware of psychics. Secondly, I don't have my amulet. That's what lets me communicate with those in the spirit realm. The bastard Duncan took it when they took me. Did you see what he did with it?"

"No, but he took something from both of us. I'll look for it since you're helping me. I say let's nail the prick."

"She wants to nail Duncan too," Hailey relayed the content if not the anger behind it.

"Are you all psychics?"

"Right now, I'm the only one who can hear you, Melody." Hailey wasn't about to divulge team secrets, even to spirits. "Can you tell us anything about VP Jenkins? Have you had any contact with him?"

"No. Not really. I've only talked with him once, and even that was strange."

"Strange, how?" Hailey wondered what could get stranger than talking to a spirit in an empty school kitchen.

"He's weird, and his secretary is a real bitch, just so you know. Like, drill sergeant type. When I finally did sit down with him, he wanted to talk general stuff. What I liked to do, where I liked to go, that kind of thing. There was no mention of academics, future plans, current education, stuff like that."

Hailey relayed the message then nodded to Casper and Noah. "Either of you two have like conversations?"

"Not hardly." Casper shook her head. "Guess we weren't on his radar at the time."

"Not with me," Noah confirmed, then asked, "Melody, did anything unusual happen *after* you spoke with Jenkins?"

"Well, that was the first week of school, so, it's been a while. Though, I did meet Benjamin Nickerson the next day. He's my... was my boyfriend."

"Your boyfriend. I never considered that angle. Is he a student here?" Hailey asked then conveyed the conversation.

"Yes. He's in calc with Casper."

Repeating the message received a snort from her partner.

"That guy is a total douche. Thinks he's the original Casanova." Casper made a face and mock gagging noise. "I remember him at the party acting like he was all that."

"I think it'd be best if a badge or two took a shot at talking with the boyfriend since your body has just been discovered. It'll appear more natural," Trenton suggested.

"I should go with them. I might pick up something through touch." Hailey wanted nothing more than to include her young partner, but her own presence would push the boundaries of any police policy.

"I'll pull up background information on him first. Let's see what we can find as far as leverage." Trenton, quiet for the most part, had absorbed the information and would devise further plans moving forward.

"Tell us everything you know about your boyfriend, Melody. We'll take it from there." Hailey listened and jotted down notes on her phone, feeling like a voyeur.

"If it's all right, I'll tag along. I might be able to help."

And just like that, Hailey had her own personal spirit guide. She'd become accustomed to sensing their presence but couldn't see them without Casper's amulet.

The essence and mood of Christmas portrayed in passing homes decorated with enthusiasm left Hailey in a subdued type of anticipation.

She studied Leigh's profile from the back seat of Colson's unmarked sedan. At the very least, she expected recriminations from her best friend for withholding information detailing her advancing abilities. At worst, a week's cold shoulder.

What she got was a big bear hug from the woman who'd taught her to navigate dangerous waters while shooting down class V rapids.

"Damn. All this time. You know I have a million questions. And I won't quit until you've answered them all." Leigh smiled from the front passenger seat. "But I'll bide my time till we can talk over a quart of praline crunch."

She'd seen the light of burning curiosity both when Leigh swiveled in her seat and when meeting Colson's gaze in the rearview. Yet Dante hadn't flinched at their first meeting, nor was he taken by surprise by any of their psychic gifts. Of the group, he remained the biggest mystery.

"I feel like a perp sitting back here. Why couldn't we take my truck?" Hailey noted the smell of things best left unidentified.

"Give me a break." Colson pulled off the secondary road. "It's a police car. We don't often play chauffeur to the cream of society.

Leigh snickered. "We're in this vehicle because we don't know this family, and they don't know us. It's better if we present an official approach. You can play the whimpering aunt."

Dante, sitting beside her, gave a conspicuous sniff. No doubt he preferred his BMW. "Melody has an aunt this young man has never met. You can pull this off."

It still rankled that Clannahan hadn't divulged Dante's past when inserting him into the task force. It was obvious the two men were on the same page, but neither shared their reasoning.

Her entire frame tightened when seeing the mansion ahead. "Hell. More of *this* type. Let me guess, entitled, arrogant, and condescending. I'm not wearing sunglasses." If they freaked out when seeing her striking eye color, so be it.

"Don't worry, they'll get over it. Maybe it'll throw them off balance for a bit." Leigh chuckled. "I never get tired of seeing that reaction."

"If this guy is part of a psychic family, they might not react at all. That will be a tell of its own," Dante agreed.

"Is Melody still with us? You might need her to verify particular details or have to otherwise prove your relationship to her."

"Yes, she's nervous, but hanging in there," Hailey confirmed after hearing the spirit's low moan.

"Ah, I feel that." Leigh smiled and touched her cheek. "Thank you, Melody."

"She appreciates you for helping get her justice." For once, Hailey was glad spirits couldn't read her mind. If this one knew they suspected the boyfriend of using her along with others, he could have a ghost haunting his days and nights for eternity.

Dante cleared his throat before unbuckling his seatbelt. "For those who are interested, Yamato's funeral is set for the day after tomorrow."

"I'll go." Hailey wanted to support their mysterious team member as much as find out more about him.

She hadn't misread the frustration in Dante's face after Casper's kidnapping. He'd claimed to know Casper's parents, except she'd dug up records placing him in Italy when Casper was young. Maybe they'd betrayed him on some level.

"We should all go. Yamato gave his life for this case. It's the least we can do," Colson declared.

Hailey steeled herself for the part she intended to play. Depicting a grieving yet determined relative wasn't difficult, not after discovering her father's body in a root cellar and investigating his murder months prior.

Several questions burned in her thoughts, but she was hesitant to ask Melody for concern of offending their best source of information. It'd be more than bad manners. It could stall their investigation if she fled out of shame or rage.

If the young man manipulated Melody into a relationship for the purpose of obtaining information for Jenkins, she'd figure that out for herself in the coming minutes. They'd have to deal with the fallout on the fly.

Meanwhile, she could do a little investigating on her own. "*Melody, have you had a problem with or know of other spirits who've had problems with maintaining stability?*"

"*What do you mean?*"

"*Like blinking in and out, changing realms. I don't know enough about your world to be more specific.*"

"*I haven't talked with many others, but I'm starting to. I did meet Addy.*"

"*Good. My sister would be a good teacher, a guide moving forward if you're looking for one.*"

"*I-I guess so. She seems kinda cool... Looks like we're here.*"

Colson parked beside a Lexus and pocketed his keys. "Leigh, you and I can distract the parents while Dante evaluates for signs of psychic status and Hailey interviews Benjamin."

"They won't think three cops and a relative showing up for a routine accident is strange?" Leigh asked.

"Not when the student attended the GE school, and that said student was *connected* to other concerns." Dante, who'd kept his own council for most of the ride slid from the back seat.

Of the four, he appeared the one most apt to wear a badge, or at least a gun. If any of Hailey's questions touched an unguarded nerve or provoked a hostile response, it was good to have him by her side. Melody claimed her boyfriend had a temper and impulsive nature.

In Dante's presence, any weapon without moving parts could turn into an innocuous item. He could render them, however innocent, to dust.

The front door opened to emit a young man tugging a suitcase on wheels over the threshold. His foot paused in midair before descending to the first step with an awkward jolt. "Who are you?"

Medium height with dark hair and green eyes, he looked back to the door, as if regretting his timing. Blue jeans, flannel shirt, and tennis shoes relegated his trip a casual affair.

"Police, investigating your girlfriend's death." Colson pulled out his wallet and flipped it open to reveal his badge.

"It takes four cops to investigate an accident?" A mask of confusion quickly replaced his irritation.

"Who said it was an accident? We haven't released details." Dante moved to block the teen's path. "We have questions for you."

"Me? Why me? I didn't know her that well. Everybody's saying it was a car accident."

"And who is *everybody*?" Leigh asked, flipping out her badge as well. "School is closed, and the students have gone home, to whichever state they reside."

Dante took possession of the youth's luggage and pointed to the door. "Let's take this inside. This is going to take a while."

"My father's brother is a lawyer."

"Good, then I'm sure they'll both have phones." Colson's smile held no hint of warmth. "Since you just turned eighteen, we can take this to the nearest station and set you in an interrogation room if you'd prefer."

The teen took a step back, his change in attitude arrived with an air of nervous anxiety. "Here is cool."

The door opened again, this time revealing an older, barrel-chested man with graying hair, a hooked nose, and shrewd gaze. "What's the meaning of this? Who are you four?"

Leigh and Colson took the lead, with Colson again showing his ID.

Genetics and a disapproving twist of his lips declared the elder man Benjamin's father. "All right. Let's go in and have a seat," he said as he directed all into the house.

Dante handled preliminary explanations after accepting his seat in a wing chair facing a leather couch and overstuffed recliner.

The parents claimed awareness of the death, word having spread through the student population via social media platforms. They denied knowledge of details and asked the same questions as their only son.

"It wasn't an accident." Dante's words as well as his monotone put the family off guard. He waited a beat for that to soak in before suggesting, "My associate would like to take a look in your son's room."

Leigh followed up immediately with, "If you'd prefer us to get a warrant, we can go to the local police station and ask questions there while it's being written. Since Melody was a student at the GE school, everything will be expedited."

"Fine," Benjamin proclaimed with sullen mistrust. "But not alone. I'll go with you."

Hailey took that as her cue to stand. "Right, then. Lead the way."

"Melody? Are you with me?"

"Right beside you. I've only been here twice. His parents didn't approve of me. The snobs."

Hailey wasn't so old or out of touch to misjudge Benjamin's teenage attitude for guilt, but waited until they were up the stairs and heading down a long hall until initiating conversation.

"Quite a house." She imagined children playing all sorts of games in such a mansion, then realized the parents downstairs were nothing like her own.

"You haven't shown your badge." Benjamin stopped to confront her face to face. He wore mistrust like a glove.

"Because I'm not a cop, although I am working with them on this case. I'm Melody's aunt."

"Her aunt lives in North Dakota." Benjamin opened the third door on the right. "With the rest of the middle-class wannabes." His tone carried boredom and a smattering of regret.

"*No, Nora lives near Billings,*" Melody refuted the statement with a huff. "*She's a dentist, but he doesn't know that.*"

"No. I live in Montana, near Billings. And I'm trained to investigate. I came to take her home, but unfortunately arrived too late."

"Since when do cops let family members participate in investigations."

"Since we have *connections.*" Emphasizing the last word produced the desired effect. "Why do you think there're four of us?"

The teen paled and steadied himself with one hand on the door jamb.

"You all right? You look like you just got cornered carrying drugs." Hailey gripped the young man's upper arm in the guise of steadying him and prepared herself for the instant flood of visions.

Specific statements usually directed her quarry's thoughts to illicit activities and shortened the time needed to sift through useless situations.

She wasn't disappointed. One after another, images of Benjamin sitting across from Jenkins and an unknown woman flooded her mind.

"You spied for Jenkins."

The youth lost all semblance of arrogance and took a step away, jerking his arm free. "You're one of *them.*"

"Them?" Hailey parroted.

"Mind readers, or whatever. I didn't believe it at first. Shit. This is crazy. Melody never said anything about *this* crap."

It took all of Hailey's strength not to cringe from the other-worldly screech in her ear.

"*He knew all this time? He was spying on me for that no-good vice principal? I'll kill them both!*"

A moment of silence ensued where Hailey rubbed her ear and worried she'd moved too fast. "What did Jenkins want from Melody?"

"Um, she had a knack with numbers, and he was up to his eyeballs in gambling debt."

"Who else was there?"

"His secretary."

"Why was she there for an after-hours talk?" In her visions, Hailey saw stars sewn in the velvety sky through the window.

"Um, I think they were having a thing, you know, an affair. She was always in there, even when he wasn't. That bitch is crazy. Maybe she was his bookie? I dunno."

"What was Jenkins' connection to the local crime syndicate?"

Benjamin held both hands up, palms out. "Crime syndicate? Oh, no. I don't know anything about that. I do know that Jenkins is no genius. In fact, I'd say he's barely average, the idiot."

"You don't have to be a genius to have psychic talent." Hailey knew all of her team members would score above average on any IQ test, but that wasn't the point.

"What? What are you—" Benjamin's body jerked like a marionette on a string. "Hey, what's happening? I can't control my arms."

If he thought his life was strange before, he now entered a new dimension. Of its own accord, his fingers fisted and rammed into his jaw, repeatedly, before he turned to the wall and banged his head against the wallboard. He left several dents.

"Melody, wait. Let him talk. We need answers to find your killer and prevent others from suffering your fate. You can deal with him in your own way later." Her appeal to the spirit rendered the result she wanted without denying her vengeance.

The youth's face turned red, then purple, his mouth opening and shutting after his hands went to his neck and made scrabbling motions.

"He's going to die."

The choking voice belonged to Benjamin, but it was Melody's anger that took physical form.

"Melody. No. We can't get the answers we need. Stop this."

Seconds later, Benjamin fell to the floor on hands and knees. "What happened? I felt, I'm not sure what I felt, but it wasn't me controlling my body."

"That was your girlfriend showing you how upset she is for your betrayal."

"But Jenkins said he was going to help her, that she and her family would earn tons of money with what she could do. He wanted her to help him out of his gambling debt and would make her rich in return. Her family doesn't come from money like mine. I thought she'd want that, then she'd feel like an equal."

"You didn't know Jenkins is connected to the local crime hub?"

"What? No. No way. I wouldn't do that to her. She was the first nice smart girl I've found." His demeanor changed in an instant, from wary to wonder. "Melody?" He touched his cheek, then his chest, over his heart.

"She's listening."

"Melody, I'm sorry. I really didn't know. I finally realized what a snob I've been, but you... you're different, kind, loyal, funny, and damn smart. Regardless of what my folks say, you're the real deal, a diamond in the rough."

"How'd you know about psychics?" Hailey asked, marveling at the change in the spirit's voice from abject rage to cooing.

"Jenkins met with me last week. Said there was something strange going on, and that I should keep my ears and eyes open. I guess now he was right. At the time, I thought he was losing it."

"No, there's a lot going on you don't know about." Hailey held out her hand. "At least, I don't think you do. There is one way you can prove it and help us at the same time."

"Anything, but first, tell me how you know someone killed her."

"She was dead before she was put in the vehicle." That much was true. "She was found with slash marks across her chest and neck."

"Like, from an animal?"

"Yes." Hailey divulged the truth, despite skipping pertinent details. "Take my hand, Benjamin. Show me your interactions with Jenkins and anyone new you've recently met that felt weird or off in some way."

The young man hesitated then gripped her hand and closed his eyes in concentration.

Another flood of images invaded Hailey's mind. Some took place at the school, others in a different and undefined environment.

The latter was a massive office with rich wood tones, a desk larger than any she'd seen, and four men beefy enough to call enforcers.

Further consideration dictated the latter images foreshadowed the future. Hailey knew this to be true due to the length of Benjamin's hair and a physique filled out with time.

She saw Duncan hand him a gun with which Benjamin fired, point blank into the shifter's heart. He then killed the others in the room, saving the older man in the executive chair for last.

When they broke contact, she sighed. In a few words, she conveyed to Melody how her boyfriend would dispense justice.

"Listen, Benjamin. The man you met, the one with red hair, calls himself Duncan."

"Um, I don't know his name, but I saw a big guy leave Jenkins' office once when I went to give a report. I never got past the bitch, so I don't know who was in there."

"Then you met Melody's killer. He's going to ask you to join his cause. I believe—"

"I'll do it if it gets me close enough to kill him."

"No. You don't understand. He has, let's say, unusual powers. He'd kill you in an instant, before you could think to draw a gun."

"How do you know this? Do you see the future?"

"It doesn't matter. Let us handle this. It's what we do."

"Damn. And I thought I was special. Hell, I'm nothing in the grand scheme of things."

Again, Melody's screech filled the hallway.

"Ah, Melody. Please stop. I'll convey your message." Hailey released the hand now gripping hers tight.

"What's she saying? I have to know," Benjamin pleaded.

"She says you *are* special. Now so more than ever. She also says you shouldn't waste your life on revenge and to not adopt your parents' attitudes."

"The thing about my parents is that they think they're at the top of the food chain. Hell, they've barely reached the bottom rung. Now that I know psychics exist, I can do more to help."

"No, Benjamin. You're not equipped for the job. Believe me. I think Melody just proved that. Live your life. Be a better man. Be what you want others to be."

"But... Melody."

"I'll figure it out, one way or another. She'll have justice, as will the others who've died in this cause."

"If Jenkins is trying to connect psychic kids with the local mob, I can help. I'm a student and can spy on him."

Hailey listened to Melody's strong objections then relayed the spirit's concern. "Your girlfriend doesn't want you involved. Leave this to those of us prepared to handle the situation. She wants you to move forward, just as she will."

Melody's revelation was insightful and heartfelt, and made Hailey blink in quick succession to avoid a sappy face.

Chapter Thirteen
Casper

"Damn your thick-headed skull. This is the best way to catch Duncan with the least amount of risk. We still can't physically tie Jenkins to any of this." Casper twisted her phone's charger cord around her fingers, wishing she could wrap it around Trenton's neck.

She had better luck trying to change a gator's mind than the damned fed.

"Jenkins doesn't have the intelligence to mastermind even a section of the power plays we've seen. Going after him is meaningless." Hailey made her point, an obvious attempt to bring Trenton to a logical conclusion in making Duncan their next target.

"When Duncan killed Melody, it was spur of the moment and happened without consulting the VP. The tiger answers to a higher authority. If we get him, we get his boss. I can damn well assure you of that. Right, partner?" Casper held her hand up for Hailey's high-five.

Her mentor Nicholai advised that an expanding team experienced minor setbacks. The significance here was that they didn't all stand on equal ground. They hadn't trained and fought side by side. They didn't know each teammates' strengths and vulnerabilities. They weren't prepared to fight as a group.

Here in Texas, Hailey was the only one who saw her as an equal. The rest of them viewed her as a kid needing constant supervision.

"No. You and Noah are not staying in the mansion alone, not without proper support." Trenton stood firm in his decision. "I don't care how much electronic security you have, it's not enough. Duncan's pack consists of God only knows how many members."

Colson sat across from her and nodded. "I agree, and no disrespect meant to your mountain lion here, but he'd be no match for a streak of tigers."

Leigh swiveled to frown at her supervisor sitting in the adjacent chair. "Since when did you become an expert on tigers, knowing a pack is called a streak."

"Since a mountain lion knocked me over and startled me shitless. I've done a lot of reading and, jeez, I've learned I have so much further to go. What I am certain of is this—Noah, you are no match for them. And they won't come in singles. They proved that behind the movie theater. Consider how your enemy operates."

"That and you would've gotten the better of Duncan without his reinforcement there, which surprised them all," Trenton reminded them. "As leader of his men, he won't let that go. He can't. He'll want your head above all others."

"Factor in his disgrace on his own turf where he had to tuck tail and run while you stole his prize from under his nose." Leigh grimaced as if continuing pained her. "Duncan's put you two at the top of his shit list. He won't spare any advantage or take any chances. He'll want to make examples out of you both."

Clannahan, for once, remained silent.

"Damn it. All Noah and I have to do is hang together, which we're doing anyway. With supervision." Casper glared at Clannahan.

"Not enough," Trenton reaffirmed his position.

Casper ignored the jibe. "Noah will sense their approach even if our security systems don't. Once they come for us, I'll phase both our bodies except for Noah's paw. Between us, we'll have two weapons they can't beat."

"Two?" Trenton questioned. "Do they not teach basic math to the GE kids?"

Casper drove her phased hand through the table up to her elbow. "Yeah, two. He can slice and dice. I can remove hearts, kidneys, pieces of lung tissue, whatever. Won't be the first time I've done it."

Trenton sat back in his chair, his expression a mix of shock and horror. "Damn."

"If I might interject here." Clannahan took a deep breath before beginning. "I have spoken with Nicholai, and he agrees with me."

"Aw, come on. This can work." Casper slammed a solid fist on the table.

"Yes, it can. As I said, he agrees it could. It *could* also backfire."

"How?" Noah asked. "Looks pretty foolproof to me."

"As you all know by now, Nicholai sees *possibilities* and *probabilities*. You'd be successful as long as neither of you got distracted." Clannahan turned a hard stare on Noah. "One of you has extreme battle experience. The other, not so much. It only takes one to distract the other, then you both die."

"Oh, I thought you were gonna reference sex," Casper murmured, her cheek's temperature equivalent to molten lava.

Noah chuckled, then straightened under Clannahan's glare. "I-I learned my lesson. I won't get distracted again. No fooling around. We'll stay alert, watch movies, and fall asleep on the couch. That way we're together."

"As in fully dressed." Trenton arched a brow.

Casper rolled her eyes. "Jeez, you think of kids as bags of hormones, but you adults are just as bad." Her gaze flicked to Hailey, whose face flamed crimson.

"You aren't seriously considering this, Clannahan." Trenton pinched the bridge of his nose and pursed his lips. "This is the very definition of insanity."

"The best way to avoid falling to prey status is to take down the predator. Duncan isn't going to stop coming for these two. His pride won't allow it." Clannahan gestured to the two teens. "We have to take him out of the game before he attacks again. It's the only way to keep a semblance of control."

"By using kids as bait?" Trenton's voice pitched higher as he spoke.

"Listen, fed. I've killed more people than you've arrested or fought in the military. I'll survive this, and so will Noah."

That brought the room to total silence.

"Seriously? Like who?" Leigh rocked back in her seat with outstretched hands. "I'm not challenging you, Casper. I'm just curious about your experience. We're taught in the academy to know your partner and anticipate how he or she will react in any given situation. That's the ticket to survival when things head south."

"Fine," Casper huffed. "There was a war fought over several years where psychics were captured, their parents killed or imprisoned underground, and all were served up for experimentation—many to death."

"Holy shit." Colson's expression held new respect. "How old were you when this started?"

"Well, it's gone on in the background for years. My parents were killed, somewhere down here, and my adoptive parents were killed when I discovered they were spying on me." Casper glanced to Clannahan for permission to continue, receiving a nod in return.

"They should know at least a little of what you've survived, young'n."

"I was caught and imprisoned underground. A woman I barely knew gave her life so that I could escape. She saw the future." Several deep breaths helped her composure before continuing.

"Once free, the psychics who'd taken me in redoubled their efforts to locate the three main facets of the organization sanctioning extermination. A senator was involved, but he was the easiest to take down."

"Son of a bitch." Trenton pointed to the major. "That's where you came in?"

Clannahan nodded. "I've spent years working with *and* beside psychics and never knew of their abilities. Now that I do, I make every effort to protect them. I also value their talent and know when it's time to let them do what they do. I, along with Nicholai, agree this would be the best course for now."

"Why?" Colson asked, clearly befuddled.

"Because we won't have a clear shot at Jenkins with Duncan's interference. I won't approach him until we have some kind of evidence. We've got plenty on Duncan after he kidnapped one of our own," Clannahan explained with as much patience as Casper had ever seen.

"Once we get Duncan, we get his superiors," Casper explained with a smirk. "The rest can die for all I care."

"Fine." Trenton scrubbed a hand over his chin. "It won't be the first time I've spent in the woods near her house."

"No. Not this time. Duncan's men would sense your presence and take you down long before you could draw your weapon." Clannahan pushed back in his chair, the debate settled. "Trenton, you and the others can wait in the van. Kiera will be on call and can provide backup when the attack comes. And believe me, it will come."

The sun had long since hidden its face below the horizon when Noah and Casper finished the dinner dishes. It was nice to have him near and the house to themselves.

Casper wiped down the counter, thinking how ordinary the action when, in fact, they waited for the inevitable attack.

As a strictly human guardian, her handler would be of little help in a supernatural fight. Sarah Garner's instincts were to protect at all costs, hence Clannahan had summoned her back to Pennsylvania for the rest of the week.

Noah plopped down on the sofa beside Casper and picked up the remote, nodding toward the seventy-two-inch flat screen on the wall. "TV?"

"Nah, I wanna hear what's coming at me. Trenton and Colson are probably having cows about now, with us being *alone* and *defenseless.*"

"Cass, you've proven yourself anything but defenseless."

"Ah, but nobody's invulnerable. I've learned that lesson more than once. There's always a way to overcome the insurmountable. Might not be the method you'd prefer, and you might not see it coming, but there's always a way."

"You've lived through so much, and I know you don't want to talk about it now, but someday, I hope you'll open up to me. I may not be a warrior like Ouray and the others of your family, but I'm a good listener and a fairly quick study."

"I'm surprised they're giving us this much rope, to be honest. Wyatt's probably glued to the security system."

In response to her statement, the living room lights blinked several times. They both chuckled.

Knowing the location of each camera, Casper flipped him the bird.

"From what I understand, you've got cameras in each room except for the bathroom, I hope?" Shifter status diminished his sense of propriety, but he maintained certain boundaries.

"Correct, but each bathroom has a panic button located behind the roll of toilet paper."

"How convenient. Your guardians think of everything. I am wondering, though, since Nicholai has visions and knows we'll make it through this, why doesn't he give us more information? You know, like a time when all hell is gonna break loose?"

"See, it doesn't work like that, Noah. He says we *can* make it through, not that we necessarily *will.* The way he once explained it is like this. Knowing some specific little detail can change the outcome of a situation."

"So, he doesn't want to jinx us."

"Exactly." Casper picked up her laptop and opened the lid. "I want to do more digging into Dante's past. It bothers me to have someone on the team that I know so little about."

"I don't like that he's withholding vital information about family, but I understand his reasoning. On the flip side, maybe spilling it will lessen his animosity toward us both, like popping a zit."

"At least he revealed his psychic ability. Converting matter is pretty cool. What I don't understand is why he isn't here. When they attack, he could just turn their claws into rubber, or whatever." Casper opened up a window and typed Martie Schrader in the search bar.

He hadn't explained whether it was a close or distant relative, or located nearby, just that this person existed. The search returned zero results. She tried spelling variations and reached the same outcome.

"Maybe sheer numbers would overwhelm him, or maybe it taxes his energy reserves to convert large masses. Who knows since he's not forthcoming. Infuriating man," Noah all but growled.

"I wish they'd come on. Waiting is getting old quick. Christmas is less than a week away, and I really want this over before then. I'd love for you to meet all of my family. They're pretty cool and Pennsylvania is beautiful this time of year."

"Yeah, I'm ready for this to be over too. I think I need a long run to stretch my legs."

"Must be nice to shift and run through the forest without a care in the world."

"Uh, that time's not as carefree as you think. We're still susceptible to the same dangers, stepping on snakes, running into larger predators, like poachers. They're the biggest problem we face."

"At least you won't have to deal with the last part soon. Clannahan swings a pretty big bat and the five hundred plus acres he's looking at will be designated as Cat's Paw Reserve, under federal jurisdiction. Meaning, it'll be for you and any visitors you have."

"He's been talking to my family. My dad's cautious but seems to respect him. That goes a long way in my pack."

"Something else is on your mind, Noah. What?"

"I was just thinking. You have all this experience with different types of abilities, and mine is very limited. How do you think Duncan's gonna come at us? I mean, you have family that deals in portals, throwing bolts of electricity... hell, you've seen someone slow time, for God's sake. What do you think Duncan's side of the equation holds?"

"Don't know till we face it. But I do know this, I'd rather face it on my own terms, whatever it is, than on his."

"Have you ever run across anyone who can negate psychic talent?"

"*Hmm,* no. Actually, I never thought about that. Phasing is such an integral part of my life; it just didn't occur to me."

"Do you think Duncan's part of this other organization Dante hinted at? Maybe like what you've already faced, but a faction just forming? Maybe some with loose connections in the past and didn't appear on your radar?"

"Possibly. They did toss out fifty grand on the *possibility* of locating psychics. They hired a professional to kill Yamato. That shot required experience. They killed Melody on the spot and without a second thought. It all indicates money and power."

Casper paused and listened to the low tick of the grandfather clock. Some change she couldn't define prodded her to reach for Noah's hand.

He took it and squeezed gently in understanding. "Seems so quiet here. I love it."

Phasing both their bodies except the soles of their feet and butts, she snickered when he leaned *through* the sofa back before jerking himself upright.

"Yeah, it does take getting used to. Sometimes it's too quiet." She squeezed back, willing him to be ready. It wasn't the first time she'd felt watched, but her heart rate doubled, and goose flesh rose on her forearm. "Not like now, but different."

Shadows felt deeper, the silence more ominous. Battle had come to her many times, without warning, without preparation. That wasn't new.

She closed her laptop and slid it onto the seat beside her. No need to risk good electronics since they were such a pain to set up.

"I was thinking about asking Kiera and Ouray to come over and play bridge," Noah spoke the words as nonchalantly as if he'd asked to go fishing.

Casper understood the coded message to their surveillance team, making it clear they both felt some change. "Play bridge, what's that? A building game with Legos?" There were times when he outdistanced her so far in social etiquette, she felt she might as well exist on another planet.

"No. Cards. You know, a few hands of that, or maybe canasta?"

"Clearly you come from another world." She felt her body deflating with the gulf yawning between them.

"Hey, don't sweat it. I'll teach you." The last words murmured accompanied his light touch on her chin, turning her to face him.

His kiss was gentle, sweet, nothing like what she expected from the courageous animal bound within. His fingers drifted to her cheek, then her temple.

It wasn't her first kiss, or the first time Noah had kissed her. It was, however, the first time they'd connected on such a deep level.

Lights around them blinked furiously, their flicker creating a strobe effect.

Casper offered Wyatt another one-digit salute, knowing he was behind it. Kiera would be laughing. Ouray would groan, and Nicholai would shake his head on a deep sigh.

"They really like to get their message across, don't they?" Noah retreated several inches but kept his palm on her cheek.

"Did you do that to piss them off?" Casper could see the glint in his eyes.

"No, I did it because I wanted to."

In her peripheral vision, she saw Noah lifting his hand to wave at the tiny camera on the bookshelf.

Then, he kissed her again, giving her his full attention in a way that made her heart swell.

If not for the cracking sound from the side, she would've mistaken the tingling sensation bursting in her head as stemming from deep emotion.

She knew better, because she knew that specific feeling. A bullet passing through the body incited a unique tingly sensation that created a shudder. Whether due to speed or its material, it was distinctive.

Noah must've felt it, too, for he released his grip and pushed forward to stand.

"No. Stay connected." Casper glanced at the window to see the small hole, head high. "And so it—"

Before she could complete her sentence, windows crashed all around the house. Glass shards fell to the floor to create a mosaic of light reflecting from the chandelier.

Three tigers leapt through the front glass wall forming a portion of the living room. More shattering in distant rooms declared the invasion underway from many angles.

"Well, hello, Duncan. Long time, no see." In fact, she had no idea which of his clan she addressed as she and Noah stood. "Well, I guess you're Duncan. Maybe? You know you all look alike. Maybe we could arrange for different colored strings around each of your necks so we can tell you apart."

From the short hallway leading to the den strode a man bigger than any she'd ever seen. Well over six feet with reddish hair, his brown eyes and flat face would make him stand out in a crowd, not in a good way.

Damn.

She'd taken down formidable men, but not without family present.

With arms bigger than her thighs, he stopped six feet from her position. "Well, this is certainly interesting. If I'd known you were impervious to bullets, I might not have been so hasty with my orders. Seems you're the bigger prize." His gaze flicked over Noah in dismissal.

"And it seems you're the biggest idiot. But I do have a bone to pick with you." Casper settled into a fighting stance, feeling Noah do the same.

Duncan frowned as if truly confused. "Well, then, maybe we do have a chance to do business after all. I'll even let you keep your boy toy."

Noah took a step forward, halted with the squeeze of her hand. The tiger shifter had already proven he knew which of Noah's buttons to push. He held an advantage over the younger shifter. Experience.

Distractions were deadly.

As the leader spoke, more than a dozen tigers gathered in a loose circle around her. Some sat, others yawned as if bored. They kept their eyes on Duncan.

"You took something from me. Something of enormous value." Damn if she'd let him die without obtaining information on her amulet's whereabouts.

"Oh?" he asked, still not catching on.

"Yeah, my necklace. You know by now I'm an orphan."

"Ah, the sentimental type. Surprises me from one so young. Whatever, I'm sure we can reach some type of agreement after we find it. Why don't we go somewhere quieter where we can talk without your security cameras? Which, by the way, the external ones are dark, and the rest are jammed."

Noah shrugged. "Doesn't matter, asshat. We can still find you. When I bested you in your own home, I also got your DNA. Remember my claws slicing out part of your arm?" Noah snorted and gestured to their leader's bicep where no scar remained. "I see even big cats can heal themselves. Good to know you're not as helpless as you are stupid."

Casper nipped both lips between her teeth. The plan was to stall until Kiera opened a portal and brought reinforcements, not goad the enemy to attack. It seemed their intruder had stung Noah's pride, which demanded satisfaction. Maybe it was more of a shifter thing than a personal vendetta.

"Rip the boy to shreds if she doesn't start moving in the next ten seconds." Wrinkles around Duncan's eyes appeared with his grin showing perfect white teeth, which seemed a little too large for the space provided.

Casper unphased her right hand and Noah's left fingertips in preparation to fight. "Remember to stay linked."

The first shifter took a short running leap from behind, then soared through the two teens.

Casper raked his side from flank to chest with her right hand, snagging and ripping internal organs with her fingertips. The animal crashed through the coffee table and landed on the floor amid glittering pieces of glass tipped with crimson.

Coarse exhalations spewed bloody foam as the tiger tried to shift, succeeding in only transforming one hand before succumbing to his injuries.

"Wyatt? Are the grounds surrounded?" Casper asked the room at large.

The first hint of uncertainty crossed Duncan's face. "Wyatt's in Pennsylvania."

"Ah, so you have some type of intelligence operation. Shame it's not worth shit." Noah crouched, waiting for the next attack.

He didn't have to wait long.

"Take them now, before their reinforcements arrive." Duncan charged to meet Noah head-on, his body shifting mid-leap.

It wasn't supposed to happen this way, not this fast. Casper excelled at goading an enemy and knowing when to back off, not that she usually did. Each member of her family would confirm that as fact without a second thought.

Her boyfriend was new to battle and the world of psychics, other than shifters and healers. In time, he'd learn finesse.

They needed it now. The unpredictability of Noah's restraint definitely needed addressing and could cost them both their lives. Realization that his need to protect stemmed from caring more than pride wouldn't help them now.

The tigers converged like a swarm of bees after having their nest disturbed. She'd use her ability to kill anything within reach. The enemy quickly learned to avoid her.

Even Duncan.

Their leader was larger and more formidable than anyone in his pack. He shifted, but sat to watch the proceedings and studied how his enemy fought.

When he shouldered the others away and approached from Noah's side, she kept her eyes on him and waited to see what course he took. This adversary necessitated the use of caution.

From a distance that allowed only his extended claws to connect, he swiped at Noah's hand, phasing through his body, but locking their claws together.

One hard tug and he pulled Noah off balance and out of Casper's grip before she could phase his nails. His body was no longer protected.

Realizing his vulnerability, Noah shifted, but not before Duncan opened a foot-long gash down his thigh.

At the same time, a silver ring ten feet in diameter appeared along the south wall, its reflection on the flat screen blinding in intensity. Thick mist filling the center shifted like fog before Kiera, then Ouray, stepped through. It surprised her to see Dante on the Native American's heels.

"Someone call animal control?" Kiera asked with knife in hand. Remnants of her gateway disappeared after four more men dressed in leathers arrived via accelerated transportation.

The first two shifters who attacked Kiera disappeared into the next portal erected. Whether she sent them to the top of a frigid mountain on the other side of the world or an underwater ice cave in Switzerland, they wouldn't return soon. It was hard to tell with her.

Noah's grunt drew Casper's attention after she ripped the intestines from a shifter intent on snapping his neck. She reached down to phase all but his mid-back, where the others wouldn't think to aim.

Yet, Duncan figured it out.

His attack came fast, but not directed at Noah.

It was a calculated risk, and he must've realized his timing required perfection. With jaws open wide, he came in fast and low when another tiger leaped for her chest.

She thrust her hand through the leaping animal's side, feeling something squishy burst from her effort.

She wasn't prepared for the sense of agony that tested her resolve to remain phased.

Duncan's strong jaws passed through the top of her boot and latched onto the sole that anchored her to the floor.

She screamed in rage as her metatarsals crunched in his massive jaws. Loss of focus released her hold on their phased bodies and left them both open to whatever attack the enemy orchestrated.

Casper was no stranger to battle. She'd faced enemies with greater strength and cunning. None had ever deciphered her weakness so fast and with such brutal consequences.

Noah rolled to his feet and used the short space for a weakened launch at their leader's greater bulk.

The momentum rocked Duncan hard and wobbled his balance, a quick sidestep recovering his balance. He remained on all fours.

"Move, Noah. You're blocking my shot." The male voice yelled from somewhere to the side.

Casper shook off the pain, realizing Noah had just saved her life. More than ever, she wanted Duncan dead.

A bolt of electricity from her favorite uncle's hand flew true to target and nailed a tiger whose mass had just reached the top of his arc. Trajectory changed with his body's spasms. He fell on his side. Muscle spasms twitched and contorted his limbs for long seconds until he finally slumped without moving.

Injured and unable to use both hind legs for better leverage and position, Noah was no match for Duncan. It didn't stop him from taking position in front of Casper.

The tiger leader scanned the room and took in the carnage. One third of his pack lay dead or unconscious. A split-second of utter stillness followed where the harsh, raspy breathing of those injured defined the tide of the battle. His intended victory failed.

The roar he sounded ceased hostilities and changed the pack's focus from attack to retreat. Each intruder fled out the window, as quiet and deadly as the night.

"Well, hell. That didn't go as planned." Casper knelt by Noah's side and took note of his injuries. Looking around, two of her family had sustained injuries, one serious enough for Ouray not to reposition before applying his talent.

Kiera was the first to address the situation. "Sorry we didn't come sooner. When the outdoor cameras went down, it took Wyatt a minute to switch to your phone's audio. Whoever they have working their electronics is good, damn good at coordinating audio and visual signal interference."

Casper grunted with the pain in her foot. "We'll all survive. But damn if I didn't miss that bastard tiger again. He figured out my weak spot quick. Only one other person's done that before."

"Let me guess? Trenton," Kiera offered with a grin.

"Yeah." Casper grabbed the afghan off the couch and covered Noah. "Shift back, Noah. It'll help you heal. Ouray will be with us as soon as he can."

"Learn anything new while you were entertaining new friends?" Kiera gestured to the broken windows. "At least now you can say you've had a wild party."

"Kiera, they knew about Wyatt. That he's in Pennsylvania, *and* that I'd have reinforcements coming."

"Aw, hell. Wyatt's gonna shit a brick."

It wasn't the first time an organized group had hunted Casper, but she prayed it was the last. They now faced another agency of unknown origin, unknown numbers and talents, and unknown ultimate objectives.

Guess we did learn something tonight.

Life tossed her yet another curve ball just when she'd started to find her groove.

Chapter Fourteen
Hailey

In Hailey's limited experience with funeral services, most held a modest and somber atmosphere. Unlike its cultural counterpart in New Orleans, Hamchet more often than not laid its citizens to rest with subdued dignity.

On one such occasion years prior, she'd witnessed a widow seated in the front pew whispering her grief without censure. Parishioners likely chalked the murmurings up to despair from a grieving matron. Maybe there were more psychics present than suspected. Prior to meeting Casper, she'd not met another with supernatural talent.

Yamato's ceremony equaled a mixed conglomeration of several traditions. His wife's heritage included customs found in New Orleans, her relatives steeped in Creole practices. The victim hailed from Vermont and didn't subscribe to any strict cultural norm.

In concert with Dante's promise to look after Yamato's widow and his obvious knowledge of both, he'd helped the widow coordinate today's service.

Yamato hovered off to Hailey's side and added running commentary regarding each part of the sedate affair along with his perspective of each relative and friend. According to the spirit, things were about to get lively.

"My wife's sister has opened her home and welcomed my Beatrice as I'd hoped she would."

Hailey nodded, unable to say much due to continued glances after accidentally speaking to him directly. It would take time to unlearn the life-long habit of looking someone in the eye when addressing them. Even though she couldn't see spirits, she marked their positions by sound.

Sitting on the end of her pew, she endured dark and questionable looks from those on the other side of the aisle.

Her mother explained how, in Haitian rites, practitioners believed that although the soul entered the spirit world at the time of death, it stayed close to the body for a week or better thereafter. Yamato's wife glanced left and right frequently from the front pew.

Dante's eulogy divulged much about his own life while expounding on the victim's virtues. Heartfelt words detailed a long history of three friends determined to right a great injustice. The specific instance remained unvoiced, but the emotion behind it numbed her soul.

Occasional pauses, hands clenching the podium, and a gaze that looked into the past signaled Dante's deep reservoir of restrained grief and remorse.

The fact he was the last of the trio standing added weight to the heavy burden already carried. Each of the task force members would understand his determination to see the joint mission to its conclusion regardless of the consequences.

He spoke of family in both present and past tense, yet none knew his current relatives. Perhaps he referred to non-blood ties. He rarely spoke of the past and never about siblings or extended family.

After prayers inside the church concluded, guests gathered outdoors to escort the horse-drawn hearse to the site of internment. This is where the service deviated from expectations.

Members of the second line carried traditional handkerchiefs and parasols behind the carriage bearing the casket. A mix of flowing white dresses, brightly colored suits, and traditional black clothing delineated the various mourners coming together to celebrate Yamato's life.

A small jazz band led the funeral march to the grave site, their respectful and somber dirge contrasting the bright red and green leis around their necks.

Each gathered around the resting site with Yamato's sister-in-law sitting next to his wife. Their quiet sobs reminded Hailey of life's fragility.

A woven belt cinched the alb worn by the priest with a slight wind breathing life into the long white robe. His words lent comfort to the grieving widow who rested her arms on her swollen belly, a damp handkerchief twisting in her fingers.

Hailey stood beside the seated family and across from Dante, whom she'd never seen so grief-stricken. A question not answered prior, now stuck forefront in her thoughts. *"Yamato, did you have any psychic ability?"*

"What? Like mind reading? You really want to question me now? Here?"

She didn't bother explaining there existed many kinds of talent. Instead, she asked silently, *"Did you know others have them?"*

"I often suspected things were weird both with Dante and... well, I'm not discussing the rest. Dante knows." A moment of silence followed, then the spirit blasted her with, *"Is Dante psychic?"*

She saw no reason to withhold those details, yet it surprised her the Italian would hold out on someone considered a close friend. Nothing should have surprised her about their aloof team member. He still withheld information from the task force.

"Yes, in fact, he is, but he can't hear or see you. He can affect matter, although I'm unsure of his limitations or the extent of his ability."

"All this time, and he didn't tell me?" A low rumbled growl morphed into a dull roar, growing more distant as the spirit moved away.

In the next instant, Dante stretched his head to the side and rolled one shoulder in robotic fashion. He resembled a marionette coming to life.

He raised his right hand and left foot parallel to the ground. The shock on his face couldn't be mistaken for anything else. Then, he squealed. Jerky increments moved both limbs to resemble a mechanical soldier. The chain he wore on his wrist reflected light over the gathering like a disco ball.

Casper coughed to suppress her giggle while Trenton's horrified expression turned to Hailey. No one knew of proper etiquette for dealing with vengeful spirits during their funeral.

Hailey shrugged and pulled both lips between her teeth then covered her mouth with her hand. As if understanding her plight, Trenton turned her toward him and wrapped his arms around her back.

Shaking shoulders would be mistaken for overwhelming grief. It took several minutes to gain control over herself, especially after hearing Dante squeal like a pig.

When she looked up, tears streamed from her eyes. She turned in time to see Dante wheel around and rush toward the church's parking lot.

She didn't have it in her to chastise the spirit. *"Yamato? Are you finished?"*

"Not by a long shot. I'm just getting the hang of possession. I had no idea how many other spirits would be here. Damn talkative bunch."

She hadn't heard other spirits talking, just the priest and the wind whispering through the willows. *"Really? I haven't heard much."*

"They're being respectful, but promise to party afterward. Hey, you wanna see my sister-in-law do a jig? She's always been such a stiff-backed matriarch."

"No," Hailey snapped, then realized by the stern looks turned her way she'd made another mistake in speaking out loud.

Trenton edged her away from the grave site and escorted her back the way they'd come. A conciliatory pat of her shoulders noted his understanding.

Bending to whisper in her ear, he asked, "Are your ghost friends done pulling pranks?"

"No. I-I'm sorry. I didn't mean to appear rude or disrespectful of the dead. I would never do that on purpose."

"I know, Sparkles. I know. Just promise me something. If you leave this world before me, please don't possess my body. Join me forever... that's fine. Talk to me, let me know you're near, but please, spare me the humiliation we just witnessed. I don't think Dante will ever live that down. Does he know what happened?"

"I'm not sure what people feel when they're possessed. It's never happened to me. Addy just talks to me or brushes her fingers across my cheek when she's nearby."

"I can't imagine what Casper is feeling. You said she and Simon have been together for several years?"

"I believe so, though he hasn't been a spirit for long, I don't think. It's not something she talks much about." Hailey tried to think solemn thoughts in approaching Dante.

He stood beside his car with his crossed arms on the roof of his BMW, his head resting on his forearms.

"Dante?"

He groaned. "That was Yamato, right?"

"Um, yeah. It was. I sorta told him you were psychic. I thought he knew since you two were close."

Dante whirled; his eyes wide with some unnamed emotion. "We were close, but that doesn't mean I'd divulge family secrets. *That* can get you killed."

"Look. I'm sorry. I didn't know he'd fly off the handle like that. Or, um, fly into you."

Dante released a pent-up breath and shook his head. "That was just the type of stunt he'd pull, thinking it funny. Not so much for his wife and family."

"I can't claim to know much about his world now, but I'm glad he's not steeped in grief."

"How do you know he's not covering it by acting out?"

"He said he's met a bunch of other spirits who're supporting him. I think they're planning some kind of big to-do after most of the guests leave."

"I'd like to be gone before that happens. Does that mean he won't be present during the wake?"

"I-I don't know. He didn't say. I'm afraid if I ask him, it'll—"

"No. You're right. Don't give him ideas. Please."

Trenton gave her waist a light squeeze. "Dante, how about we meet you at the house? Hailey and I can start preparations for the gathering."

"He always said he'd have the last laugh." Dante's eyes focused on something far away, in another time, before a bittersweet smile slid into place. "I guess he did."

"Why don't you come back with us? You can tell us tales of old," Hailey suggested.

"No, thanks. I've seen your driving. I'm not ready to meet Yamato again so soon."

Clannahan had overseen window repairs, accomplished in record time. He likely included a few upgrades in the process.

Preparations for a large gathering after the service were well underway. Tables laden with covered dishes awaited their guests with cloth-covered picnic tables arranged on the patio for an overflow of mourners.

Hailey took a seat beside Dante after setting a cold drink in front of him. "You miss him a lot."

"Yes. I never realized death wasn't the end. It's unfair that I'll be able to speak to him through you or Casper, but his wife and child never will."

Trenton took a sip of his own drink, then offered, "That's if we find her amulet. We still have no clue where it is and no idea how to find Duncan. I think it's time we pay a visit to Jenkins. I've seen first-hand Casper's interrogation style. She *will* get answers."

Not much made Trenton shudder.

"Or... we could follow the leads going in the other direction." Hailey knew her partner's hacker friend had located the recipient of Jenkins' emails. Even if Jenkins turned out to be a dry well, they'd still have leads.

"Wyatt get a name? I thought dark web mail was hack proof." Dante sat straighter in his chair.

"My understanding is that yes, that's pretty much true unless you have either the starting or endpoint." Hailey reached for a bottle of water from the table.

"Good. The sooner we get Noah and Olivia out of that damn school, the better."

"You always call her by her given name..." Hailey hedged with the leading statement hoping to gain insight as to why Dante was so surly toward both teenagers.

Dante harrumphed with a crooked grin. "Those kids were both born defiant, two peas in a pod. It should be each of their middle names."

"You knew her when her parents lived in the area?" It was the first real snippet of information she'd obtained about his connection to anyone local. "You know she's desperate to find at least one living relative."

In lieu of answering, Dante said, "She'll have to survive this tangled mess first. And damn if she doesn't keep sticking her neck out." The rise of his voice drew the attention of two caterers arranging trays of covered dishes.

Anger accentuated the scar over his right eyebrow. "Sorry. I'm just trying to keep the little idiots out of harm's way."

"She was raised to stand her ground, or at least, that's the lesson she's learned," Hailey murmured.

Trenton rapped the table with his knuckles. "She's learned it well. Maybe too well. Although, she maintained her body phased even while Duncan's jaws broke the bones in her foot. You should be proud of her, whatever your relationship to her family entails." He held both hands up. "I'm not asking, not prying, and won't repeat a word. I just recognize the need to protect."

Musical chimes announced the first of what would be many guests arriving to reminisce over a meal about their missed loved one.

Dante paled when Yamato's sister-in-law made a straight line for his table, his apology stumbling out before she leaned over and placed both hands flat on the table to stare directly at him.

"Jesus. I'm so sorry. I don't know—" Downcast eyes could not meet the other woman.

"For giving my sister great comfort? For confirming our beliefs and bringing her back into our fold?" Clear mocha skin denied the ability to hide puffiness around the older woman's eyes.

A slow grin overtook her expression. "If not for your uncharacteristic display, she would be lost. As it is, you've confirmed her husband's presence, such that she's decided to continue with the move and purchase the property you both visited."

Yamato's sudden outburst in Hailey's ear signaled the most recent animated awareness of his position. Her startle response diverted the older woman's attention to her.

"*No big decision should be made during heightened emotion.*" Dante continued to voice his objections.

"I see we have a psychic among us. Good."

Hailey's jaw went slack. She didn't openly discuss her abilities with strangers. "Um..."

"Do not fret. Your secret is safe with me. Nor will I reveal it to my sister, for she would forever hound you and not move forward as she eventually should."

"*Jaylene has always believed in the old ways. Tell her I will watch over my family, but that, in time, Beatrice will need to open her heart.*"

Spot decisions were rarely good ones, but Hailey relayed Yamato's message and received a nod and smile in return.

"Thank you, Hailey. I appreciate your gift and have one question for you."

Hailey inhaled sharply then leaned back into Trenton's arm around her shoulders, who pulled her in protectively.

"Can you get justice for Yamato?"

It was Dante who intervened. "I will not rest until we've done so. I give you my word, Jaylene."

The sister-in-law nodded once. "Thank you. If ever there is something I can do for you or yours, please do not hesitate to ask. We Creoles take care of our own." As she turned to greet other guests, a knowing gaze took in Dante,

Trenton, Casper, and the others who'd filtered in to sit at their table. Yamato's relatives valued family.

Hailey released a pent-up sigh.

Casper smiled when her gaze landed on Dante. Instead of avoiding him, she'd taken a seat next to him. "Did she just call you an undignified swine?"

One corner of Dante's mouth kicked up in a small grin. "She never did like Yamato. Blamed him for taking her sister away from the fold."

"How'd it feel? Your first time being possessed." Casper elbowed him in the side with a smirk.

Dante rolled both shoulders as if removing an uncomfortable weight. "Strange. I saw myself doing things, felt the movements, yet had no control. A peculiar buzzing in my ear made me think of Yamato, but I heard nothing specific. I guess it was his way of telling me how pissed off he was."

"Why would he be pissed off at you?" Leigh asked.

"I never divulged the truth about psychics, or much else. I kept both my friends in the dark trying to keep them alive."

"Ah, I understand how the other side of that feels." One corner of Leigh's mouth tipped up in closed-mouth understanding.

"Did he get it out of his system, or can I expect more of the same?" Dark pain-filled eyes turned toward the only one who could now communicate with those in spirit form.

"Not sure. Dealing with spirits isn't the same as dealing with humans. They see things differently," Hailey replied with as much honesty as she could.

Casper seemed to weigh his words, then said, "There's a lot of mistrust going around. I've dealt with it for as long as I can remember, from one side of the coin or the other."

"And your conclusion?" Dante asked with obvious interest in what the teen thought.

"That you either trust someone or you don't. I don't see a middle ground."

Hailey understood the subtext of their abbreviated conversation. On one hand, Casper felt the sting of mistrust from Dante since he remained aloof and wouldn't divulge his backers. On the other, he protected others by keeping his secrets.

"Guess we'll have to agree to disagree, then." Dante selected a bottle of flavored water and handed it to her, a peace offering.

Guests filed in by couples and small groups, each greeting the family and offering condolences. It didn't take long for the great room to fill and for the overflow to spill out into the sixty-degree sunshine warming the patio tables. Family and friends had come in from Yamato's hometown in Vermont along with his wife's kin from New Orleans.

Hailey circled the guests and mingled, adding commentary supplied by Yamato himself. If the small deceptions offered a measure of comfort to those he loved, she'd accept them as little mercies.

Casper tugged on her sleeve when guests began leaving. "Is he here?"

She didn't need to name the person she sought. Hailey nodded.

"Ask him if he's met Melody. If not, send him to the school to see if they can connect. They have something in common and might be able to help each other *and* us."

"Okay. They're both still learning to navigate their realm, but I think it would behoove us all if they joined forces. Maybe together, they can find the amulet."

In a corner of the room, Hailey spoke softly, glad when her other-worldly new friends gathered around her. Perhaps the new circumstances overwhelmed them both, or maybe navigating the spirit realm existed as a new level of confusion, but they agreed to assist however possible.

If Casper still had her amulet, she could assist them in their endeavors by enlisting aid from older spirits.

It was time to find Casper's treasure and reunite her with Simon.

Chapter Fifteen
Casper

The lightest of caresses brushing Casper's cheek let her know Simon hovered by her side. Having spent the night in Hailey's spare bedroom, she now sat on the window seat in the massive great room and watched a squirrel scamper across the street below.

Instead of painting fingernails and styling each other's hair, her girls' night with her partner consisted of brainstorming about the investigation and planning for Christmas. It wasn't the first holiday season she'd wondered if her family would live to see Christmas Eve.

No news from Nicholai was better than the bad news from Trenton. Ballistics of the bullet lodged in Yamato's chest failed to match anything in their databases, either officially or from Clannahan's files.

Meanwhile, she lingered between the zones of frustration and sorrow. Losing that most precious link between her and the spirit world wasn't just a professional hit. It tore away one of her oldest and dearest friends.

While it was great Hailey could relay messages between the living and the spirits, they'd gained no ground in solving the mystery.

On the street below, Casper watched as Colson parked behind the FBI's SUV. "Trenton's here. Looks like he brought breakfast for the entire group."

Hailey strode from the hallway with Gunther bouncing at her side. "Yum, I'm starved. Let's go on down. I think we're gonna make great progress today." The smile playing about Hailey's lips offered hope. The blue denim shirt she wore matched her eyes and accentuated the waist-length contrast of midnight-black hair. "Been up long?"

"A while." Casper felt Simon's tug on her hair. It was his way of offering support.

"You're itching to get your hands on, or should I say *in,* Duncan's chest. I think we're gonna find him soon."

"I want to end this mess." Casper tilted her head to the side and frowned. "You know something new. What is it? Did Melody find my amulet?" She was on her feet in the next instant with both hands out to stop Hailey's progress.

Hailey never could hold out against another person's desperation when able to alleviate it. Yet she smiled and shrugged, saying, "Let's go downstairs and meet with the others."

Casper dogged her heels with a hand on Gunther's head, excitement lighting a fire in her soul. At the base of the stairs and off the hallway running the building's width, she caught the rich aromas of breakfast through the open side entrance to the office.

Leigh helped Trenton set out food leftover from the prior day since Yamato's widow left to visit with family. Various savory dishes spread down the table offered a variety from which to choose.

Casper selected several mini quiches and Cajun-style baked chicken wings before sitting beside Noah. "Breakfast of champions."

"I see Nicholai did not instill a sense for a proper diet." Dante's comment earned a serious case of side-eye from all when he took the seat beside her.

"He believes in picking his battles, a wise approach not shared by all, I've come to learn." Casper smiled around a mouthful of food.

Dante grimaced in looking around at each person present. "What? Somebody's got to make sure those two stay out of trouble. Might as well be me."

Bright-eyed and brimming with energy, Leigh sat across from her and waited until everyone was seated to ask, "Any news from the spirit world? Other than Yamato obviously got his revenge yesterday?"

Dante huffed but remained mute.

"I have news." Hailey grinned wide. "And we need to act on it post haste."

Colson leaned forward in his chair to add emphasis to his comment, "Who says that anymore? Have you made friends hanging around for centuries?"

Hailey lifted her chin. "Actually, I've been talking to a few. We now know the whereabouts of Casper's amulet."

Casper shoved her chair back and stood, the thud of its landing on cement silencing other comments. "Well? Where is it? Who found it? Melody?"

"Yes. I know Clannahan's men searched the area, but Duncan and his pack took a meandering path when leaving school grounds."

"Clannahan," Casper began with a frown at her legal guardian. "Your men are very thorough."

Hailey held up one finger. "They are, Casper. I mean, they were. See, whoever took the amulet carried it for quite some distance. And with so many tracks running through those woods," She smiled at Noah, "...there's no way to delineate the difference. It was found miles from the school."

"Well, what are we waiting for?" Noah stood and made a "hurry up" gesture with his hand. "Is this another ambush? Did Duncan leave someone behind?"

"No. Not that they can tell, anyway." Hailey stood, along with Dante and Trenton.

"Yes, well. First things first. Let's retrieve this thing and reconvene this afternoon for our meeting and a training session. It's time we all worked as one." Clannahan pushed his chair back and stood. "My men are ready to provide backup should it be needed."

"I think the fewer that go, the better. We'll finish quicker." Casper pointed to her partner then Noah. "Hailey, you can guide us via Melody, and Noah, well, you're pretty handy in a fight and can sniff out trouble before it arrives. I can phase the three of us."

"Four of us. I will also go," Dante proclaimed without hesitation.

"No. What can you do in a fight that we can't?"

"From a short distance, I can convert Duncan's boot into lead, at which time he will neither shift nor run." Dante waited for someone to refute his claim.

"Then why didn't you do that before?" Casper turned to face him.

"Because he was not within sight, and I thought the boy could resist a few taunts. I will not make that mistake again."

"What are your limitations?" Casper asked with defiance. They'd spent precious few hours training together, and she didn't like entering a fight with an unknown.

"No moving parts, no great change in mass."

"Hold on, guys. Let's back up here a second. Phase? What does that mean?" Colson also stood, ready to go. "And why didn't I know we had our own personal alchemist?"

"These are what you'd call growing pains." Casper sighed. "No, Colson, you can't go. However, I will show you why during our next training session."

"Damn," Colson said. "Behind the eight-ball again."

"Not for long, son. Not for long." Clannahan grinned and waved them out with the promise of full disclosure.

Casper breathed in the morning air with a lighter heart and the promise of better tidings to come. "Wanna take my car?"

"No. We'll take mine," Dante said, his BMW chirping when he pushed the button on his key fob. "I prefer to arrive in one piece."

He drove the foursome per Hailey's instructions. It seemed the Italian grew more like the old Trenton with every passing day—overbearing, territorial, and unbending. Hailey maintained a buffer to keep the peace while relaying Melody's running commentary.

School grounds channeled a silent desolation despite the colorful decorations. It reminded Casper of a ghost town described by one of her older acquaintances. Would that change in the coming school year?

Ruts in the dirt road circumventing the grounds contained puddled water from the previous night's rain and tossed the car's occupants to the side at intervals. The current area would support more of the creatures they all wished to avoid.

"Pull off to the shoulder, here," Hailey said from the front passenger seat. "We're close."

Each slid out from the car, Hailey and Dante with pistols in their back waist, and Noah with claws extending from his fingertips.

Casper took center position and prepared to phase them all.

"And here I'd thought they took my amulet because they knew what I could do with it. Good thing they turned out to be total idiots." Brisk wind blew Hailey's long hair across her face before she retrieved a band and corralled it.

"Sometimes in life, you get a break for no apparent reason," Dante confirmed when pocketing his keys.

Casper nodded and held both hands out to her sides. "This will go a lot faster if we link up and walk side by side. We can travel the same path as the spirits do and save time."

Hailey directed their movements from the roadside. "Wish I could see them as well as hear them."

"I don't think I'll ever get used to walking *through* trees." Noah chuckled and lightly squeezed Casper's fingers, remembering to retract his claws when she flinched.

Striding in step allowed Casper to coordinate phasing and releasing her talent. A chuckle escaped her lips. "And this is why we need to train more together. These things need to be second nature, not seen as a novelty. Ouray and Kiera are gonna come down and work with us."

With Hailey and Dante on one side and Noah on the other, Casper followed Hailey's relayed directions.

"We could all benefit from their experience," Hailey agreed then inhaled quickly. "Oh, Melody says she found it 'bout a hundred yards ahead, she thinks."

"She thinks?" Dante parroted.

"Things are different on the other side, or so they all tell me. Time, location, travel, everything. It's like a whole new world, well I guess it actually is. And since most spirits don't communicate much with others, it's not like there's a continuing education class to help them."

"Who else is here?" Dante asked.

"Addy and Yamato. They're arguing over the morality of possessing the living. Yamato doesn't understand that Addy has never lived, so she never absorbed the cultural norms ingrained in some spirits."

"So I guess his taking over Dante was a quirk." It felt eerie, like Casper stood on the verge of a great discovery. Each remained wary and ready for attack despite their unseen lookouts.

Thick vegetation proved no barrier, nor did the two coral snakes or copperheads present a problem when they tried to strike.

"I don't understand why Duncan's man didn't come back for it. They must have taken it as some kind of trophy." Casper stopped when Hailey pulled up short. "He's proven very cunning so far."

"Melody says it's close by. She can't remember which tree base, though."

"One of them probably lost it during a shift. As far as not coming back for it, they probably figured Clannahan would have these woods under surveillance twenty-four-seven at this point."

"There it is!" Noah released Casper's hand to brush aside a tangle of briars and grab the gem reflecting a sliver of filtered light. Holding it aloft, he turned to hand it over. "Here you go."

Casper snatched the lanyard and slipped it over her head. "Thank God. I've missed so much."

Noah's next step paused with his tennis shoe inches from the ground. "Nobody move." Retracing his step, he crouched to study the tangle of vines. "There's a trap hidden in the bush."

"How'd you see it?" Casper moved closer in disregard of his order.

"Light reflected off the pan of the trap." Noah grabbed a fallen branch and jammed it toward the ground through a patch of thick viny growth. "Ha."

A loud snap accompanied the springing of thick sawtooth jaws closing tight and cutting the limb in half.

"Whoa. That could've been my leg." A slight coating of perspiration dotted Noah's face.

"Okay. So, why didn't we set one off before now? You know they've got to have a bunch of these scattered around. Clever bastards."

Casper examined the thick metal. "We took a route through the trees and heavier brush instead of using the deer trails. These were probably set before they knew we could phase through objects."

"I haven't seen any cameras. If they're watching us now, they must know they don't stand a chance," Dante said in scanning the trees around them.

"Either way, I suggest we leave... now. Casper?" Hailey held out her hand.

Dante retrieved his cell with one hand and took Hailey's hand with his other. "I'll let Callahan know to clear these woods of further traps."

Casper breathed deep. "*Simon? Are you around?*"

She felt it the second he settled on her shoulder with a loud, "*squee.*" His weight, once familiar and so comforting, restored a piece of her soul. Instead of the light brush of butterfly wings at his touch, she felt his tail wrap around her neck and his arms squeeze her head tight.

"I'm not quite sure how to interpret that sound," Hailey murmured. "I'm hoping that's a happy reunion? Maybe with a little chastisement to not lose the amulet again?"

"Yeah. He's glad to see me."

The capuchin monkey cooed softly against her hair.

"I missed you, too, buddy. Thank you for not leaving me."

A solid round of chittering communicated Simon's glee over their renewed connection. He stood to his full eighteen-inch height with arms held up in a victory stance before reaching out to give her a noogie.

"*Hmm,* this has been a bit anticlimactic." Hailey stepped through a downed tree covered in ivy. "Not our usual style, huh? Let's go back and give Leigh and Colson a colossal migraine. We can have all kinds of fun giving them a proper introduction to the spirit world."

Addy floated in time with the group's pace, her backward movement through a large boulder disconcerting. "You know, I feel better since you put that amulet back on. One of Duncan's psychics must have been fiddling with it, because I feel like I'm all here now."

The fact she drifted through the trunk of a large oak instigated a few chuckles. Each could hear as well as see the spirit while linked with Casper.

Casper's steps back through the woods grew lighter than she'd felt in months. She couldn't stop talking on the drive back.

Each Christmas, she and her family gathered at Nicholai's house, which, of course, she'd do this year. But she also wanted to start a new tradition of her own. A darker thought occurred, could she remain at Clannahan's house after graduation? They'd not discussed their plans that far in the future.

By now, Clannahan had formed plans A, B, and C.

Leigh and the others were sitting at the conference table when they returned to the loft.

"Ah, and so they're back. That was quicker than expected." Clannahan nodded at the quartet with a raised brow. "Anything unexpected other than the bear traps?"

"Not really." Casper beamed a bright smile. She'd feared losing one of her oldest friends. She'd met Simon at the time Kiera's family adopted her. He'd moved to Texas with her rather than stay in Pennsylvania, and she couldn't imagine life without him.

"I take it by your grin that your amulet is intact?" Trenton asked. "How 'bout you all finish eating and tell us about it."

"Oh, yes. I'm starved." Casper sat and began filling a paper plate with biscuits and crawfish gravy.

"Spoken like a true teenager." Dante ambled over to where Clannahan stood in front of their murder board. "Any news on Wyatt's end?"

Clannahan shook his head. "Not much. We have surveillance on the local boss, and can follow him down the food chain, but not upward."

Trenton shrugged. "So, we work with what we have. At least we can cut off the supply of information and maybe prevent any more kids from getting taken with the start of the new year. I do have one suggestion."

"Fire away," Dante said then moved to Clannahan's other side to study the board.

"Since they have their own hacker and have proven adept at circumventing security systems, I suggest we do a bit of hands-on surveillance."

"I second that," Dante agreed. "But we should be careful of how we divide into teams when we go."

Casper brushed crumbs from her hands and stood when finished. "It's also time to integrate our skills. Now, we start training together. Full disclosure, no secrets."

The grim smiles plastered on Leigh and Colson's faces didn't come close to reaching their eyes. Hailey took pity on her friend and said, "Don't worry. You're gonna love this part. I promise."

Clannahan had spared no expense in remodeling the first floor of the converted warehouse. Thick mats lined the area designated for training, which gave each leave to utilize their special talent.

Each team member had specific skill sets and strengths, but they hadn't learned to meld together as a whole. That took practice, field experience, and time.

Colson took Casper by surprise when stepping up to her. "Let's see what you've got, kid."

"Seriously? A norm?" Casper smiled, looking forward to this particular sparring session.

"Is that what you call us?" Colson took a tentative swipe to gauge his opponent's skill.

They'd sparred before, but not with the no-holds-barred expression he now wore.

"You'll get used to it," Clannahan replied as he watched from the edge of the mat. "What she hasn't *fully* learned yet is that even us *norms* can take a psychic by surprise on occasion."

"Oh, I learned that when Trenton first stepped through my phased boot to hold me in place by the sole of my foot. Damn clever, that one. Then, Duncan got me too. Yeah, I'm learning all right."

"Even feds can learn," Trenton replied with a snort as he faced Hailey.

Casper landed a glancing blow to Colson's shoulder but took one in the gut in exchange. He proved superior in both reflexes and strength.

But that wasn't the only way she fought. "*Addy? How 'bout a little help? How scary can you be?*"

When she feinted a straight punch with her left fist, Casper grabbed hold of Colson's wrist with her right hand.

The spirit of Hailey's younger sister manifested inches from Colson's face in a form not previously seen and one Casper could not have imagined. It did, however, give her a great idea for next Halloween.

Floating between the combatants, Addy took shape as an ogre with wild, flowing red hair and pointy teeth. Claws extended from her fingers as she manifested a size double her normal appearance.

"Holy shit. What is that?" Colson stumbled backward to land on his ass with a thud and breaking the connection.

"You see, when fighting with a psychic, you need to be alert for *different* styles." Casper smirked and held out her hand.

"A little more description, please?" Colson tentatively took her hand again, this time with a new wariness.

"Sure." Casper launched into her past experiences with the spirits. They'd become so much a routine, she rarely thought of spirits as different.

This time Addy appeared her normal size wearing jeans and a t-shirt. Though still translucent, dark hair hung in waves down her back to her waist.

"Well then, Addy. It's a pleasure to meet you." Colson held out his other hand but didn't suppress a shiver when Addy touched him. "Damn. I've felt that before. That was you?"

"Yes. I'd like to consider myself an honorary member of the team and as such, will endeavor to protect my allies."

"Thank you. In the woods when we arrested Frederick. That was you?"

"Yes. I owed that prick a bit of payback on behalf of Hailey. Matter of fact, I still do. He tried to kill her."

"Damn. Remind me to never get on your bad side. From what I hear, the hospital has Frederick under constant surveillance. At first, they thought he was faking a lot of nonsense, that no one could be that bad. They've come to learn differently." Colson nodded to Casper when she released him and stepped back.

"Shall we continue with today's lesson?" Casper smiled sweetly.

Colson narrowed his eyes and smiled. "Why, yes. Yes, we shall." Instead of settling into a fighting stance, Colson stepped forward with hands at his sides. "Well, Casper. Now I understand the nickname." The smile curving his lips didn't signal attack. In contrast, he extended one hand slowly until touching her wrist. "You've grown into quite the young woman, haven't you?"

Casper noticed the others who'd been sparring stop to stare, having obviously noticed Colson's change in tone and demeanor, sexual in nature. She looked to Leigh in confusion.

They are a couple, aren't they?

She hadn't been the only one to notice the two sheriff department detectives growing closer. Hailey had come to the same conclusion in the loft last evening during a late-night discussion.

In the next instant, she flew ass over tea kettle to land on her back. Colson had twisted his body and yanked her off balance before using his body as a fulcrum.

The mat underneath her wasn't a new feeling. Though, usually it was Ouray or Kiera who put her down.

From the sidelines, Clannahan chortled. "And that is why Nicholai says to always remember you are neither at the top or the bottom of the food chain. The minute you forget it, someone will remind you."

Casper grumbled but accepted a hand up. "It's not like I consider arrogance a virtue. I know we're supposed to fight with our mind as well as our heart."

"We all can learn," Colson replied with a wink, all suggestion gone from his mien. "I guess us norms aren't so bad after all."

****

Duncan

Duncan prowled the small confines of his kitchen on two legs and growled. Small equaled a relative word when the average tiger shifter weighed well over two hundred pounds. If not for his shifter status and ability to heal during transformation, carrion creatures would be enjoying a large feast on his body.

Half his pack was either dead or missing, presumably fled in the face of a stronger adversary. He'd been a mercenary too long and in too many situations to not protect his reputation now.

This job offered the biggest payday of his life, bigger now with less members to share it. The unknown boss on the other end of his email had promised nearly unlimited resources with a fat paycheck and other perks along the way.

In return, he had to deal with the two teens and stifle their little rebellion. He should have been told about Clannahan's reinforcements. It made him wonder if the mystery boss knew about them.

In his back pocket, his phone dinged with an incoming message. He'd requested more resources and the signal to proceed as planned.

Finding the student with the incredible and near-invincible ability to walk through any danger equaled the golden prize. Containing her, and training her to obedience, might be an issue, but worth it in the end. He kind of appreciated her mouthy responses.

He'd enjoyed taking her down a peg and crushing her foot even more. The fact he'd seen video of her walking normally soon after meant the enemy camp employed a healer.

"Hey, D, are we good to go?" His second in command transferred his weight foot to foot in anticipation of the next battle.

Duncan checked his message. He had no clue of the puppet master's identity or how they were connected to the VP's office. As long as they paid well, it didn't matter.

You have failed again. We're tired of your dawdling, regardless of their psychic abilities. You have forty-eight hours to capture or kill the girl, the shifter, and the PI. After that, our contract is terminated.

"We've got two days to finish this assignment. Since our target can't find us, they'll go after those they suspect are involved."

"Chopper says they're on to Jenkins."

"So that's where they'll show up next, and they won't be expecting company. We'll hunker down for a few days for everyone to heal. Then, we kill them all."

Chapter Sixteen

Dante

Afternoon breezes failed to sweep away Dante's concern over continued meetings held in secret. The men he, Burke, and Yamato worked for had proven themselves powerful and connected. They also intended to safeguard the right for psychics to thrive in a world where they weren't hunted.

Both Burke and Yamato were dead, yet somewhere along the line, he'd adopted these strange bayou aberrations as family. He still hadn't figured out how that happened. His boss warned him that having feelings for others, however unintentional, equaled a danger which could spell their doom.

In their own way, each member of the task force embodied the honor and integrity required for employment with the Hachiman, an organization dedicated to the psychics' freedom.

Olivia's family in Pennsylvania thought they'd rooted out those wanting to either eradicate or enslave the supernatural, but they were wrong. The elimination of radicals on US soil created a void, one filled mostly by Viets and southern Chinese.

The difference in the new upstarts stemmed from their objective. The new regime didn't necessarily want to destroy from what they'd determined. They wanted to take control of major political and economic resources from the inside.

Never had he considered non-psychics a valuable asset, but the norms of this group—as Olivia called them—had proven their worth. Still, that wasn't the life he wanted for them. Did he have the right to sideline anyone willing to fight for their beliefs?

He stood shadowed under the concealing leaves of the hardwood canopy to await his contact's arrival.

The Hachiman predated his family and new friends by hundreds of years. Most of his old friends were now dead, fallen in the tidal wake of the war to come.

If destiny chose these misfits from hell to fight by his side, he wouldn't interfere. First, though, they had to survive.

With the loss of Yamato came the necessity for backup communications since telepaths were rare in his experience. His friend had lied about his ability in an attempt to keep Hailey and Olivia out of danger. It didn't bear thinking about what would happen if they discovered the truth.

Both women held valuable if raw talent and were now targets of a group they knew nothing about. Olivia had been right, they needed full disclosure. Secrets protected no one.

But the ones I hold aren't mine to share.

Assassinating a high-functioning telepath was difficult, but the faction they fought had proven better. Yamato was skilled and always kept his mental shield up. Perhaps he was targeted due to a slip by someone close to him.

"You are late," a deep voice from behind chastised.

"For good reason," Dante replied to the one who'd recruited him as a young man.

The psychic known only as Kaito stood straight, his brown eyes assessing everything around him. "She has found the amulet, then?"

"Yes. Her spirit is strong and her will equal to her mother's. She will make a good addition to the cause."

"She has little restraint, more mouth than sense, and is subject to her hormones. She is impatient, arrogant, and stubborn." Kaito offered his opinion without malice.

"As was I at that age, if you remember."

"How could I forget?" Kaito paused to consider whatever he intended to say.

A man of few words, when he did speak, others listened. It wasn't his ability to teleport with a thought that made him invaluable. No, he'd proven himself a clever strategist and ruthless during battle.

"Both she, the shifter, and the private investigator can help tip the scales in the future. That is, *if* they learn to integrate their abilities. Hailey will be particularly powerful." Kaito's perspective had evolved since their last meeting.

"The PI is a late bloomer, although I believe she will inherit her full potential with the right guidance." Dante had watched Hailey's progression with a sense of pride, as if she were kin.

"See that she does, but do not lose sight of your goal. Even the humans must play their part."

Dante knew it was too late to exclude any of the bayou mavericks, as they'd gained the attention of both the Hachiman and those wanting to destroy them.

"I didn't think such a diverse array of character traits could work as a cohesive unit, but they are learning to do so. Progress is difficult but steady. Their allegiance to each other is strong and smoothing the way for the addition of non-psychics. We cannot take one without the rest, or at least offering them the choice."

"Yes, but now is not the time for revealing the threat to us all, Dante. The ultimate battle is far in the future. Like our enemy, we must prepare. We must plan and take small wins where possible. If we can root out their infrastructure, we'll collapse their effort before it gains a momentum none will survive."

"We need time and experience to form a cohesive unit. Also, the group from Pennsylvania who adopted Olivia could be of great help." Dante considered what he'd learned about Nicholai and his band of diverse warriors.

Kaito nodded and crossed his arms over his chest. "Yes, they will be needed one day. They think their battle is over. What is to keep them from becoming complacent and... starting families of their own? I've seen it happen more than once. Psychics have been hunted since the dawn of time."

"Family is what makes them strong and will increase their incentive to join us when the time comes. Members of the task force do not share blood ties, but they've proven they'll stand together." Dante had never planned on calling anyone family, ever again, not after shifters murdered his relatives.

"I do not believe Nicholai has had a vision of myself or our cause. It is better I don't interact with them for now."

"But I can? I'm told it is difficult to hide anything from him."

"Reveal only the barest necessities and not until necessary. Nothing more."

To keep vital facts and history from trusted friends could cause an irreparable rift when Dante divulged the truth. "They are preparing to cut the ties between the GE school and those pulling strings behind the scenes."

"Then help them, but keep Noah, Hailey, and Olivia safe. The boy in particular is untrained and untested. Take whatever precautions are necessary, but don't let that trio divide in the coming skirmish." Kaito's forewarning came with a nod. In the next heartbeat, he vanished.

Damn.

He'd need help to accomplish his task *and* avoid exposing vital knowledge of a war yet to be fought.

Guess it's time to bring Clannahan into the fold, if only to the outskirts.

Just because Kaito didn't name Clannahan didn't make him unimportant. The major was a master strategist and clever as hell. He'd help guide the group, but only if given sufficient reason.

Inviting the semi-retired officer for a beer required a clear head to balance the flow of information. When Clannahan entered the house, he looked around and smiled.

"This isn't where you live. No pictures, no personal items of any kind, it's almost sterile. I take it this is where you met with Yamato and Burke?"

"Didn't take you long to figure that out, yet you nor your men have visited."

Clannahan chuckled. "Didn't need to once you contacted Hailey and fired up Casper's curiosity. I can see that duo as a force to be reckoned with one day."

"You have no idea." Dante offered his guest a beer then sat in a wing chair.

"Nicholai has indicated the same thing." Clannahan took the offered beverage and sat on the leather sofa. "Are your employers ready to show themselves?"

"No. Not yet. They want this local mess cleaned up and our unit blended to work as one. I *can* share this. There is a war coming, deadlier than what you and Nicholai's men and women dealt with last year. We have time yet."

"Preparations?"

"Our goal is to fracture their underlying foundation to help facilitate internal collapse when the time comes. For now, we can stunt their growth, as it were."

"By preventing them from connecting with some of the best minds the US has produced." Clannahan nodded his agreement. "Good strategy."

"There are other factions in play. Not schools for gifted children, but psychics who could play pivotal roles in their regime if turned toward their goals."

"I won't back unity until meeting your commander or administrator."

"And you will, but not yet. For now, I need to see Hailey, Casper, and Noah safe. To that end, whatever divisions the task force deems necessary, those three must stay united."

"Your *other* team has a seer. I'm surprised Nicholai hasn't caught wind of them. Then again, maybe he has. He keeps everything close to the vest."

"As does Kaito." By revealing that tidbit of information, Dante hoped to gain the major's cooperation. "We *all* want to see the world safe from autocrats, psychic or otherwise."

"And from which side of the coin is this next threat coming?"

"Both," Dante replied. "Which is why we'll need a mix to combat them."

"You've indicated your force is experienced, but not their size."

Dante recognized military strategizing flowed in the man's blood.

"I know of roughly two dozen. There could be more." He couldn't give specific details regarding Kaito or individual talents, in part because he didn't know them all.

When obviously satisfied he'd gain no further details, Clannahan nodded and stood, having taken only one sip of his drink. "All right, then. To ensure the trio remain together, I'll need Nicholai's help. Understand, I will not lie to him, but I will promise him full disclosure at a later date."

From what Dante had heard about the warrior leader, Nicholai would see it all coming.

Chapter Seventeen

Casper

Something about being tossed to the mat by an overbearing tyrant edged the needle higher on Casper's frustration.

Just because Dante had earned his place in the group didn't mean she had to like it, but she did have to suffer his presence. He seemed particularly focused on her non-psychic combat skills, criticizing any wasted movement or perceived weakness and, in general, proved himself a gigantic pain in the ass.

In cahoots with Clannahan, they'd commissioned special boots for them all, an innovative design preventing penetration of the sole. Next generation material protected the instep, vamp, and shaft of their footwear. She could protect anything above that with phasing.

The matted training area maintained ample room for four sparring couples. Switching partners periodically kept each member focused, mentally agile, and helped ease her desire to maim.

Hailey currently faced off with Noah, but Addy enjoyed adding her own element to the match. The young shifter swiped intermittently at his face, causing Hailey to smile and Casper to giggle.

"It's not funny," Noah complained. "It's like fighting two, except you can only see one."

"Hey," Hailey failed to dodge his leg sweep and landed with an, "oof." Again. "We all have specific strengths and need to learn to use them to our best advantage. It's not like our enemies are gonna fight fair. 'Sides, I'm the one who's gonna be sore. I'm on the light end of psychic ability."

"At least you have something," Leigh retorted after landing a solid punch to her brother's gut.

"Hailey, you're sore because you lack specific experience against shifters, just like the rest of us, well, except for Casper. That's why you need to train every day," Clannahan piped up from the sidelines where he pored over several files.

"No, I'm sore because I keep landing on my ass." The morning's session saw her knocked down more often than not. "I'm not asking anyone to take it easy. I just wish I was faster."

"*Then, might I suggest you not take point on future missions?*" Yamato Takahashi's advice was as unwelcome as his untimely arrival.

"Don't badmouth my partner, ghost. Fair warning." Casper grinned when Dante failed to land a punch to her solar plexus. "Frustrating, isn't it?"

"Good." Leigh stopped and bowed to her brother. "Next time, brother. Next time."

Trenton merely smiled.

They'd all reached an unspoken truce yet remained competitive to the point of utter concentration, except for the two most stubborn and vocal of the group.

The verbal cease-fire between Casper and Dante occasionally stretched the boundaries of tolerance. Those sparring paused to observe the obstinate teen and aloof Italian clash.

When Casper phased her hand into Dante's shoulder and wiggled her fingers, he countered by converting the sole of her boot to melted rubber. It was a toss-up as to which of the two growled the loudest.

"Enough, you two. Get along," Clannahan warned.

"If she doesn't accept her vulnerability, she'll get herself and others killed." Dante took a step back and rolled his shoulders.

"I do accept it, but I don't give up, you overbearing boot-slinger." Casper stripped off her boots and socks, ready for another round despite the pain in her foot.

"I'll have you know Italian boots have the finest craftsmanship and style in the world. I'll be sure and order you another pair, if your closet isn't stuffed with high heels."

The slur on Casper's perpetual jeans and boot casual wear hit its mark, yet she remained stone faced. Until she smiled.

"Damn. I sure wouldn't want to be on the receiving end of that. Might bode ill for a good night's sleep. Many nights in fact." Hailey inserted herself between the pair. "I think it's time to switch partners."

"*Hmm,* if I can't sleep, I'll practice converting matter, like a mattress pad to water, or perhaps vinegar." Dante gave no quarter nor would he back down.

"All right, then, Dante, how about you and Leigh work together for a while. You both have skill, but Leigh is exceptionally fast." Hailey urged her partner away. "Casper, why don't you quiz Yamato on what he's been doing lately. Maybe he'd like to join us for breakfast in a bit. I was beginning to think he'd given up on us."

"*Gee, thanks for the vote of confidence. I see you've retained your sense of humor, PI.*"

Rolling his shoulders once more, Dante questioned Hailey, "Yamato's here?"

"Yep, and I'm hoping he has something for us." Hailey turned in the general direction of the spirit.

Casper pursed her lips then covered her mouth with her hand. "What's up, Yamato, and why are you wearing a dress?"

"*This is my formal Umanori Hakama.*"

"Is that like a formal gown?" Casper had seen the traditional clothing in movies. "What do you wear underneath?"

Hailey laid her hand on the younger woman's forearm to see what the fuss was about. When connected, she brightened and said, "Very nice, Yamato. Why the formality?"

"Guess formal doesn't include shoes?" Casper quipped. "I was beginning to think you'd moved on."

"*I will not move on until knowing my killer is vanquished and my wife is safe. The former, I can help you with. The latter, I will need Hailey's help, hence the extra concern for her safety.*"

"Okay. So, we're trading favors now?" Casper set one hand on her hip, a sign of belligerence to come.

Hailey intervened with, "How can you help us with locating Duncan?"

"*I know his location at this very moment.*" With head held high, straight back, and hand resting on his Tsuka, the katana's handle, he appeared every bit the samurai warrior.

Casper's translation to the team members included a few added comments, unappreciated by their informant. Each began unwrapping the thin layers of tape and gauze from their hands and removing protective gear.

"Way to bury the lead, old friend, but I'd like to see you when we speak." Dante approached with outstretched hand, accepted by Casper. Whatever their personal differences, they subsided when it involved work.

Turning to face the spirit, Dante added, "I will see to your wife and child. You know this. They are still with your sister-in-law, west of New Orleans."

"*Thank you, Dante. As to our business, we need to move now. It seems Duncan fancies himself a great leader and has set a trap, or probably several by now.*"

"I say we go pull the tiger's tail." Casper smiled and raised her hand for Noah's high-five. "Where is the douche?"

"*Where he thinks he has the greatest advantage, of course. His home in the bayou.*"

"Then, let's lay this out and go." Casper headed toward the meeting room where they divvied up assignments.

The sooner they cut ties between the GE school and whatever faction wanted the students for their special projects, the sooner life could return to normal. Though, having Noah stay at her house was a perk, even under Sarah's watchful eye.

Dante's suggestion of the entire task force remaining together struck a discordant note for Hailey. If not for Clannahan backing the proposal, the group might have rebelled.

Casper voiced her own concern. "That's not the way we do things."

Clannahan made a low noise in his throat. "You mean that's not the way the *other* half of your family does things. This is a new team, hence new tactics. You all haven't worked together long enough to anticipate each other's reactions. You each have very specific but very different talents, and that takes time to assimilate."

Dante inserted commentary ending with, "Hence, we go together so that one can pick up the slack if the need arises."

"You calling us slackers?" Casper challenged.

"I'm calling the team, as a whole, inexperienced. For instance, the last time we split into two teams, your first instinct was to move to your downed teammate and phase him, yet it was more effective for me to convert his knife into a harmless piece of rubber. In some cases, it'd be more effective for Leigh or Colson to shoot an enemy than to challenge one physically. *These* are the things and the situations we need to iron out."

"Our non-psychics have proven themselves every bit as valuable as the rest of us," Clannahan agreed, moving to stand. "They also seem to view situations with more logic than emotion."

"'Cause they're older." Casper grinned at Dante.

"Hence, have more experience," the Italian fired back.

"These armored shin guards are the devil to get used to." Hailey bent to readjust her right boot shaft. "Though, the thought of having my foot eaten off does add motivation. I don't think I could stay linked very long through that kind of pain."

"We'll get used to them. I like moving in during daylight. The strap on night-vision goggles always gets caught in my braid." Casper took center position on the team's approach to their target with Hailey on her left and Noah on her right. This left Trenton and Dante taking end positions of the single advancing line.

According to the plan, they'd put Leigh and Colson's sniper skills to use. She'd phased each one, along with two of Clannahan's snipers, to within sight of the target house and waited until they'd secured themselves high in the canopy.

Casper's questions regarding the assignment remained unspoken due to the probability of creating uncertainty in the team. Clannahan was a genius with strategy and would've consulted Nicholai on such a mission.

Still, it rankled. She might have kicked a loose stone in the paved driveway a little harder than necessary. Conforming to group standards required patience and restraint, but mostly patience.

Beside her, Hailey squeezed her hand. "Think of this as a new beginning, your fresh start. You're part of an official task force."

It didn't help.

"Who puts a half-mile driveway to their home like this? I know it's not like they're gonna have to shovel snow, but still, it just screams tacky with all these flower beds. What does this even say about Duncan anyway? I figured him for more of a manly man."

"Men can like flowers," Dante argued.

"To me, it says an assassin job pays well," Noah replied, snorting when Dante made a rumbling noise in his chest. "What? *I* wouldn't mind living in a mansion like this. Look at it. Two floors with sliding doors opening all along the balcony. How many bedrooms do think he has here?"

"Enough for his kitty pack, I'd think. With lots of room for visitors." Dante scanned the thick woods on his side. "We should be coming parallel to Leigh's position soon."

In answer, two clicks over their ear mics signaled both snipers ready.

"Speaking of living arrangements, you can't go back to the dorm after the holidays. It won't be safe until we've settled the school's issues." Dante's proclamation aired with a sense of finality.

Casper grinned. "Oh, we already figured that out. He's gonna stay with me."

A round of snorts and chuckles arose from the group—except for Dante.

"Um, no. He won't. I've already spoken to Clannahan, who's made arrangements for you, Noah. With your family's blessing, of course." Dante's words contained a challenge.

"Let's settle this later." Trenton, the voice of reason, pointed at the final bend in the driveway with his free hand. "Stay focused."

"Why haven't they attacked?" Casper asked, startled when Yamato appeared and floated before her. "They have to know we're coming. It's broad daylight, for God's sake."

As if on cue, a single shot fired from the second story passed through Hailey's chest and ricocheted off the asphalt.

"They've watched you all since you parked down the road. They know you're linked. And, no, they don't know about our two teams positioned in the woods." Still dressed in his traditional, formal garb, Yamato pulled his sword from its scabbard.

"Hey, translucence is nice, but do you mind? It's still distracting," Casper didn't duck when the spirit made a sweeping motion with his blade. "How about telling us what's going on in there?"

Yamato nodded. *"Duncan is on the main floor. He's set up a command center in the living room. It's all open, so that'll give them less places to hide."*

"Numbers?" Dante asked after Hailey translated the conversation.

"Nine inside."

To Casper's right, Addy and Melody floated side by side, each dressed in jeans and button-down shirts. Apparently, the two got along well, as Melody appeared more determined, her silhouette glowing brighter, a factor wrought through heightened emotion.

"You've got two more outside. They shifted and divided after leaving the house. They're making their way to Colson and Leigh," Addy advised. *"Can you tell them each to make ready?"*

Again, two taps on their ear mics signaled the response to Casper's relayed message.

"How high up did they climb?" Yamato asked.

"Thirty feet minimum," came Clannahan's murmured voice in their ears. *"I have drones on each. Shifters may pick up human scent, but they won't pick up the mechanical devices."*

"Why is Duncan keeping the fight inside?" Leigh whispered in their ears. Slight crackling sounds from rubbing branches where she perched muffled her words.

"He must know we've used military drones in the past. He's not one to rush into battle without studying his enemy. He won't come out until forced." Clannahan then spoke to one of his men in the background.

They'd set up their staging point two miles down the road.

"Unless he has something else up his sleeve. I feel like we're missing something," Trenton cautioned. "Not sure what, but we'll know it when we see it."

An unattached garage as long as Hailey's loft sat cattycorner to the home proper. No light seeped from the windows on the front.

"Think he realizes his own mortality?" Casper asked. "His arrogance seems limitless."

"Reminds me of someone else," Dante muttered.

"Hey, I'm not arrogant. I'm just good at what I do." Casper smiled when hearing each of her companions either giggle or grumble.

"Listen up. Our job is to capture Duncan. Alive. Please keep that in mind." Trenton's caution derived from military experience.

Chapter Eighteen

Casper

Welcoming the visitors inside, the front door opened before they reached the porch's foundation. The interior mimicked the style of a classic southern mansion.

The line ascended marble steps in perfect sync, one of many exercises practiced until perfect. If Hailey or Noah noticed a slight bit of moisture coating Casper's palm, neither offered comment. She'd survived numerous fights battling other psychics when her teammates all had some type of talent.

Trenton called the shots in today's assault, depending on her to offer different tactics that might be employed.

Behind them, a dozen micro drones flew waist high then immediately rose and spread out once through the doorway, the assemblage split into three groups.

One set peeled off to soar down the long hallway under the stairs, another went to the second floor and split up to search each hallway. The third searched the perimeter of the first-floor open area.

Smaller size increased their agility when Duncan's men shifted and leaped to swat them out of the air. It also negated the ability to carry weapons.

"Wow, I thought there'd be, like, more of a fancy feel to the joint. How disappointing." Casper scanned the open space.

Duncan stood straight, his arms loose at his sides. "It's a shifter thing you wouldn't understand."

"Do you, like, grow your own version of catnip?" Casper wanted to give the two remaining shifters outside a chance to approach her from behind—and receive sniper's lead for their effort.

Duncan's flat stare was answer enough.

"I keep a supply of the same drug used on you to find perfect specimens. A shame they never last long. My men play a little rough. And since they've been restricted since moving here last month, well, they're ready for some fresh meat."

The team faced four oversized hulks wearing sweatpants with no shirts or shoes, split up to flank their leader. Either bald pates or buzz cuts coincided with military bearing. Casper hadn't seen such a line of bulging muscles since the war of psychics.

In less than ten seconds, each shifted and stood ready at Duncan's command.

Casper chuckled. "Wow. Kitty cats that all look alike. How do you tell them apart, Duncan? Or doesn't it matter? I mean, you're leading them to their deaths, so I guess it's better not to get too familiar."

If they faced men, Casper could discern much from watching their eyes and facial expressions, like the moment before they decided to strike, which way they'd go, and more. One could anticipate much from studying an enemy in human form.

"Wow, they do look the same. I agree with Casper. Not very sporting of you, Duncan." Hailey pivoted slightly to take in the entire room.

Forty feet to the back slider in the kitchen would take them outside to a deck spanning the home's width, according to prior drone surveillance. Dozens of stacked deck chairs cleared space for the coming fight's overflow.

A massive staircase to the right led to the second floor where four brutish men stood with automatic weapons. Each caressed their triggers with longing and hunger in their eyes.

"Ah, I see his plan. He wants to shoot each of us in the foot before they attack." Casper nodded respect to the ginger-haired leader.

"Everyone has a weakness. Exploitation puts us on equal ground. Firing from height gives us the advantage."

"*Hmm*," Dante hummed. "Give me a minute." Closing his eyes, he tilted his head to the side then opened them with a smile.

"Dante, handguns?" Trenton asked. He'd proposed this possibility during training as an ambush tactic.

"Neutralized, but their knives have moving parts, switchblades. There's nothing I can do with them."

"So do automatic weapons. How'd you manage that?" Casper asked, still confused over how the Italian utilized his talent. Changing matter was great, the limitations not so much.

"I didn't touch the guns, just what's inside. Each bullet has no moving parts within it. Duncan must acquire his ammo in bulk, which makes me grateful, as they are all the same composition." Dante nodded toward the homeowner. "And the same weight."

"We still outnumber you. If you surrender now, I'll let your human playthings in the treetops and down the road live." Duncan removed his t-shirt and waited for an answer.

"Do you guys buy shirts in bulk too?" Casper asked, genuinely curious. "I'd think you'd go through them at an alarming rate. I understand how you can keep the sweatpants on, and by the way, they look absolutely ridiculous."

"Maybe he makes them wear different colors to tell them apart?" Hailey suggested.

"They're not telepathic," Noah confirmed. "At least I've never heard of a pack that is."

"Then what good are they? It's like using a blunt instrument. Not very effective."

Duncan shook his head and heaved a sigh. "*You* might be more trouble than you're worth. I've been ordered to kill you, Noah, and Hailey. However, I'm willing to make an exception for the right trade."

"I guess the bigger they are, the smaller their brains. That sound about right, Hailey?" Stalling was usually Casper's strong suit but, today, she just wanted this to end.

"Kill them all." Duncan raised his right hand and indicated his men on the second floor. "See, we know your weakness. In order to remain on this floor, you have to have physical contact, at least with the sole of your boots, which gives us an entry point, from the top."

Instead of a hailstorm of bullets raining down and through them, four gun barrels exploded. Each of the men lining the interior balcony screamed and threw up their arms to protect their faces.

Too late.

Barrels split with the detonation when the firing pin struck the material which replaced the primer.

Two men fell over the balcony to the first floor. The other two fell to the side. All carried metal remnants from the explosion.

If death didn't immediately find the two falling fifteen feet and landing on polished hardwood, it secured its hold with broken necks. The others lay on the balcony, failing to shift or move.

"Well, that went swimmingly." Casper made a face when viewing the angle of head to chest of the closest fallen mercenary. "Damn. At least he's no longer in pain."

"Wonder what his spirit will be like," Hailey quipped. "Do you see him yet?"

"Nope, they're usually confused for a while. It takes time for them to realize they're dead, longer to adjust to the new environment." Casper shrugged. "We have our own contingent of spirits to counter any mercs who prove fast learners."

Tiger shifters stood beside their leader, slack-jawed. So sure of his plan, they remained flat-footed. Two on his left side looked ready to turn and run.

"So, it's true. They say you talk to spirits." Duncan took a fighting stance. "Do you command them or offer them compensation for services rendered?" His sly rejoinder coincided with him scratching his chest, now starting to sprout hair.

"I've never thought to ask, does it itch when your fur stars to emerge? And do you have to use a special shampoo, like, from a veterinarian?"

Simon launched himself from her shoulder toward the leader now sprouting hair on his face. Spirits didn't suffer the effects of gravity, but navigating the spirit realm required shedding mental restraints.

If Duncan's slow transformation equaled a form of distraction, it worked.

A light haze accompanied the change, enough to block the finer details of the shift. Each psychic cringed with the snapping and crackling of bones and tendons.

Clinging to the lead shifter's shoulders with his prehensile tail and otherworldly force, Simon clawed at Duncan's chest. The man frowned but continued his shift.

"Yeah, fortunately in this instance, you men won't learn much just from crossing over, so you can't use them against us," Casper replied. "Any word on the rest of the structure?"

"Clear," came Clannahan's voice in her ear.

"Well, then. Shall we? Mindful of their knives." Casper let go of Hailey and Noah, then indicated the others do the same.

She was well aware of their enemy's fighting style. Shifters had faster reflexes, were more powerful, and fought with a hive mind mentality, despite lacking telepathic ability.

Duncan had even greater strength and good deductive reasoning. He was not an enemy to engage lightly.

Unlike fights in the movies she'd watched, most skirmishes lasted minutes, usually less. She'd been party to one stretching out over an hour when a small army attacked her family in Pennsylvania, but here, she knew the score. Brutal, fast, and deadly.

Her friends were untried in a team effort, but each proved they could adapt on the fly. One shifter, three other psychics, and a war-tested veteran made a good team.

"The two who were outside are coming in," Clannahan informed them.

Two gunshots sounded at the same time the first shifter leaped at her. The loud crack to her left was from Trenton. The tiger's arc changed after receiving a splitting headache for his effort. Literally.

Her first opponent either hadn't engaged her during the earlier fight or acted on instinct. He leaped from ten feet away.

Casper had phased all but the soles of her feet then timed her fingers' entry into its skull.

Yuck.

Beside her, Hailey had drawn her gun but not fast enough. A second tiger rushed from beside Duncan.

Casper sidestepped to intervene, remembering her first deadly fight.

The tiger bolted forward and opened its massive jaws low to the floor. He'd learned from his boss and aimed for the bones in her foot.

There wasn't anything she could do. Picking up one foot would instigate him going after the other. Considering time and reflexes, he'd be faster. That took mere seconds to work out in her mind.

It ended with crushing pressure but wasn't as debilitating thanks to the boots' unique construction.

When the animal failed to bite through its target, it switched tactics and yanked her off her feet.

Casper switched gears and solidified her butt where she landed and phased to kick the brute in the head. By the time he gathered himself to leap, she'd rolled to her knees to attack.

"Casper, down. I'll shoot him," Hailey yelled.

The beast struck at her midsection then moved lower when finding his jaws phased through. Using her solidified feet to push off, she phased her entire body, except for her fingers delving through his back on either side of his spine.

In effect, she did a handstand on its spinal column. Its roar of pain morphed into a strangled cough as it went down.

Hailey's shot ended its struggle.

Twisting to the side before her feet touched the floor, she used the dead tiger's body for cover in fighting her next opponent as she lowered one foot at a time until between the animal's neck and the hardwood.

More shots fired.

Casper checked her partners to see who needed help. Both Hailey and Trenton emptied a magazine during their quarry's mid-leap, sidestepping to allow the dead bodies to crumple on the floor behind them.

It took Duncan less than a minute to determine the battle's tide. He pivoted toward the stairs and ran underneath them. His tail disappeared down the hallway before anyone could stop him.

"Damn. Clannahan, can—"

"I've got eyes on him. Down the hall, fourth door on the left. Ran into a closet and closed the door. Heat signature shows he went... down."

"Down? As in secret passageway-type down?" Hailey asked, standing over a wounded tiger with her gun at its head.

It didn't move. She didn't shoot.

Trenton also had an injured animal at the end of his Glock. "You can shift back to human form, and we'll take you into custody, or you can die like an animal. Your choice."

On Casper's other side, both Dante and Noah stood over inert tigers. Neither had shifted back to human form. In her experience, when a shifter died, their body reverted back to human status.

They'd have prisoners to interrogate.

"You guys got these clowns? I'm going after Duncan." Casper visually checked the scene before turning toward the hallway.

"Not alone. We'll go together." Dante had already taken the lead. "Noah, stay with Hailey and Trenton in case they have reinforcements coming."

Casper bolted down the hall toward the large bedroom and followed Dante into a walk-in closet. A three-foot square hatch covered in the same carpet lining the closet sat open. Apparently, Duncan didn't figure anyone was fast enough to catch him.

A set of stairs led down to a tunnel.

She saw nothing move in the black void but did hear intermittent splashing. Grabbing Dante's arm, she hauled him back. "No, I go first. I'll hang onto you once I descend and keep you phased."

Dante grumbled something she couldn't decipher.

Metal treads of the ladder pinged under her steps in entering pitch-black nothingness. "For the record, I hate snakes, spiders, and all the biters waiting for us down here."

"Then move back to Pennsylvania."

She descended the first three steps then decided to jump. A splash preceded the shin-high water seeping into her boots. "Aw, gross..."

"We're in southeast Texas lowlands. You should've expected water in any kind of subterranean passage."

"Disgusting." She retrieved her phone from her jacket pocket while Dante scurried down the steps.

He jumped the last third and landed with a splash before accepting her hand.

"Clannahan, we're heading west. You might want to send out drones to see where this comes out." She didn't know if he could hear her or not. Knowing his foresight and his experience with psychic talents, he'd probably thought through this scenario.

"Been surveying the land in all directions, concentrating on the west side now. Vegetation is thick. Working as fast as we can. I've got armored drones topside and men closing in. They'll hold until we find the exit."

If good news existed, it was the fact they kept traveling straight for each short distance her phone illuminated. "Whoever heard of tunnels in lowlands like this?"

Either tiger shifters had excellent night vision, or Duncan had supplies waiting in case of an emergency exit.

The phone's app allowed communication with whomever listened in on their progress. No doubt Wyatt heard every sound while watching through the drone's camera he would've hacked.

They were family.

"Seriously? You carry your phone to a fight? Dear God, no wonder psychics are doomed to extinction." Dante made a grab for her phone, missing when she phased both through his reach.

"Later, dinosaur. Wyatt?" She led her not-welcome partner through ankle-deep water, no longer hearing Duncan in the distance over the noise she made.

"*Yeah, kid. I'm scanning topography via satellite and drone. Looks like they've got two man-made dunes a quarter mile northwest and northeast.*"

"And?"

"*Clannahan's men are closing in on both. Duncan won't escape either way. I don't see another avenue for escape. Careful. He might double back on you.*"

Like many caverns she'd seen in northern climes, the tunnel branched off at forty-five-degree angles. "Think this is their way of a diversion? If we take the wrong one, our guys upstairs might not be prepared for his return."

"*Hmm.*" Dante urged her aside to take the lead.

"Well, shit. How many dead ends do you suppose he has? There could be a maze down here. If it were me, I'd have quite a few tunnels branching off." She stopped at the first bifurcation. "We can't split up unless you're willing to return. You can't fight what you can't see, and he's too fast for you to take on alone."

He couldn't deny her claim and didn't try. Whether because he understood the validity of her statement or had determined to protect her didn't matter. At least they agreed.

Dante tugged on her arm and pointed left. "This tunnel is wider than the other. Makes better sense if he's evacuating a large number of residents."

She'd never been claustrophobic but didn't appreciate the dank and musty smell or the low ceiling reinforced with an unidentified material. She couldn't remember the species of algae and fungi that could grow in dark zones, not requiring light for photosynthesis. At least the slickness didn't arise from bat guano.

Intermittent splashes ahead signaled movement growing closer. The fact she hadn't heard it a minute ago meant Duncan had reversed course.

She had trouble maintaining her gaze on the lower half of the tunnel, the result of too much education. "There's a cave in Mexico, Kantemó Cave, where snakes dangle from the roof."

"It's also called Bat Cave." Dante pulled her to a stop. "Listen."

"Yeah, I hear him. If I see him, I'll phase us through him."

"No. Don't do that. We would leave the others topside to deal with him and possibly get caught off guard. Duncan's story ends here. Now."

"So, you hate all shifters. Why?"

Dante cleared his throat. "I've come to accept Noah, although I don't know his family well enough to say the same about them. Yet."

"And here I thought you'd pulled a Clannahan move and had them all investigated ten ways to Sunday." Casper crouched, listening.

In the distance, bipedal splashes grew louder. The man had speed as well as agility.

"He's on two feet, not four. And he's moving toward us. Guess he found his exits blocked." Casper wanted to let go of Dante to face Duncan but couldn't take the chance. Her instinct to phase would put him in danger due to the shifter's size and speed of transformation.

"He probably has a gun."

"So, do your thing with his gun. Which by the way, what was that back there?"

"Not now. I have to see that which I'm affecting, and your phone doesn't give us enough distance."

"At least I thought to bring a light," Casper countered.

"Who'd think to find a tunnel in bayou country?"

"Shifters, obviously." Casper crouched, ready to drop her phone and unphase her free hand. It'd require split-second timing and she'd ruin her cell, but she wanted justice for Melody and Yamato.

The splashing stopped.

Dante moved to her non-dominant side and laid his hand on her shoulder.

The hair on her arms rose, the warning clear. "There's no safe passage for you out of here, Duncan. Give up and survive."

"Even if I fail, others won't. None of you will survive what's coming."

"So, tell us more about it. You assholes love to gloat." Casper's goading came natural. If she could learn more, it might protect other students.

"No need. You'll find out when the time is right."

"But you won't be alive to see it, shifter." Steel edged Dante's words.

She couldn't hear Duncan's breath or stealthy movement. If she gave him more time, would he think it through and opt to live?

Soft crackling, popping sounds echoed in the confines. The light she'd come to associate with the shift contrasted the dark surrounding it and marked his general position. He'd made his choice.

If he leaped at her, she'd have to time unphasing of her hand perfectly in order to stop him from getting to or past Dante. This is why Nicholai and Clannahan insisted they train while depriving them of critical senses. She relied too much on sight.

Casper slid forward as silently as possible to put space between her and her partner. Hearing the damn Italian move likewise to keep a consistent distance made her want to scream.

She didn't dare speak to warn the others and miss her chance to eliminate the threat. Instead, she thought, "*Yamato, are you near?*"

"*Yes. The creature has shifted and is waiting... for something.*"

"Go tell Hailey to block the exit with her gun in hand. We'll stay out of her range."

"*On it.*"

She couldn't hear or see the spirit move behind her but felt it when he'd left.

The sound of water swirling caught her attention a second before she saw the tiger's form flying through the air. She'd heard a low grunt. Tiger shifters could leap thirty feet, outdistancing her light.

The second she saw a glimpse of fur and gleaming white teeth, she dropped her phone and phased her hand.

Her timing was off. The tiger passed through their phased bodies before she could latch onto anything solid.

Damn, he's quick.

Now standing in ankle-deep water surrounded by pitch black, the only light seen was a shaft at the entrance to the tunnel. It didn't matter. They both heard him making his way out.

Duncan splashed toward the ladder and stopped.

There was no need to search for her light.

Dante yanked her back the way they'd come. "Hurry. I need to be closer and see him better on the stairs."

"For what? It's too far to be accurate." Casper tapped her mic as they raced for the entrance. "Hailey, Duncan's headed your way. He's in tiger form... still wearing his sweats."

It was curious that the tigers kept their sweats after shifting, whereas Noah and the others she'd known disrobed first.

Expediency?

Backlighting from the ground floor entrance revealed the shifter had again transformed to bipedal movement. Light from above reflected off the metal barrel in his hand.

"Gun! He'd had a gun in his sweatpants. That's why they don't undress." Casper bolted forward but knew she wouldn't be fast enough. "He's coming out."

Duncan fired twice. Whether preliminary or seeing his target, he didn't hesitate to start climbing the ladder.

From the bottom rung, he moved up quickly, sure to be listening for signs of his enemy.

"He's not going anywhere," Dante assured.

An agonized growl echoed down the tunnel when both of Duncan's feet passed through the middle rungs of the ladder.

In the next instant, solid metal encased both of his legs. Dante's psychic talent had converted straight stair treads to circular cuffs.

Not admitting defeat, the man glared his hatred over his shoulder. "You have no idea what's coming for you. When it does, you'll both die in ways you can't imagine."

Duncan shifted to beast once more, allowing his lower legs to slip through the restraints. He splashed down on all fours and faced the passageway. A low roar gained volume.

"Can you change the water to solid form?" Casper asked.

"No. It's already moving, hence, is beyond my power."

"Fine. I'll do this the old-fashioned way." Casper jerked out of Dante's grasp and started forward.

"No. He's mine. I have an old score to settle." Dante urged her aside and removed his jacket to meet Duncan face to face.

The tiger's next roar reverberated off the walls and shook Casper's resolve. She steadied herself and leaned heavily against the tunnel wall. Firsthand knowledge of the damage his bite could do slid forefront in her mind.

The leap with outstretched claws would've taken any man down upon contact, but Dante pivoted to avoid the brunt of the approaching force. At the same time, he tossed his jacket in the tiger's face and shoved against its massive body.

The tiger jerked and contorted before landing but couldn't dislodge the garment quickly enough. Dante punched out and caught the tiger's flank, shoving his shoulder into the opposite wall.

Collision only created anger as Duncan slid down to land, splashing into the water on all fours.

Mindful of his temporary advantage, Dante swiveled to coil his jacket around the animal's head, effectively blinding him but not negating his power.

A second later, the tiger wore a granite mask with an enraged Italian shoving its head under water.

"Dante, don't. We need him alive. You're going to drown him."

"This is for Natalie Mandler, Yamato Takahashi, Clarence Burke, and Melody Gingham." Using his weight and position for leverage, he held the tiger's head below the water line.

Ahead, Hailey hopped from the middle of the ladder into the tunnel. Her dash forward included the flashlight app on her phone and lit the scene for all to witness.

Casper stood transfixed, never having seen their newest teammate so unbalanced.

Pure. Seething. Rage.

When bubbles stopped floating to the surface, fur receded from the animal's skin, replaced by the finer vellus hairs covering Duncan's now-human form.

He no longer struggled.

"Well, damn. Feel better?" Casper asked, not sure what else to say.

Dante looked up and met her gaze. "That's been a long time in coming."

"So, who's Natalie Mandler?" They'd hunted together and survived a tiger's attack. Maybe he'd be forthcoming.

"Not now, kid. I need to regroup."

Casper got nothing further, nor did she prod, having learned the futility of it.

Once upstairs, they saw Clannahan and his men had contained the surviving shifters in cages. What surprised her was seeing Noah and Clannahan in what appeared to be a deep conversation, which was not going well according to Noah's tight expression.

She was too tired to get into it. Debates on timing and procedure could wait until after they'd eaten and debriefed. On the positive side, she'd wanted a new phone and could now justify its purchase.

Chapter Nineteen
Hailey

Hailey awoke early the next morning to a very distinct vocal screech. The alarm cleared the grogginess from her brain in an instant.

A glance out her window declared it well past her usual rising time. After yesterday's success, the team deserved a break, not the hundred-plus decibel shriek capable of breaking glass.

Gunther whined. Not one to see spirits, he was sensitive to their presence and agitation. His degree of restlessness usually changed with a spirit's rise in emotion.

"Okay, boy. Let's go see who's harassing Casper now." It was the only explanation for Simon's vocal outburst.

She donned her robe and puppy dog slippers in hopes the entire gang wasn't present. She caught enough hazing about her dress code from Trenton. Gunther pawed at the door, his tail brushing the rug where he sat. He bolted through as soon as the door opened.

"Well, don't mind if you do, fella."

The entire team had gathered in her living room. "Since when did we start meeting in my loft?" Her amusement dwindled when seeing Noah and Dante in a heated discussion despite their voices remaining low and taut.

Trenton and Casper looked on, with the latter stepping forward to intervene until Trenton held out one hand with a firm, "No. Never disrupt an argument between your boyfriend and another man."

Trenton's acknowledgment of Noah as both a man and her boyfriend successfully stopped Casper's progress and indicated the agent's ability to learn tact.

The high-pitched squeals didn't stop until Casper held out her hand, accepting Simon's weight with a *shooshing* noise.

In the kitchen, Colson and Leigh prepared breakfast, ignoring the drama.

"What's the ruckus about?" Hailey accepted the cup of coffee from Leigh and started for the door to take Gunther out. "On second thought, never mind. I'll leave you guys to it while I'm gone."

"Wait, Hails. Colson and I can take him. You might want to stay for this one." Leigh patted her thigh and opened the back door. "C'mon, boy. Let's get some fresh air."

"Strangest task force I've ever encountered," Colson muttered in following Leigh.

"Well?" Hailey asked. She started to take a seat then thought better of it. It'd be best to remain close in case the argument got physical.

"Mr. Italian here has a problem with me staying at Casper's house."

"Technically, it's not *her* house. When you're old enough to pay your own rent, then you can decide who sleeps under *your* roof," Dante countered. "You two need to cool off and take a break."

"We haven't *done* anything," Casper yelled. "And besides, Sarah makes rounds every night. She's like a damn robot."

"I don't care. Still not gonna happen. He's too much of a distraction for you." Dante stood firm with both hands fisted on his hips.

"Screw you. You're not my keeper. We'll do what we damn well please." In full defiance mode, Casper pulled Noah close and kissed him full on the lips before smirking at Dante. "So, there."

Noah's hands went out to his sides, his eyes wide and stance unchanged.

"I'm trying to save your life." Low and controlled, Dante's tone held a world of unnamed emotion.

"You're trying to control my life," Casper countered. "There's a difference and I won't stand for it."

"That's what your mother said and look where that got her," Dante shouted before pivoting and stalking out the door.

"Oh." Casper's form deflated with a *whoosh*. She turned to the others, stock still with mouths agape. "What did he mean by that?"

There was no one else to ask, except for Nicholai and Clannahan. From what she'd learned to date, prying secrets from either required more strength, stamina, and cleverness than any of them could muster.

"I don't know, Casper. I just don't know." Hailey wrapped her arm around the teen's shoulders and guided her to sit. "Noah, get her something to drink, please."

"Doesn't matter. That tight-lipped dago can keep his secrets for all I care. It's not like anything can bring my parents back. It's time I accept that and move on."

"As in physically?" Hailey asked wondering if Casper would fold and leave, going back to Pennsylvania.

Casper's wan smile failed to reach her eyes. "No, my home is here now. It'd be nice to boot *him* out, though." She hooked a thumb over her shoulder in the door's direction.

Leigh, Colson, and Gunther returned just as they heard the roar of an engine and a car peeling out of the parking lot.

"Guess that didn't go well," Leigh surmised. "Come on, guys. Let's eat and hash this out or eat and leave the talking part for later. Whaddaya say?"

"She's right," Colson agreed. "We need to strike fast. If we can get to VP Jenkins before he restocks his crew, we might be able to track his command up the line to the organizer of this mess."

"Then I'll meet you guys downstairs in thirty minutes. Did anyone bring food for this morning's meeting?"

"Got it covered," Leigh said. "I've made fresh coffee and will take it down."

No one speculated on the connection between Dante and Casper. Her folks died years ago in Pennsylvania, with their identities confirmed through the teen's DNA.

Of all the sparring matches with the aloof psychic, Dante had always worn gloves and shielded his thoughts. More than once, Hailey had considered the option of alcohol to loosen his tongue and inhibitions.

Dante refused to drink with them.

Once downstairs, each took a seat at the table and passed around the carry out containers of Creole mini quiches, beignets, and fresh pastries. They were warm, gooey, and smelled like heaven.

Clannahan cleared his throat at the head of the table. "Dante will join us later. He's, ah, otherwise occupied." No one addressed the previous argument, having the sense to pick their battles.

"Yeah, probably turning the Gatlin Bridge to molten slag." Casper took a bite of her pastry and washed it down with coffee.

"Do we have enough intel on Jenkins to move on him?" Colson asked, sitting beside Leigh.

"I believe it's time. Yes." Clannahan addressed them all. "From our surveillance and what I can determine, he has no psychic talent. I believe he's been placed in that position for the mere purpose of easy manipulation."

"What about the captured shifters?" Colon asked. "Did they know anything about the chain of command above Duncan? Since he's, uh, unfortunately dead, we have little from that direction."

They each knew of Dante's temporary loss of control. Hailey wondered if this morning's outburst signaled the beginning of a downward spiral. If so, there'd be difficult times ahead.

Colson and Leigh had spent the prior afternoon and late into the evening filing reports appropriate for authorities to read. Both human and experienced officers, they had the best handle on how much diversity from the truth locals could swallow. The world wasn't ready to know about psychics.

"No," Hailey replied. "They took orders from Duncan and knew nothing that went above their own heads. I'm afraid that information died with him."

"We do, however, have a lead on where these shifters came from. There's a consolidated group near the west coast where residents claim to have seen tigers." Clannahan opened a folder and passed around photos of their target's house. "I'll be keeping an eye on them to see if anything else develops. There's no way to know if those men were selected at random from like-minded mercs or if they were the only ones who took assignments."

"Looks like Jenkins lives on a quiet street in a middle-class neighborhood." Casper wrinkled her nose. "Having strangers within a stone's throw of where I sleep would keep me awake."

Hailey agreed. *Probably from years of looking over her shoulder in expectation of a deadly threat.*

"Surveillance shows Jenkins is alone in the house this morning. I suggest we keep our entry group to two." Clannahan nodded as if confirming the plan forming in his head. "Casper and Hailey. You two have worked together longer than anyone else here."

"I'd advise a badge of some sort accompany them," Trenton suggested. "If he's concerned about appearances, it could help."

"Either way, we need to go into this phased. Me holding the hand of a man your age is gonna look a little weird." Casper's smirk received a quizzical frown from the federal agent.

"No stranger than a mid-twenties young woman holding hands with a teen," Trenton responded.

"All right, fine. You can come. But if your hand sweats, I'll have Simon perched on your shoulder and screeching in your ear for the next two days."

Trenton merely shook his head. "Fine, but you can tell Simon I only mean to keep you safe. Team members look out for one another. Remember?" He smiled and touched his cheek. "Thanks, fella. We all know you're part of the team as much as Gunther."

Details of the upcoming mission included the resident's habits, daily routines, and known contacts. His recent schedule comprised trips to private gambling sites, the grocery store, and a local bar.

Callahan was as thorough as he was determined.

* * * *

Casper

Casper slid from Trenton's SUV parked on the road's shoulder. Some might call the dead-end street quaint or even cozy with its interconnecting branches overhead forming a sheltered passage.

To her, it felt cramped.

She accepted Hailey's hand, then Trenton's on the other side after he rounded the hood. Considering all the crap she'd given him in recent months, he remained wary but now accorded her more respect and always considered her opinion as he would any member of equal standing.

"Ya know, I'm glad you two finally decided to get together. I really couldn't see Hailey with Dante."

"And you wonder why your instructors always harped on you to focus." Trenton paused when a car turned onto the road at the end of the street, until it pulled into the second driveway and parked.

Small but well-kept lawns marked the caliber of the neighborhood. Colorful light strings waited for sunset to provide a dazzling display of holiday cheer.

"Nah, I know why they do. They just don't realize how good I am at multitasking." Casper kept them phased up the stone walkway and to the bottom of the front stoop. "Hang on, guys. I'll take the lead. Jenkins knows my face."

"Wait. Casper, where's Yamato?" Hailey firmed her lips into a straight line and waited silently.

"*I'm here. Hold on, I'll check to see if anyone else is in the house.*" Yamato floated through a support pole to make a beeline through the front door. It was considerate that he didn't go through his teammates.

A minute later, he returned.

"*He's got company of the brutish variety. Might I suggest a faster approach if you want him to maintain the ability to speak?*"

Hailey ignored the brass knocker in favor of her fist. "You hear that, Clannahan?"

"*Yeah, I got it. Not sure how visitors got in there without our knowledge.*"

"Yep, the side of your fist is a subtle method of introduction." Trenton blew out a slow breath. "Why bother knocking at all?"

"It's so we don't startle anyone into rash action. It'll help them focus." Casper chuckled at flipping Trenton's words back.

They expected Jenkins to open the door but didn't expect to see a face used as a punching bag. His right eye was swollen shut and blood oozed from his split lip despite him wiping it on the sleeve of his shirt.

"What happened to you?" Casper asked.

"What do you want, Olivia?"

"*Hmm,* you remember my name. Good. Well, for the record, I'd like world peace, a house of my own, and to find out what happened to my parents. Not in that order, mind you."

"Go away." The door would've slammed in her face had she not thrust her steel-toed boot against the jamb.

"That's no way to treat someone who's possibly here to help you." Hailey stepped up beside Casper and held out her right hand, keeping hold of the teen with her left.

"We're here to help this douche?" Casper murmured low, a deep frown taking over her expression.

Jenkins ignored Hailey's gesture. "It doesn't matter. I'm beyond help, and I can't help you. So..." Jenkins arched a brow at Casper's lower leg. "You mind?"

Trenton flipped open his credentials to reveal his badge then returned them to his pocket. "We need to talk, Jenkins." In lieu of waiting, the agent shoved the door wide with his free hand and stepped inside, tugging Casper and Hailey along.

Jenkins had no choice but to move back, his posture a mix of disgust and defiance. His gaze flitted toward the kitchen.

Hailey gripped the homeowner by the hand at the sound of footsteps coming from the kitchen.

The size of the intruder carried more significance than the gun in his hand when rounding the corner. Standing close to six and a half feet, he wore blue jeans and a denim shirt. His balaclava denied visual identification, yet his brilliant golden eyes declared his genetic oddity. Most of Duncan's pack carried the same physical marker.

He fired four shots in quick succession, his gun barrel swiveling the slightest with each.

One by one, the bullets passed through their targets to strike the living room wall.

The intruder grunted and shook his head.

Jenkins tried to pull free until Hailey jerked him closer. "Stay still. We're trying to protect you."

Trenton returned fire, but his reflexes were no match for the shifter.

The back door slammed seconds later.

"Great." Trenton holstered his weapon.

"No, Trent. He's not our objective." Hailey urged Jenkins to sit on the worn leather couch. "Let's have a chat about what I've seen. Shall we?"

"What, the man wearing a mask? I have no idea who he is. Not that it matters. How did he miss us all? Was he shooting blanks?"

"Of course," Casper said with disgust. "Guys like that always fill their guns with blanks. They even buy the kind that leaves holes in your walls."

Hailey closed her eyes, a sense of calm overtaking her features. "Were you part of their plan to collect unique individuals?"

"Collect? What are you talking about? These kids are prodigies, not *things* to be accumulated."

Hailey lowered chin to chest. "*Hmm,* you're telling the truth, at least in part. He didn't find out until he was deep in hock to them."

"Really? He's that dumb?" Casper asked in disbelief.

"They were leveraging his gambling debt to make him their puppet. He met with a black-haired woman. He's shocked about... her demand for him to interview certain kids. He thought at first they wanted to help those with special talents."

"The woman is Beverly. My secretary."

"You're screwing your secretary?" Casper shook her head. "Old men are so disgusting. Way to go. Like any horndog, led by his horn."

"No. That's not our relationship. Never has been." Jenkins shuddered.

"What specifically did she want you to do?" Trenton asked, visually scanning the perimeter for threats.

"She wanted to know more about them. What they did in their spare time. What they liked. Who they liked. Places they wanted to go. I thought if these kids could get a leg up, so much the better. I didn't see her goal at first. By the time I did, it was too late."

"What? You're saying you're not behind Melody's murder and my kidnapping? What the hell?" Casper's outrage simmered in her mind.

"I had no idea. It was all Beverly's doing. I overheard her one night, talking on the phone when I was coming to meet her. Jesus. She planned to kidnap one of the kids to get to another."

Trenton asked, "Why didn't you go to the authorities then? Accepting a bribe is nothing compared to kidnapping and murder."

"It was too late. She already owned my soul. I had no idea they were going to kill anyone."

"So that fifty grand from Melody's uncle *was* to gain her entrance to the school." Casper pieced things together but not all seemed to fit. "Is her uncle part of this scheme or not?"

"Not," Hailey said. "He just wanted his niece to have an advantage after graduation."

"I was trying to pay off my debt with that money when I realized they meant to get their hooks into the students. I figured they were corporate headhunters at first, which was a problem for their parents, not me."

"They were headhunters all right. Just not the corporate kind," Casper responded.

"You thought you found a way to dig yourself out with the money, but let me guess, it wasn't enough." Trenton nodded like he was taking mental notes. "Who approached you about Melody's acceptance, her uncle or the ones holding your marker?"

"Her uncle. He wanted her to have a better life. That's all."

"What about all the emails between your computer to Duncan? Using the dark web, no less." Casper nodded to Hailey, hoping for a new set of images and more information.

"What emails? Dark net? I don't know how to navigate that. Oh, hell. That's what Beverly was doing at my desk."

"And Duncan?" Trenton asked.

"Oh, that Neanderthal? He came to deliver a message, said either I cooperate or die. That was before Melody, and before..."

"Before what?" Casper asked, her breath coming a little faster.

Hailey tilted her head to the side, eyes closed and a frown creasing her brow. "You found out they wanted to kill Casper, Noah, and me."

"Yes. I overheard Beverly talking yesterday when I went to her house. I was desperate to get out from under them. I won't be a party to murder, but they said they had incriminating evidence that would put me in the electric chair."

"Melody might still be alive if you'd come forward at the start," Trenton berated the sweat-soaked VP. "What about the local crime boss? We know he's trying to make connections here with Beverly's contacts."

"What? I don't know. I'm not involved in local crime."

Despite his knowledge of events and the fact he'd facilitated criminal activity, Jenkins continued to claim innocence.

Hailey nodded, affirming what truths were spoken. "Looks like with Jenkins out of the picture, we're cutting those ties, at least for now."

"There's one thing left to do, and one way to save your life, Jenkins." Trenton retrieved his phone from his shirt pocket and checked his settings. "I've got his statement recorded."

"What? You can't do this. It's illegal entry. And I didn't kill that kid. I've done nothing wrong."

"We can't pin a whole lot on him legally," Clannahan advised through the mics. *"Find out what other individuals were targeted."*

"Jenkins. The guy who just used your face as a punching bag then tried to kill you... how long do you think it'll be before he comes back?" Casper acknowledged Clannahan's statement in her ear with a tap on her mic. "Tell us who else is at risk."

Jenkins sputtered and looked around, his gaze settling on the bullet holes in his drywall. "I'm a dead man."

"If we let you go, you'll endanger the lives of other students first."

"No. They said I could keep my place as long as I cooperated. I told them I wouldn't be a party to hurting any of the students."

"They're trying to kill Noah and me. We're students," Casper countered.

"Well, you're different. I'm talking about the normal students. You've got no proof. If you did, I'd be under arrest. Now, get out of my house."

They had one chance to cut the ties between Beverly's boss and the students. If they waited, it'd be too late.

Casper smiled. "I have an idea." She grasped the pendant around her neck. "Hey, Yamato. You still around? I have a job for you."

"You all finish your Christmas shopping?" Casper sat on a sofa beside Hailey in the loft. "It's only three days away." She didn't mean to whine, but last year it'd become the most important day in her life after sharing a home with those considered family. Her present companions were no less so, and she wanted to express what she couldn't verbalize.

A chorus of, "No," filled the air.

She accepted a cupcake and made room for Noah in eager anticipation of the evening's local news. The performance could have significant bearing on many lives, not to mention their entire investigation.

Trenton sat on Hailey's other side with a beer in hand. "You think Yamato can pull it off?"

"I think he's very determined and won't quit until he succeeds. I just hope while he's possessing the creep, he remembers to leave Beverly out of it. Both Wyatt and Clannahan are monitoring her moves to see when and where she contacts her boss."

"What about Jenkins' computer? Didn't they trace the emails back through that?" Colson asked from the kitchen before returning with two slices of cake, giving one to Leigh before sitting beside her.

"No. The connection was terminated, or whatever. It's a dead end," Casper replied, disgusted with the situation and failure to finish closing out the case.

On screen, VP Jenkins stood behind a podium on the steps of the GE administration building. Bruises on his face had already started to darken. His right arm leaned against the platform and supported his weight. He likely had broken ribs.

"Thank you all for joining me today for this very important announcement. I'd like to make a statement before answering questions." Stilted speech with a distinctive northern accent didn't alter the small gathering's enthusiasm.

If not for the advertised subject matter, only a fraction of the news teams would attend. As it was, a dozen reporters and their cameramen waited, each checking their notes or equipment.

On screen, Jenkins tugged at the collar of his shirt before detailing his spiral into gambling debt and his part in Melody's enrollment at the school. He omitted incriminating his secretary as requested.

By the time he finished, sweat beaded his brow and his breath came in labored heaves. The fight against Yamato's influence was taking a toll on his mind and body.

As one, each reporter inched closer and asked their questions. All wanted details the VP didn't have. Cameras clicked, and video recorders honed in on the now-pale face.

The outcome—the public learned an unknown organization attempted to infiltrate the school and gain access to the prodigies.

As a result, one student was murdered and another kidnapped. The latter student rescued. Names were withheld due to the ages of the teenagers.

Even if the school didn't close, parents wouldn't be the only adults vigilant and concerned for the kids' safety and well-being going forward.

When finished, Jenkins collapsed to the marble steps. Still, the reporters didn't grant a reprieve. Each pressed closer with more questions, their mics inches from his face.

"Well, then," Colson patted Leigh on the thigh, "...I think I'm ready to call it a night. How about you?"

"Yep." Leigh stood and collected empty dishes to take to the kitchen. "Tomorrow, we go after the secretary. That should be interesting." With a pat on Gunther's head, she said, "Be on guard tonight, fella. Watch out for your mom and her guests."

Casper watched them go, amazed at how they'd adapted to the psychic world and interacting with everyone on the task force.

No one had addressed the fact they were down one team member, or the fact it was her fault. She'd acted impulsively in challenging Dante. Again.

The aloof member of their team had never made an inappropriate move on her. He genuinely cared about her safety as much as the others even if he was a stiff curmudgeon.

What is his problem?

There existed something between them she couldn't define. A DNA sample sent to Neah, a geneticist married to Ouray, yielded nothing.

So, she addressed the elephant in the room. "Anyone heard from Dante?"

"No, but Clannahan's still insisting you and Noah stick with me until we finish sorting out this mess. The major and Dante know *something* they're not telling us." Hailey leaned into Trenton when he laid his arm along the sofa behind her shoulders.

"Don't look at me like that." Trenton gave her a little squeeze. "I agree, but I'm not in the loop either."

"Since they're still keeping secrets from us, how are we supposed to trust them?" Casper punched the pillow beside her in disgust. "I won't work with people I can't trust. If they don't come clean after we nail the secretary, I won't work with either of them anymore."

"What about your family?" Noah offered his girlfriend another pillow for good use. "Isn't Clannahan tight with all of them?"

"Yeah. He and Nicholai tend to be a little cagey at times, but I do trust Nicholai. Let's see how tomorrow goes and decide from there." Casper's suggestions received nods from the other three. She didn't necessarily want to split with the major and Dante, but she agreed with Hailey. Trust equaled an essential part of any working relationship.

Chapter Twenty
Hailey

"Who doesn't love chasing down a homicidal woman who may or may not be psychic two days before Christmas?" Hailey appreciated how diverse activities had fast become the team's new normal.

Not for the first time, she wanted an ordinary day with no bullets, claws, or ghostly possessions. Maybe she'd step out of her comfort zone and enjoy a spa day, taking Leigh and Casper along for the inevitable fireworks.

Fate never took that direction.

Clannahan brought an abundance of tasty food for today's meeting. When asked why he always had food with meetings, he'd said it was the psychic way and left it at that.

Casper dished another spoonful of breakfast casserole onto her plate and said, "This isn't as good as your mom's. If she ever wants to give lessons, I'd love to learn how to make... whatever this is."

"I'll tell her, but be prepared to make cooking your most consuming pastime." Hailey laughed yet knew her partner and mother enjoyed their times together.

"Yes, well, back to the matter at hand." Clannahan used his laptop to pull up a map on the big screen. "It seems our secretary gave us the slip last night."

"I thought you said she'd tucked into bed when we last spoke around midnight." Trenton folded his paper napkin and placed it beside his plate.

"Of course, you'd be up at that hour and still working." Casper pointed a finger at his chest. "Man, you need a hobby, girlfriend, and... I don't know what else. I thought you played the guitar."

"I do, and I have hobbies, thank you." The fed smiled at Hailey, who blushed under his scrutiny.

Clannahan cleared his throat. "We did have her home under surveillance. She's a clever one. I sent men into her house when her heat signature faded around two a.m. Turns out, someone used chemical warmers around a mannequin to simulate her presence in bed."

"Damn." Casper set down her fork. "I've seen that before, except it was a life-size anatomical model with a battery-operated mechanism that simulated slight movement."

"Yeah?" Colson asked. "How long did it fool you?"

"'Bout till the moment the bomb inside went off. We're dealing with professionals."

"A bomb?" Noah asked. "Jeez, your life never lacks for meaningful events, does it?" The shifter obviously didn't have a comfortable word choice. "Then, how'd they not pick up on the heat signature leaving the house?"

"I suspect she used an insulated cold suit. It's what I would've done if I lacked the psychic talent to do otherwise," Clannahan replied. "It makes sense if she had a second vehicle stashed close by."

"Anything of note in the house?" Colson asked, blowing out a deep breath.

"Yeah. There were signs of a skirmish and her blood smeared on the bedroom carpet. Looks like someone took her by surprise and didn't bother cleaning up." Clannahan duplicated his laptop's window on the wall.

"What about her computer?" Noah asked, wincing at the newest photo.

"We have prints and another name for her. Also, her emails revealed the order to terminate Casper, Noah, and Hailey, but that was before canceling Duncan's contract."

"That's code for assassination," Hailey assumed, wondering what rabbit hole she'd fall into next.

"Correct," Clannahan affirmed. "I think she saw the writing on the wall and knew they'd come after her next to close the loop, especially when Jenkins exposed their plan. It also revealed a name in the local organized crime faction we suspect will try to take over their efforts."

Another photo of the master bedroom marked the disparity of the rest of the home. Clothes lay strewn about the floor with a small suitcase lying open on the settee against the footboard.

"This means they're cutting ties and leaving everything to our homegrown thugs. Wonderful," Casper said, washing down her last bit of pastry with coffee.

"If she bled that much, she might be dead," Hailey suggested with a side glance to Casper, the proposal clear.

"Fine. I've got a picture, but her other alias would help." Casper set her plate aside and pushed her chair back.

Hailey watched her partner close her eyes and repeat the name Clannahan tossed out, knowing Casper could call the secretary forth if she existed in spirit form and hadn't crossed over.

The major had kept the meeting moving forward and avoided mentioning Dante, still absent. Tomorrow was Christmas Eve, with the deadline to divulge secrets fast approaching.

In order to avoid catastrophic consequences, she intended to pull Casper's legal guardian aside and have a heart to heart. He clearly respected each member of the team, which meant the secrets he held were monumental.

He'd either be forthcoming and keep the team intact—or lose them altogether. Either way, she'd stand beside Casper, and knew Leigh and Trenton would too.

Restless energy forced Hailey to stand and gather the trash. When she turned from dropping the plates into the trash can, an apparition made her gasp. "Oh, shit. Who are you?"

"*Ah, so the witchy bitch has finally opened her eyes.*" The spirit gained in death what she'd reportedly lost in life. Clarity of vision.

"My eyes are just fine, thank you very much. And yes, I can see you just fine, Beverly. You don't look much like the secretary type to me." For the first time when not in contact with her partner, Hailey saw a spirit.

A dark malevolence darkened her aura.

"*I played the part for that buffoon. Damn thing is, I can't find Jenkins now. Navigating this realm is a pain, but I ran into someone willing to help. From what I've seen so far, it's about time someone organized the idiots on this side.*"

Hailey repeated the spirit's words verbatim.

Casper stood immediately and strode to confront the secretary. "*Hmm, don't dress much like a secretary. More like a madam.*"

"So, she is dead?" Leigh asked. "Does she know who killed her?"

"*I know exactly what's going on. You've ruined everything with your clever Vodou cover. I was just about to get everything they promised me.*"

"Who promised you what? Who's backing you?" Clannahan pushed back in his chair after Casper relayed the conversation. Though he couldn't hear or see the entity, the major inserted himself in the turmoil.

"The ones who will bring you all down. Your paltry Scooby gang will never stand against the tide of forces heading your way. When they attack, you all will join me... and I'll be waiting."

Even without much experience with the spirit realm, Hailey understood the threat. It turned to face her, the light from its aura darkening even as it flickered.

"I knew you were trouble the minute I heard you'd joined with those damned teen brats."

The entity's hazy outline disappeared then reappeared within arm's distance. Its translucent expression changed, the smile transforming her face into something hideous and frightening.

"Hey, I'm not a brat," Casper snapped back but didn't release the amulet in her hand. "And for the record, we've obviously made the right moves, as we're alive and you're not."

Aggravating an angry spirit probably wasn't the smartest move. Then again, Casper could control them with the power in her amulet.

No one else could.

The spirit faced Casper. *"Yeah, I'm dead. You and your bitch friend are the reason. It's time for a little payback."*

The spirit flew directly at Hailey with hands outstretched and claws extending from ethereal fingers.

Every childhood nightmare Hailey ever experienced couldn't compare to the horrific terror invading her senses. She felt the effects of fingernails raking her skin with maniacal laughter filling her ears.

Then, she felt something else, something different. It was akin to the listless feeling when the anesthesiologist injected a sedative prior to anesthesia. The difference, she was aware of the drugged effect but was powerless to stop it.

"Wow. I heard about this but didn't think I could pull it off. Hey, brat, watch this." Hailey heard her voice but had no control over the words spoken.

Hailey saw her arms move in robotic fashion and felt her legs stiffen in taking an awkward step back.

When her shoulder blades smacked against wallboard, she felt the handle of her Hellcat punch her at her back waist.

Her head tilted side to side as if experimenting with movement. Her jaw worked up and down with little more than a groan escaping.

"Love this body. It's stronger than mine. Now, one of you gets what you deserve. The other suffers years of remorse."

Now that she was speaking through Hailey, everyone could hear Beverly and understand her intent.

The guttural words emitted from her mouth instigated expressions of horror on Trenton and Casper's face. She tried to close her jaw tight but lacked control.

"Get out of her. Now." Casper grabbed her amulet and repeated, "I order you to leave her body."

A strangled giggle erupted from Hailey.

"You can control me when I'm free but not while I inhabit this bitch." To emphasize her point, the spirit ran Hailey's hands over her chest and down her flanks, a suggestive eyelid fluttering when smiling at Trenton.

Hailey felt the intent, understood the meaning, but couldn't stop her hand from moving.

Her next words, along with a malicious grin, centered on the federal agent. The gun pulled from her back waist centered on his chest. "Move another inch. Any of you. I'll kill the fed first, then I'll kill the kid."

Without Dante present, the spirit could make good on her threat.

If Casper could connect with Hailey, she could use her amulet and remove the spirit. Her partner had described such an invasion of a teammate the prior year. Removal required physical contact.

Casper released her grip on her amulet and started around the table, until the spirit forced Hailey to rack the slide on her gun, effectively making sure the chamber housed a bullet.

"What do you want?" Clannahan asked, calm as ever and not moving.

"For this bitch to suffer. I think killing her soon-to-be lover then her partner would give her enough grief to last a lifetime."

Hailey felt her finger slide along the cold, metal trigger guard. She felt the clamminess of her skin and saw the horror in her friends' faces.

Trenton stood but didn't pull his gun. He made it clear he'd rather die by her hand than bring her harm.

She saw the love in his eyes mixed with regret, the same consuming her soul. With all her might, she tried to force the barrel pointing at his chest to the side.

Her finger twitched. The coinciding crack reverberated off the walls.

No!

She watched Trenton rock back and spin to the side with the bullet strafing his bicep. She'd managed to avoid a direct hit.

The brush of Addy's fingers along her cheek a split second later signaled both support and help.

"I'm coming in, too, sis. I'll give this bitch hell."

Hailey could feel her mind and body exploding from the inside. Her skin felt too tight to house her organs.

The battle for control raged between her sister and the squatting spirit. Pain racked her mind, her chest, her entire body. Every nerve ending fired at once, inflamed and growing hotter.

Tears tracked her cheeks. Her jaws clenched tight. "I can't control my actions. Trenton, I'm sorry. I-I just can't."

The gun dropped from her hand, but her fingers then clenched her throat. The vengeful spirit held dominion over her hands and was cutting off her air supply.

Her vision clouded.

Sounds dimmed, the boxed Christmas decorations in the corner lost color as everything turned to hazy gray.

Somewhere in the distance, Casper shouted Yamato's name.

Multiple streams of conversations blurred in the background, undefined when two were shouting in her head.

Her sister screamed the rage Hailey felt.

"Addy?"

"Not now, sis. I'm trying to keep you alive. I could use a little help here. Yamato's on his way."

Her lungs burned but didn't compare to the stabbing pains in her head. Rubbery legs gave way, and her knees hit the floor.

Trenton was the first to her side, preventing her face-planting on the cement floor. He repositioned her on her back, his pallor worse than a cadaver.

Strong hands pried her fingers loose. She was aware of the burbling nonsense syllables coming from her throat but couldn't control her speech.

The pain was too much to bear. If death waited for her, it was preferable to what she currently experienced.

"*Hailey, relax your mind. Stop fighting us,*" Yamato commanded.

His voice sounded like it was piped through her ear buds, but closer. The last thing she felt was Yamato's soothing calm invading her senses.

Murmured voices.

Hushed commands.

No more agony in her chest, but residual pain kept Hailey from opening her eyes.

The groan she heard came from her own lips, and a cool cloth rested on her forehead. A familiar warmth pressed against her side, hard and unyielding.

"Hey, sleepyhead. If this is your way out of Christmas shopping, you'll have to do better." Concerned humor laced Casper's voice.

Unseen arms had picked her up and were holding her close. Trenton's scent surrounded and welcomed her back. Hailey opened her eyes to see him smiling.

"Hey. How're you feeling?"

"Probably better than the person I shot. Um, sorry?"

"Already taken care of." A piece of cloth wrapped Trenton's upper arm showed blood stains seeping to the surface.

"You carried me with an injured arm."

Instead of settling her beside him on the sofa, he sat with her cuddled on his lap.

"She's observant for a private investigator. Do you remember what happened?" Leigh hovered nearby, watching.

"Well, I think there were too many people in my body to keep track." She didn't know what else to say, not wanting to utter the word possession.

"Yeah. That about sums it up." Casper stood from across the coffee table and offered her a soda. "Want some caffeine. I hear it helps."

Trenton accepted the can and held it while she sipped.

"You've experienced this, Casper?" There were still so many things Hailey didn't know about her partner.

"No, I'm immune, but one of my friends did. Actually, a bunch of them did. No residual effects in case you're wondering."

"Addy and Yamato booted her out. I remember them arguing, but it was so damn weird. Where is the evil body snatcher now?"

"Well." Clannahan stood from the table separating living space from the kitchen. "Your sister and Yamato carted her off, according to Casper. Something tells me none of us will ever have to worry about that one again."

"Wow. What a way to end a case."

"Over? *Hmm,* I doubt it. But over for now, yes. You all are safe, but we still have work to do." Clannahan nodded as he turned toward the door.

"I think it's time I finished my Christmas shopping. Who wants to go with me?" Casper grinned at her boyfriend. "I have the perfect gift in mind."

"I'm game." Noah smiled and took her hand. "Let's head to the mall. There's something I need to pick up too."

"Guess I'll go also," Leigh spoke up, bringing a tray of gingerbread cookies from the kitchen. "Someone's gotta keep an eye on you two." Nudging Colson in the side, she added, "How about giving me a hand in case they try to divide and conquer?"

"Sure, why not?" Colson took a cookie and hummed his appreciation. "My mom's flying in from Arizona. It's her first Christmas alone after Dad's passing. Care to join us for a while?"

Leigh hesitated, then smiled, her teeth nipping at her lower lip. "You want me to meet your mother?"

"She's been wanting to meet you, but if you'd prefer—"

"No. I mean yes, that's fine. I'd love to."

"Guys, don't forget. Christmas dinner at my mom's. Actually, let's do this here where there's more room. Who's in?"

Nods of approval included everyone present.

Yet there was still one member of their team absent and unaccounted for. Dante.

Chapter Twenty-One
Casper

Christmas morning dawned clear and crisp with the temperature climbing in the low fifties.

Shopping with Noah and the rest of her team had ended with a group dinner at their favorite local eatery, Bouchard's.

They'd all spent Christmas Eve trimming the tree and hanging decorations in Hailey's loft. Colored lights, Santa and his reindeer cutouts, and window stickers included but a few of what filled the room.

As much as Casper enjoyed the outing and dinner with friends, she was glad to sleep in her own bed, even if it was temporary and Clannahan owned it.

Aromas of holly and Frankincense from Cecile's incense welcomed visitors bringing trays of food upstairs to the loft. An extra table along with many chairs provided space to sit and eat during the informal gathering.

Casper smiled at seeing the federal agent wearing a red Santa hat. If women carried an *afterglow,* this guy radiated thermonuclear energy. His smile beamed brighter than she'd ever seen. "*Huh,* looks like somebody got some last night. 'Bout time."

"TMI, kid." Leigh coughed behind her fisted hand. "Though, I have to agree with you."

Trenton's blush didn't diminish his smile.

"How was 'meet-the-parent' day with Colson's mom? I'm sorry she couldn't stay and join us today." Hailey set about making another pitcher of iced coffee.

"She flew back last night to be with my sister and her family in Oregon this morning," Colson offered while helping set out the dishes they'd carried in.

Clannahan strode by with an armful of wrapped gifts. "I had a car waiting at the airport to drive her, so she didn't have to wait through that hassle."

"Thank you." Colson helped place the boxes under the tree.

"I see a few more presents than were here yesterday, Hailey." Casper moved closer to examine a small, wrapped box hanging from the pine tree decorated in a woodland theme.

"Ah, you're right. I didn't put that there, and it wasn't there when we went to bed." Hailey advanced and fingered the box then pointed to a few more. "These are also new."

"Love that it's *we* now." Casper poked Trenton in the chest. "You spent the whole night? You realize, don't you, that you jumped *two* levels in less than twenty-four hours. And there's no taking that back." Protective to a fault, she wouldn't see her friend and partner hurt.

If possible, Trenton's smile widened.

Hailey turned beet red. "Don't worry, Cass. He and I are on the same page."

"Among other things, I'd say," Casper retorted with narrowed eyes. She had every intention of monitoring the situation.

"Back to the problem." Leigh bent closer to examine the items in question.

"Excluding myself, I only know of two other people who've come into your loft without a key, though, it looks like Trent has one now." Casper sidestepped to avoid Hailey's mock punch to her shoulder.

Enthusiastic chuffs and yips from Gunther accompanied him bolting from the kitchen to the door. He lowered his shoulders into play-bow position when Dante walked inside. "Is the offer to join you still good?"

"Yes!" Hailey moved to his side before anyone else could speak. "I'm glad you made it in time. We have a ton of food."

Dante nodded his thanks but strode toward Casper. A slight downward turn of his lips conveyed more than the sorrow in his eyes. "I am sorry for our disagreement."

Casper eyed the newcomer and evaluated his demeanor. Whether in hopes of resolving their previous argument or burying it to move on, she accepted his outstretched hand.

"And?" It was then she noticed he wasn't wearing gloves. She arched a brow and waited for him to dictate which way the wind would blow.

"You suspect I've withheld information, and you're right. I thought it for your own good, but maybe I was wrong." Sincerity, remorse, and grief radiated from the newest guest.

"You were. Trust me."

"Seventeen years ago, you lost your parents. Although I wasn't in the area, I, too, lost those I loved."

She'd never seen him so raw, so earnest, and lacking his usual air of arrogance. "You knew my mother, personally."

A statement she was sure to be true.

"We've not been formally introduced. My name is Martin Schrader." Dante wrapped a tentative arm around her shoulders and led her to the window seat overlooking the street below. "Let's sit for a few minutes."

The others continued their conversations in the background, yet the air remained subdued and expectant. Words stuck in Casper's mouth. There were so many questions she wanted to ask but couldn't figure out where to start.

Dante was a relative of some sort. Reviewing past interactions in her mind assembled pieces of a puzzle that formerly didn't fit.

Dante began in hushed tones, his thoughts years away. "When I turned sixteen, I thought I had the world by the tail." His smile was wistful. "I told my parents I wanted to go abroad and study. I thought they'd flip."

"So, you're not really Italian?" Hailey asked, moving closer, as did Trenton.

"Not hardly. My older sister was the one who paved the way for my overseas adventure. I had no idea at the time why. Not until later."

"You... my uncle?" Casper guessed.

"Yes."

"But your DNA doesn't match mine."

"Like you, I was adopted. I was six at the time. My new family moved to Texas, although my parents never said why. My adopted mother, like your grandmother, had a very special gift. Though, I see now it could be considered a curse. She passed it down to her daughter. Your mother was my sister."

"My mom saw the future?"

"Yes. I'd been living near Lake Bracciano in the Lazio region and studying, albeit having more fun than working, when I got a strange letter from Natalie. She told me to stay put until spring. It was early December, and I was making plans to come home for the holidays."

"She knew..."

"Yes. She insisted it wasn't safe to return. She and her husband were packing and taking you north. Said the rumors were true and that someone hunted us. They wanted to protect you."

The weight of that truth crushed Casper's heart. "What happened?"

"I don't know the specifics. I do know they intended to travel with a pack of shifters, a ragtag group that'd come together from all over the country to settle in southeast Texas. Safety in numbers and all that."

"How'd they die?"

"One of the shifters was a spy, which Natalie discovered too late. She was a seer but could never discern her own future. In her note, she apologized for sending me halfway across the world when she knew death had drawn a bead on her family."

"She was trying to protect you. Family meant everything to her..." The discovery shouldn't have surprised Casper. Maybe it was an inherited trait.

"Yes. She'd begged her husband to leave and take you somewhere safe. When he refused, she secured other arrangements for you. I arrived too late, but swore I'd find you one day."

"My parents were killed by shifters?" Casper couldn't help her gaze from swinging to Noah, whom she'd trusted with her heart and soul.

"I would never betray you, Casper. I couldn't even if I wanted to, which I don't." Noah sidled closer and laid his hand along her back waist.

"I know that. It's just, well, a lot to take in."

"I never found any trace of them. I do know she and Alex broke off from the group to make their own way."

"Alex was my dad's name? They went to Pennsylvania." Casper's voice sounded hollow to her own ears. "I found their remains in Pennsylvania. We dug them up and gave them a proper burial. I'll take you there after the holidays."

Tears streamed down her cheeks with the memory of learning her parents were among the others who'd died at a facility where scientists experimented on psychics.

"I wanted you to know the *why* of my actions and beliefs. I, too, trust Noah. Believe me, I've used every connection and called in every favor I could to make sure of his entire pack, which isn't that large by the way."

"Thanks, Dante. I appreciate you looking out for my girl."

"*Our* girl," Dante corrected. "Everything I've found points to your pack being hardworking and dedicated to family. Secretive and protective, yes, but honest and sincere."

"Your assessment of my family is spot on," Noah assured them.

Dante offered his hand to Noah. "I'm sorry for all the grief I've caused you. But, you see, Olivia is my last remaining relative, and I swore on my sister's death to find and protect her."

"How'd you know my mom was dead?" Casper asked.

Dante blinked several times and looked away briefly. "I was approached by a group not unlike yours in Pennsylvania. They knew. I didn't want to believe it at first, but... it's true."

Casper wiped at her cheeks when another thought occurred. "If she could see the future, why didn't she stay in this realm after death? We could've talked. I talk to spirits all day long."

The grief in her uncle's eyes matched her own.

"Aw, Olivia. That's one question I might be able to answer. You see, she knew you and I would be together eventually. She sent me something to pass along to you. Maybe... I hope it helps."

Dante removed the chain he'd worn around his wrist. "She wanted you to have this."

"Why?"

"It's a bracelet with a physical reminder of every place they'd visited. See the links?"

Casper selected each piece in turn, asking for clarification of dates and locations. It dawned on her that, like other spirits, her parents could not find her, now lost in the spirit realm. "I wish I remembered them, at least some small thing."

"Look in the mirror. You're just like her. A hellion." Dante's crooked smile held grief, remorse, and love.

"Casper, you've called spirits to you once you have their name and picture or something that belongs to them." Hailey tugged on Dante's shirt sleeve. "Do you have a photo of her parents?"

Dante extracted a snapshot from his wallet. "This was taken the day I left for Rome."

Casper stood and studied the picture. Her uncle was right. She did look like her mother. Grasping her amulet on a prayer, she closed her eyes.

"*Mom? Natalie and Alex Mandler, if you're of this realm, please come to me.*" Never had she concentrated on such a heartfelt plea.

The entire room quieted. Nothing stirred. Nothing broke the silence other than the hum of the refrigerator and the mechanical Santa waving.

A minute later, she rubbed her eyes and mopped the tears streaming down her cheeks. "I guess they've moved on. Figures."

Simon's appearance included a brush of his fingers over her scalp accompanied by soft cooing. He pointed toward the window.

Casper spun around to see a woman slightly older than Dante, standing in the morning light. The crystalline form gained opacity until she saw sea-green eyes so much like her own, long dark hair, and a smile that welcomed her home.

"Simon? You found my mom... How?"

The spirit smiled. "*Call it fate, karma, whatever you like, but I'm thankful. From what others tell me, he's spent an awful lot of nights looking for me.*"

"All this time, I've been wondering where you've been going, fella."

Standing in the morning light, the spirit smiled.

"What?" Dante asked, taking hold of Casper's forearm to see who'd appeared. "Oh, my God. I never thought to see you again. Natalie?"

"Hello, Olivia. Martin."

"Mom?" Casper felt lightheaded and hollow.

"*Yes, sweetheart. I've waited an eternity for this day. I wish I could've found you sooner, but—*" Natalie looked to her brother. "*Martin, thank you for looking after my daughter. I hope one day you'll forgive me for sending you away.*"

Dante nodded. "I'm sorry it took so long to find her. Well, actually, she found me." Dante reached forward to touch his sister's cheeks. "Our parents?"

"*Are both happy and safe. They've moved on. You'll meet them again one day. For now, you need to embrace life, little brother. Don't shun the idea of having a family. You'll miss out on so much love.*"

Dante nodded, his emotions swelling as he cleared his throat.

Casper stepped into her mother's open embrace. "I know time and, well, everything is so much different in the spirit realm." She'd spent so many years dreaming of finding her parents. "Where's Dad?"

"*He's no longer of this plane and is waiting for me. I couldn't go until I saw you again. You'll understand one day, a long, long time from now.*"

"How will I find you again?" She wanted the moment with her mother to last for eternity.

"*Oh, sweetheart. There will come an irresistible tug that'll take you to where you belong. Understand this, we will be a family again. One day.*" Natalie smiled at those gathered. "*A very large family. It will feel like no time at all has passed. Trust me.*"

"I have so many questions I want to ask."

"*And I wish I could stay to answer them, but even now, I feel the force pulling me away. Know this, Olivia. I have and always will love you. Trust in your family.*"

The last words drifted into the ether, along with her mother.

"She's gone?" Casper heard Hailey's running summary of events.

"But she said you'll see her again, Casper. She waited all these years to say goodbye. She must've loved you very much." Hailey wrapped her arm around Casper's shoulders.

"*She did.*" The small glowing light beside Hailey expanded until Addy's form took shape.

Casper had much to learn about the other side of life, yet she now understood a little more. "It's not just love that keeps a spirit anchored to this world."

Addy nodded and spoke one word. "*Fate. And I can say no more.*"

They spent the next half hour and through much of the meal learning about Casper's family and ancestors through Dante.

By the time they finished and the dishes were cleared, the group had truly become family in every sense of the word. With drinks of their choice, each moved to the open space where they'd set up a dozen chairs in a circle in front of the tree.

Casper's anxiety ratcheted up to the point she began babbling. So much had happened, and she felt vulnerable like never before. Life was beginning anew.

It was Dante who tugged her to stand and wrapped her in a hug. "You are so much like Nat. When I first saw you, it almost killed me. I didn't believe it. Then, I realized the only way I could get to know you was through Hailey."

"That explains a lot," Hailey remarked. "I never could figure you out."

"I probably wouldn't have made much progress if not for... my employer, whom we'll discuss later. Suffice it to say, they are much like Nicholai and his warriors."

"Then it's a good thing we found common ground," Clannahan agreed. "I, too, have apologies to make. I've kept Dante's secret."

"And hounded me every second to come clean," Dante retorted with a grin. He released her to take his seat. "But it worked out."

Casper's gaze took in the group. "This is our first Christmas together, and I wasn't really sure how things should go. Back in Pennsylvania, well, we haven't spent many holidays together. Um, kind of only one where we weren't fighting to survive. So..."

"Casper. You're fine," Noah said and moved his chair closer to her. "This is perfect. Everything is great. You have family. Real, blooded family, along with the rest of us. It couldn't be better."

"You think so?"

"Absolutely. I come from a normal family, and this is exactly what we do. Except, I want you to open my present first." Noah handed her a small box.

"Looks like a jewelry box." Dante leaned forward in his seat across from her, his frown indicating suspicion.

Noah sighed. "Remember my dad is a jeweler? He taught me everything he knows. I made this for her."

Casper opened the box to find a necklace on a short gold chain. "Hailey said your friend took you dolphin surfing once and you loved it."

"Yes. She connected with them and asked them to give us toe pushes." Casper remembered her day at the beach and how much fun they'd had. Kiera was more like a sister than a mentor at times. The sense of freedom obtained that day had changed her worldview.

"I'm not going to ask." Dante shook his head.

"I'll explain anyway, Uncle. Hey, should I call you Dante or Martin?"

"Dante, please."

"Fine, anyway, toe pushes happen when a dolphin comes up behind you and pushes you through the water with its nose under your feet. They pick up speed and you come to a forty-five-degree angle. It's strange, but one of the best times I can remember."

The pendant was a pair of entwined silver dolphins with blue sapphires for eyes. She held her hair away for Noah to secure the clasp. "It's beautiful. Thank you." Blinking furiously didn't stop the moisture brimming in her eyes, so she quickly swiped them away.

In changing the focus, she grabbed the amulet in her hand and said, "Trent. I couldn't figure out what to get you, so, I talked to the major and learned more about your old friends in the unit. So, um, here goes." Casper stood and ambled over to where the fed sat.

He took the hand she offered and stood hesitantly.

"Some of the friends you lost overseas have stayed on this plane. Two in particular saved your life, but you never got the chance to thank them or find closure."

Closing her eyes, she silently called the two soldiers in question. A prior conversation ensured they were happy to visit.

Trenton stumbled back at seeing his friends. One cracked jokes while the second shook his ethereal head at Trenton's remorse.

It was a day of revelations, finding closure, and making peace with the past.

When Trenton mopped at his face with a handkerchief, no one made note of it. He'd earned his right to grieve.

Not to be outdone, Clannahan offered Hailey a small cardboard tube, the type typically used for keeping important documents secure.

"What's this?" Hailey asked while removing the end cap.

"The deed to your home and office." Clannahan grinned and held out two small packages. "Noah, Casper?"

Each accepted a small box and opened them to find a key in each.

"Noah, that house you found so perfect? I figured it'd be a good place for you and your family when they visit, which I can arrange at any time. As you said, and we all found out, there's plenty of room. And... there's five hundred acres of surrounding preserve that's off limits to the public. Plenty of room to stretch your legs."

"The Cat's Paw?" Noah read the inscription on the key. "Do my parents know about this? This is..." he was left speechless.

"Yes. I've spoken at length to them. They are aware of certain other factors and are considering a change in climate."

"Damn," Casper said and held up her key. "Is this to your house, Major?"

"No, it unlocks *your* house, Casper. You're eighteen and have shown you keep a level enough head. This way, when your PA family visits, there's plenty of room for them too."

"What aren't you telling us, Major?" The edge in Trenton's voice gave them all pause.

"Nothing to worry about now, but as Jenkins' secretary and Duncan indicated, there's trouble brewing."

Dante made a low noise in his throat. "That discussion can wait for another time. And when that time arrives, we will have support."

"From whom?" Hailey asked.

Dante took a deep breath and let it out slowly. "Moonpie, the family that took you in, Nicholai, Kiera, and the others, well, they only make up a percentage of known psychics. There's been a war brewing for decades, an internal struggle that split us into factions. When the time is right, I'll introduce you to the man who hired me, then Yamato."

"That's why you never come in contact with me without gloves." Hailey firmed her mouth in a straight line. "That is the other part of what you've withheld."

"Yes," Dante confirmed, "...and for good reason. But as I said, now is not the time."

* * * *

Thank you for reading *Phantom Reunion*.

Hailey and Casper's adventures continue in southeast Texas as the newly formed task force investigate a student's murder and ferret out those hunting gifted prodigies.

Read farther for an excerpt from *North Side of the Grass*.

If you'd like to know when my next book is ready, take a second and sign up for my NEW RELEASE email alerts. I only send out emails when I have a new book ready for release or a special sale. My original release dates always have time padded in for, you know, life events and such. They usually move up by several months. Plus, I don't spend a lot of time on social media. You can find a complete list of all my books at www.reilygarrett(dot)com.

North Side of the Grass
Hailey

Shadows retreating to the wood line gave way to pinks, golds, and lavender of early morning. Trekking in the bayou to capture a special photo was great. Tromping through a forest to a strange murder scene didn't make Hailey's to-do list.

Her young partner muttered something unintelligible as she rubbed Gunther behind the ears when he rubbed against her thigh. The wolf dog remained in tune with their moods and countered with energetic bounding and wide doggy grins

"This better be good." Casper phased her boot through a coral snake's attack. "I should be snuggled under a blanket with the windows open."

"Which Sarah considers a security nightmare." Hailey looked back at the snake and shook her head.

"Only because she doesn't realize how many spirits lurk around the house now. You and I are the only connections with the living world for them. I bet your loft is the same by now, especially since you can now see the buggers."

"I've noticed, but they are getting more considerate and respectful of my time and privacy."

"Since they don't sleep and have little concern for timing, it's important to set boundaries, especially for those... special times." Casper waggled her eyebrows. "That must frustrate the hell out of Trenton."

"Not near as much as you've generated in Trenton and Dante."

"I swear I don't know which one is worse. Trent takes leadership too seriously, and Dante, well, there're days he's worse than my family in Pennsylvania."

"They all mean well. It's just gonna take 'em time to realize you've become not only stronger, but more aware of your surroundings."

Casper's phone dinged with an incoming text. She read it and sighed. "Noah's disgusted with his pack. They think he's too young to live alone. Actually, I think a couple of them want to move to Texas."

"That won't go over well." Hailey accepted her partner's hand to walk through a thicket of briars.

Voices ahead redirected their focus. Hailey scooted out of the briars and onto a deer trail before breaking contact. She and her partner worked seamlessly but sometimes forgot to hide their talent from the norms.

Trenton's ever-watchful gaze picked the duo up the minute they circumvented a pine tree. His frown indicated knowledge of them using talent in the open.

The federal agent stood among five others in a small clearing. All five heads turned to watch her approach with mixed expressions. Colson grimaced, two plain clothes investigators frowned, and Leigh grinned.

Fun times in the making.

Trenton took a deep breath and briefly closed his eyes, a sign of needing patience. "Hello, Hailey. Didn't realize you'd be bringing your partners this morning."

"Seriously?" Casper stepped forward to the small gathering with hand outstretched. "I wouldn't miss a chance to give you all a migraine. Not for the aspirin in the world."

Between the women, Hailey's wolf dog sat. His size gave the two strangers pause.

"What the hell are you thinking, Agent Briner… bringing a kid and a dog to a crime scene?" A southern twang infiltrated the voice of the slim stranger wearing slacks and a button-down shirt. The slight bulge in his jacket under his left shoulder declared him a right-handed shooter.

Hailey recognized Ranger Landers from a previous case. Leigh had declared him a resolute, untrusting jackass. When his gaze climbed her body and finally reached her eyes, he took an involuntary step back. "Damn. That's intense."

She hadn't worn sunglasses to hide the unusual but striking azure blue of her eyes. It was time people got over it.

His brow furrowed with a narrowed gaze, his mind working out a puzzle he wouldn't solve.

Casper retracted her hand when the recipient merely stared. "Ya know, I heard that wearing hats all the time causes premature balding. Is that true?" She ducked a little as if to see under the big white Stetson.

The ranger huffed but didn't answer.

Gunther barked but kept his place between the private investigating duo. Shifting his weight from foot to foot signaled the desire to express himself. His lip curled up over gleaming white canines, his message delivered.

Leigh took a step back from the group, the slight dipping at the corners of her mouth couldn't disguise the smile threatening to appear.

Trenton looked skyward as if the boiling clouds might provide divine intervention.

Picking up the group tension, Gunther growled but remained seated.

The ranger eyed the animal but addressed the group at large. "That animal's a liability. We can't afford to ruin evidence."

"My four-footed partner has earned his place in H&C Investigations." Hailey stood firm. Her dog had saved her life more than once. "He also has as much sense as most people."

Landers didn't relent, his gaze skimming Casper once in dismissal.

"This is no place to bring a kid." His tone suggested disbelief bordering on condescension.

"I'm in training."

"More like a training bra." Though mumbled low and obviously not intended for others to hear, Landers made his first big mistake.

Trenton made a low noise in his chest but didn't intervene. Beside him, Leigh, his sister, snorted.

Not to let such an insult to her partner go, Hailey held her hand out in greeting. "Everyone's entitled to their own opinion. I respect that, and hey, good showing at the last MMA tournament. Your wife must be so proud of you."

After leading the conversation in the general direction she wanted his thoughts to go, Hailey took the ranger's hand, accepted grudgingly. As expected, a flurry of images erupted in her thoughts.

Maybe her quarry had a winning personality when not working, maybe he had the sexual prowess of a bull. Either way, he didn't keep a string of girlfriends in line with his hulkish looks.

Disgust and annoyance entwined for an irresistible distraction that required elimination. She wouldn't allow the idiot to interfere.

She and her partner, though neither telepathic, had found a way to communicate privately when standing in a crowd. Each could communicate with the spirit realm with a mere thought. All they needed was a spirit to relay the message.

"*Addy? You around, sis?*" Hailey's sister appeared during times of heightened emotion, and the ranger was ticking her off.

In the next instant, Addy flowed through a pine tree. Dressed in her usual jeans but with a leather jacket over her flannel shirt. "*I thought spirits didn't get cold.*"

"*We don't, but we do like to be cool.*"

"*Why are you flickering? Are you okay?*"

"*There's some kind of interference. Not sure what it is or what's causing it. It's difficult to adjust to. What's wrong?*"

"*Tell Casper this Texas Ranger fancies himself a Casanova. He's a real player and his wife has no clue. He's also making fun of her.*" The last tidbit was sure to produce a response, if not several.

A minute later, Landers' hat flipped off his head in a gush of wind that didn't exist. His reflexive twist and grab failed, the hat missing waist high vines behind him in favor of a muddy puddle beyond.

"Damn it. That's my last good white Stetson."

"Maybe you belong on the dark side." Casper giggled. "Might suit you better." The teen held her left hand out, her shoulder dipping then raising to position Simon on her shoulder. The spirit's penchant for mayhem multiplied with any threat to his friends.

Landers stood and made a show of brushing off his suit, now with a tear in the jacket sleeve.

"Yes, well now." Tall and lean, the handsome stranger next to Leigh smiled and extended his hand. "Hi, I'm Hal Burrows, state investigator."

Hailey accepted the warm greeting and appreciative gaze. A birthmark on the back of his left hand resembled a large cat on the prowl. She wondered if it was significant. She'd never noticed anything similar on Noah, Casper's boyfriend.

From his thoughts, she saw a group of men gathered around a pool table with a big screen TV behind him. It exemplified male bonding over football and beer.

"Can't say as I've ever worked with private investigators, but both Agent Briner and Lieutenant Colson swear you two get results. And isn't that what we're all after?"

Burrows stood tall with a straight, military-type posture. His green eyes zeroed in on Hailey with curiosity before flicking to Casper. Extending his hand, he continued, "I've heard good things about your colleague. "Nice to meet you both.""

Casper accepted the greeting with a slight frown. Beside her, Gunther leaned his full weight against her knee, causing her to sidestep. His continued antsyness drew Leigh's attention.

"Want me to take him for a walk?" Leigh asked.

Hailey shook her head, studying her four-footed friend. "He usually only gets like this—"

"When dead bodies are in the area?" The ranger asked.

She wanted to answer, "*only when spirits are present,*" though he'd gotten used to Addy and the capuchin monkey, which he enjoyed romping around the yard with the primate on his back. His current behavior equaled a conundrum she'd have to solve later. She rested her hand on the wolf dog's head to steady him.

On his other side, Casper shifted her weight foot to foot.

Burrows and Landers might suspect she suffered from a case of nerves. Nothing could be farther from the truth.

No other spirits hovered in the area, other than Addy and Simon. Whatever set Gunther and the teen's senses tingling wasn't obvious.

Burrows didn't acknowledge the air thickening with anger, but Hailey felt it. Landers, the ranger, was the obvious instigator, but it felt like more.

"I understand from Agent Briner here, that you're learning the ropes, young lady. Good for you." The state investigator gestured to the tree at the edge of the small clearing. "Hell of a case to cut your teeth on though. Hope you have a strong stomach."

"Don't worry, she'll be fine." Trenton led them closer to the scene. "Forensic techs have gathered what they can. They'll be back with appropriate equipment to remove the body."

Hailey looked around and saw nothing unusual other than the leafy debris missing from the base of a large dead oak tree. "Where is the body?"

The trunk rose ten feet in the air with intermittent, perfectly round six-inch holes appearing at various levels. The top culminated in a somewhat jagged, saw-tooth pattern not occurring from natural circumstances.

"Inside the trunk," Leigh advised, gesturing for them to circle the tree to the back.

"You found someone stuffed a hollowed-out tree? How'd they do it? Drop him in from the top?" Casper stepped forward with her hands behind her back to peer into one of the holes.

"Good question." Burrows asked, providing light from his phone app.

"Hikers were drawn by all the holes after their dog drew them near." Lieutenant Colson replied, handing the teen a pair of gloves and a flashlight. "Here, I know you want to see."

Hailey moved to stand beside her partner, stopped by Trenton who held out a pair of gloves, folded in half. "Hold on, not without these. "By the way, Clannahan invited us to dinner tonight."

Her friend had always been quick to think on his feet. She took the offered gloves and slipped them on with her back to the others. "Is it a male or female?"

"Burned beyond identification," Trenton responded, giving her the look that said, "*You tell me.*"

Sure enough, the second and third sleeves of each glove had a hole in the end, allowing her to touch evidence. Behind her, an argument over jurisdiction flared.

Hailey left them to it, knowing Leigh and Colson would occupy the two others and give her a chance to see what she could learn.

First contact yielded strange images that wouldn't form a coherent scenario. Then, she caught flashes of a masked man, tall, wearing black clothing and carrying something wrapped in a blanket. About six feet long, she assumed it was the body.

Next to the tree, he dropped his bundle.

New images flashed, but they were from an earlier time. Leaves on the trees were green, and surrounding foliage was lush. Someone drilled holes all around the trunk at varying heights.

"Wow." Keeping her voice low while the others argued, she spoke to Trenton.

"Guy in black wearing a mask, brought the body here, but he'd prepared the tree earlier, as in months earlier.

"How'd he get the top like that? And Why?" Trenton murmured.

"Picked a tree cut off by lightning. He' a pyro tech. I think the jagged top is to mark his spot. Maybe he was practicing his talent." Hailey shrugged. "I dunno, but he hollowed it out by drilling holes, filling them with saltpeter, potassium nitrate, then set it on fire."

"Had he already burned the body?"

Hailey shuddered at the next flurry of images. "Yeah, he did that in a cinder block building, can't see where, but he got her down to charred bones, then stuffed her skeleton in here."

"Why not burn the bones to ash?" Casper asked.

"Because it required too much heat. This was done using psychic power and the killer didn't want to spend the time or energy."

"Damn, do you have an ID?" Trenton nudged her back and indicated she remove her specially made gloves.

"No, but I have a face. It was a teen girl who's spoken with the new principal." Hailey bowed her head and turned away from the approaching ranger and state investigator. Peeling off her gloves one at a time to leave them inside out and balled, she stuffed them in her jacket.

"Damn it." Casper inhaled deep. "I thought that was over."

The Gifted Elite school Casper and her boyfriend attended housed over four dozen prodigies from around the country. The recent removal of a corrupt vice principal and his secretary cut the ties between the local faction facilitating a link between students and those seeking psychics for their own ends.

Or so they'd thought.

The facility's principal resigned after discovering his staff was involved in murder and kidnapping students. Casper's guardian had been quick enough to insert one of his own men into the VP's position, but not the principal's post.

To date, there'd been no evidence or communication from staff members concerning nefarious dealings.

Casper tapped Hailey on the forearm and staggered sideways. "I need to get out of here. Something's wrong."

"What?" Hailey reached out a steadying hand to her partner, who wobbled in her stance."

"Is our little girl squeamish?" The Texas ranger asked, ignoring Leigh's hand on his shoulder.

"Listen asshole." Casper placed her palm on her forehead and grimaced.

That one action caused a flurry of movement.

Lieutenant Colson inserted himself between the ranger and Casper, nodding to Hailey to return. "We'll catch up with you later."

With an arm around the teen, Hailey led them across the clearing and onto the animal trailed they'd used previously. "What's going on, Cass?"

"Don't know. Sudden onset of... anger, despair, frustration. No idea where it came from. The only spirits there were Simon and Addy. It wasn't either of them."

"Could there be more, like, hiding themselves?"

"Guess it's possible, don't know. All I know now is that I've got this splitting headache and have never suffered such extreme emotion."

"Let's go back to the loft. We can pull up the yearbook and see if I can identify our victim."

"You see anything else when touching the tree?"

"No. I can't even identify where she was killed, but if we can figure out her name, you can call her spirit to us."

Reilys Books

Romantic Thrillers
McAllister Justice Series
Tender Echoes
Digital Velocity
Bound By Shadows
Inconclusive Evidence
Carbon Replacements
Shattered Reflections
Remnants of Evil

Moonlight and Murder Series
Shifting Targets
A Critical Tangent
Pivotal Decisions
Seeds of Murder
An Unlikely Grave
Deadly Interception
Love You To Death

Psychic Thrillers
Mind Stalkers Series
Bending Fate
Silent Depths
Shadow Guard
Whispers After Death
Mind Hunters

Guardian Series

PHANTOM REUNION

Shadowed Horizons
Shadowed Origins
Shadowed Passages
Shadowed Spirits
Shadowed Intent
Shadowed Visions
Shadowed Deliverance

Hailey Arquette Murder Files
Perfect In Death
Deceptive Silence
Unlikely Justice
Phantom Reunion
North Side of the Grass

Paranormal Romance
Immortal Lovers Series
Unholy Alliance
Blood Union
Standalone paranormal romance
Tiago

About Reily

Reily Garrett is a writer, mother, and companion to three long coat German shepherds. When not working with her dogs, she's sitting at her desk with her fur kids by her side.

Author of chilling suspense and snarky romance, her stories span the distance of romantic thrillers, paranormal romance, and erotic romance. Regardless of genre, each book delves into a dark and twisted imagination yet is tempered with romance and a touch of humor.

Reviews by Kirkus Reviews, San Francisco Bay Review, and BestThrillers.com best describe her work:

"This could be James Patterson, Lee Child, and Tess Gerritsen rolled into one, but the dark, twisted methods used by the serial killer could surprise even those readers..." - San Francisco Bay Review

"...steamy, seductive police procedural..." - BestThrillers.com

"...well-researched thriller that remains romantically genuine throughout." - Kirkus Review

Prior experience in the Military Police, private investigations, and as an ICU nurse gives her fiction a real-world flavor.

www.ingramcontent.com/pod-product-compliance
Lightning Source LLC
Chambersburg PA
CBHW051319130726
47987CB00004B/1874